THE ELK HUNT

A novel by

Roy Mullen

Black Rose Writing | Texas

This is a work of fiction. Names, characters, businesses, places, events, and incidents are either the products of the author's imagination or used in a fictitious manner. Any resemblance to actual persons, living or dead, or actual events is purely coincidental.

ISBN: 978-1-68513-466-2
PUBLISHED BY BLACK ROSE WRITING
www.blackrosewriting.com

Printed in the United States of America
Suggested Retail Price (SRP) $20.95

The Elk Hunt is printed in Garamond Premier Pro

*As a planet-friendly publisher, Black Rose Writing does its best to eliminate unnecessary waste to reduce paper usage and energy costs, while never compromising the reading experience. As a result, the final word count vs. page count may not meet common expectations.

Praise for
The Elk Hunt

"A nail-biting experience."
–Pam Greer, Page Editing Service

"Another well-written one, with a distinct voice. Clear writing and a quiet, calm feel to the narrative. There is a good sense of place and atmosphere, and the third-person characterization feels confident but thoughtful."
–Black Rose Writing Acquisition Reviewer

"This is another keeper. It sits with you after. It will find an audience with fans of nature/outdoor adventure with a lot of reflection."
–Black Rose Writing Acquisition Reviewer

This book is dedicated to my father, Marvin L. Mullen, Sr.
You didn't make it home from your mountain, Dad.
How I have wished, many times, for one more campfire
on the mountain with you.

Acknowledgements

To my sister Sue and her husband Jim Brown. I can't thank you enough for your support, encouragement, and suggestions during the writing of this book. You were the first to believe in it and my writing. I love you both.

My sincere thanks to Dr. Glen Groben for your encouragement, advice, and friendship. It means more to me than I can say.

The cover was prepared by my niece, Jennifer Mullen. It is fantastic, Jen. Thank you so much. It was crafted from a photograph taken of me on a ridge just north of the ridge described in this story. I was then camping in the same place as described in this story.

A deep, heartfelt thank you to my son Dane for all of your hard work, advice, and your belief in me and my 'Elk Hunt.' Thank you for your very professional and loving work on it.

THE ELK
HUNT

CHAPTER 1

He woke well before daylight and lay in the sleeping bag, eyes closed. He had slept well.

He was tired from the long days of hiking the ridges to the east of his camp, but he had always slept well up here—up here being wherever the mountains are. High mountain peaks, timbered ridges, wind in the pines, clear, ice-cold streams, and fresh air accompanied him on his long, tiring walks along the game trails. Yesterday had been clear and warm with clouds coming in late in the day. Sundown had brought overcast skies and cold, but no wind.

He had shared the trails and ridges with no one, no people anyway—a few deer, an old owl napping in the high shade of a pine tree, squirrels, and one grumpy old badger. That was usually the way it was the places he went, and the way he liked it—the mountains and no people. When there were people around, there weren't many, and he could usually avoid them if he wanted to. And most often, up here, he wanted to avoid them. Up here was a hell of a lot better than down below, with its traffic jams, car exhaust, and crowds of people. Noise, noise, noise. Never any quiet. Not even in the middle of the night.

That's not to say that there isn't sound up here. There's wind in the pines and the chuckle of the creek. There's the hoot of an owl in the night, the chatter of a squirrel welcoming the day at first morning light, and the squawking complaint of the crows from tree to tree. But none of that is noise. To him, these sounds are the orchestra of life, music to that ear somewhere deep inside him. He often told people he came up here to talk with the trees and the creek and the squirrels. But the truth is he came up here to listen—listen to the whispers of the earth. He knew that even the rocks, left here hundreds of thousands of years ago, spoke to him.

Lying in the spotted, shifting shade of an aspen grove, leaves trembling above him, he heard their voices. The voices of the leaves, the wind, and the rocks sang in chorus to him. He knew that something elemental, deep inside him, understood their music and their language. The decaying old log of a fallen pine lying beside the stream, now replenishing the earth that had fed and sustained it for a century or more, told him the story of its life.

And on cloudless nights, there are the stars, the only sleeping pills he ever needed up here. Man, oh man, are there ever stars, stars that no one in any city can ever see. Maybe no one even knows they exist. If you've never gone to bed in a high mountain meadow on a cloudless night, you don't know what stars there are in the sky. Nor have you seen the beauty of the Milky Way streaking across the black sky like a smear of twinkling silver paint.

These are not things of the city. Nor are they things of the tightly packed fence-line to fence-line RV park. These things—these sights and sounds—are the reasons he comes up here. Alone. Something to hold on to with other than his hands. The fundamentals of life. His touchstone to existence.

In many ways, the hunt is incidental. Hunting season or not, this is just a good place to be. Then again, hunting season is not the only time of the year he comes up here. Whenever he hears the call sliding down from the hills on the wind, whispering across the valley, this is where he needs to be. As often as his other life will allow.

He was a big man, in stature anyway. He stood nearly six-and-a-half feet tall and weighed just over 250 pounds. With broad shoulders and strong legs, he could carry an elk hindquarter on a packboard. But here in the mountains, moving among these peaks and pines, he felt small. But despite that smallness, he knew he was a part of all that surrounded him. He may be just a fragment but a fragment that blended with the smell of the earth, floated on the breeze with the fragrance of the pines, resounded with the hoot of an owl in the dark and the murmur of the creek. He sang with the squirrel chattering in the morning's first light. He fed his soul as he watched the deer clip grass in the meadow at the fading light of the evening. Here on the mountain, he was one with all that surrounded him—all that held him in its embrace and that he held in his heart. If he lived anywhere in this world, God lived here.

Now, awake in the lean-to, he felt the cold. Not the down-to-the-bone cold, but it was more than just a nip in the air. He definitely felt colder than when he went to bed last night. He lay in the sleeping bag, his body warm and comfortable. It was a good bag, good enough for a lot colder than it is this morning. Stretching his legs and tensing his muscles, he looked up through the trees. The moon was gone, and it was very dark. No stars shined above in the black sky. He pulled his arm out of the sleeping bag, dragged his backpack closer from the back of the lean-to, and got out a pack of cigarettes and matches. He shook the pack, pulled a cigarette out with his lips, and lit it, taking that first long, deep drag of the day. It was the only one he really enjoyed. All the rest were just habit maintenance. He blew a long cloud of smoke to the top of the lean-to and watched it curl and float, hanging near the roof before slipping over the edge of the tarp into the dark of the morning. No breeze was up yet this morning. That would change once the sun was up and the day along the ridge tops warmed.

Turning on his side, he saw it had snowed in the night—not much, just an inch or so. Smiling, he knew fresh tracks would be easier to see and ground cover would be a lot quieter today where he walked.

When the cigarette was finished, he tossed it into the firepit just outside the front of the lean-to. From a small pile of branches stored near the back of the lean-to, he gathered several small branches. Scooting the sleeping bag over the cloth ground tarp, he piled the branches in the firepit. The evening before, he had smeared some of the branches with pine tar that oozed from a scar on one of the trees the lean-to was anchored to with rope. Lighting the pitch on one of the branches, he tossed it into the firepit and slid back under the lean-to. He wriggled deeper into the sleeping bag and waited for the fire to get going and reflect its heat to the interior of the lean-to.

He had chosen well where the lean-to should be. It was positioned between two large pine trees that provided a canopy of branches covering the entire camp area, creating a good shelter from rain and snow. He had trenched the lean-to on three sides to channel water away from the camp if it rained. The area for the lean-to was level, and he had swept away rocks and branches with a pine bow. Nothing will stop a good night's sleep like a rock in the middle of your back.

He had first camped in this same spot some years ago and had been back two other times. This year, he had come up three days before the start of elk season to set up camp and scout the area. It was at the dead end of an old logging road at the head of a maintained trail winding down to the big river. The road in from the Forest Service road hadn't been maintained for a few years. It was now overgrown with small trees and brush that scraped the underside of his old truck. Deep, washed out ruts had carved trenches across the road in several places. He had had to fill two of them with logs and rocks to get past them in his truck. But he had made it in, and there wasn't much chance that anyone else was going to bother him for the week. Getting out could be dicey if it snowed too deep. He had to keep that thought always in the back of his mind.

Part of his first two days was spent gathering firewood and setting up the campsite. A large cache of firewood was now piled on a waterproof ground tarp under the trees and covered with a well-staked tarp to keep the wood dry. It had been sweaty work on a warm afternoon cutting up a deadfall log with a sharp, bladed bow saw and splitting the rounds with a good axe. But as a result, he had more dry wood for campfires than he would use on this trip.

He smiled in the warmth of the sleeping bag. He was well dug in for the next week, as long as he didn't get more than a foot of snow. In that case, he would have to pack up his old truck and get the hell out of here. It would be a long walk back to the Forest Service road. Beyond that, it was more than thirty miles before he could get to some human contact. *Keep that in mind old son. And don't get stupid. You don't want to leave that old truck in here all winter and walk out.*

With his feet, he brought his rolled pants and shirt up from the bottom of the sleeping bag. They were warm from his body heat. He stayed in the bag as he squirmed into his pants. Unzipping the bag, he put on the shirt. He pulled his boots from the back of the lean-to, turned each over and slapped them on the sole twice to evict any critters that might have crawled into them in the night before he pulled them on and laced them up. Before he left the lean-to, he zipped up the sleeping bag, rolled it, tied it with the pull strings, and stowed it in the back of the lean-to.

A coffee pot, already full of water from the creek, sat near the fire ring. He added a couple of logs to the fire and placed the metal grill over the flames. At the truck, he unlocked it and dug out the can of coffee. Placing a filter in the top of the pot, he added coffee grounds and sat the pot over the flames.

Every time he made coffee over an open fire, he thought of his dad in hunting camp many years ago and how he had made coffee. He used an old, blackened coffee can crimped on one side for a pour spout and fitted with a piece of baling wire for a handle. The formula was: fill it with water, throw in a handful of coffee grounds, put it on the fire, and get it to a boil. Grounds floated on the top of the water. Add a little cold water to settle the grounds to the bottom, mostly anyway. To pour it into your cup, there was a pair of rusty vice grips always handy to clamp onto the hot can. You always got a few grounds in your cup, and it was either strain the grounds with your teeth and spit them out or chew them. Bitter and harsh were words far short of the mark for dad's coffee. But the thought of that bitter taste always brought a smile. *I wish you knew this mountain, Dad.*

He started to feel the cold and got his coat and hat from the truck. He brought out bacon and eggs, an iron skillet, a paper plate, and silverware. He left these just inside the lean-to. With a bowl in hand, he walked away from the camp and stopped beside a tree near the creek. Pushing his hat back on his head, he unzipped and stood looking at the sky as he aimed at the base of the tree. Away from the light of the fire, all was dark. The sound of the creek whispering in the dark soothed him and hinted at some of its secrets. This was a good place to sit in the evening and just listen or doze in the shade of the tree on a warm afternoon. He looked forward to hearing more of those secrets in the days to come. Above him, one lone star peeked through a hole in the clouds.

With that chore over, he zipped up and stepped to the creek to dip water into the bowl. He took it to the tailgate of the truck and washed up. The ice-cold water tingled his face and hands. "Time for breakfast," he said as he threw the water from the bowl. While the bacon and eggs were cooking, he poured a cup of coffee. Sitting on a log near the fire, hands warmed by the tin coffee cup, he thought of other hunts, other times, on this and other mountains.

More often than not, he had camped and hunted with friends or family. He really enjoyed hunting with his kids when they got old enough. Teaching them what he had learned over the years in the mountains, how to be quiet, how to read tracks and other sign, safety with guns and knives, hiking in the mountains, and patience—that was the hardest lesson for some of them. Sharing this part of his life, this part of himself and his soul, was important, vital even. But what he really liked, what renewed him, and he could never get enough of, was being up here on his own. You just can't talk with the trees while someone is listening in. And you can't listen to the secrets of the creek while someone else is preoccupied with the sound of their own voice.

You can share your appreciation for the beauty of the mountains, the creeks, and the animals. You can share the wonder of a doe and her fawn feeding in a high meadow in the evening, unaware of being watched. You can share the majesty of a bull elk silhouetted on a high ridgeline and the spine-tingling awe of his challenging bugle in the first light of day. You can teach taking care of what is here and leaving it the way it was when you arrived. You can share the calmness and peacefulness of those far-off mountains.

But you cannot teach the craving to come here. The fundamental need for this. That feeling for just you and the reality of the natural world all around you. You either have it or you don't. And if you do, there is nothing better. No job, no house, no personal relationship with another person could take the place of being here. *Excepts, perhaps, the love of a good woman,* he thought. That would come mighty close to this feeling.

The kids are all grown now with families of their own. It's hard for them to get away. Their own kids, jobs, and responsibilities get in the way. That's the way it had been for him years ago. But he'd always managed from time to time to get off by himself on a mountain somewhere. Many times in his life, he wondered what it would have been like if he were born a hundred and fifty or more years ago. Would he, could he, have been a mountain man? Living alone every day? Talking only to himself, the trees, and the creeks? Hearing only his own voice and the voices of the earth? Going wherever the mountains and creeks took him? Surviving on what the land provided? It might have been interesting to have found out. But then, he never would have known the kids.

What a tragic loss that would be, for him and for them.

And those kids thought he was nuts, going it alone up here. Maybe he was. But it was good. Real good. Always had been. It was what he wanted. No, it was what he needed from time to time; time to get into his own head without distractions, to wash away all the crap that accumulates down below. A time to iron out the wrinkles in his soul, flush all the crap of civilization from his head, listen to the trees and the creek.

Besides, the kids knew where he was. He made sure they knew that before he took off. He'd left a map with one of the boys. That was for their comfort, not his. If he didn't get back within the time frame that he had set, they would come looking for him. Or more than likely, they would send someone who knew the area to look for him.

Oh, he knew what they worried about. And he couldn't say that he hadn't thought about it, too. What if something happened to him up here alone? What if he got hurt and couldn't get out? What if they couldn't find him? What if? There are always what ifs in life. Things happen all the time in the most common of activities. People get hurt and die every day. Does that mean that you aren't supposed to do what you want to do? Or what you are compelled to do? A lot of people die in bed. Do you stop going to bed so you don't die in your sleep?

There just comes a time when he is driven to be up here. Alone. He knows the risks. And he does all he can to minimize those risks. Yes, something could happen. He could get hurt. He could even die up here. Get caught in a snowstorm. Or even get lost. He scoffs at the thought of getting lost. But he's not going to get mugged or get run over in a crosswalk. And there is no point in dwelling on the negative. He isn't here to be negative or worry about what might happen. That's just not his way.

And what if it happens? Is there a better place to die? Not by his way of thinking. Maybe propped up under a tree overlooking a deep, timbered valley and some far-off blue mountains. The sky above, the wind in the pines, and maybe the murmur of a creek nearby. His body breaking down in time and returning to the earth. That's a long stride better than lying face down in a crosswalk, eyes fixed on a chunk of asphalt. Or trapped in a crumpled car beside the freeway somewhere with traffic flowing by, horns blaring, and sirens coming from far away. And going back to the earth is a hell of a lot better than being placed in a metal box that goes inside of a concrete box, planted under manicured grass in a crowded cemetery with strangers on every side. Sure, he would have regrets. Not seeing his kids or his grandkids again. Not being able to say goodbye. But if he had a choice, this is where it would be, or some other place like it.

He always half joked with them. "When you come looking for me, bring a shovel, and plant me where you find me. Don't carry me back down the mountain."

The people of long ago believed that everything lived. Everything had a spirit. So if everything lived, did everything die? The trees, the grass, the brush, and all the plants were born from seeds dropped by older plants of their kind. Those seeds, buried in the soil, sprouted, grew, lived, spread their own seeds, and then they, too, died. They rotted into soil to feed the new plants. Rocks were born far beneath the surface and pushed up by the earth's forces to make mountains. They, too, were gnawed at by wind, rain, heat, and cold, and over millions of years would be diminished to fine grains of sand. They would mingle with the soil or be washed away by the rains, the streams, and the rivers to the sea. The very mountains themselves were eroding, shrinking, dying. All things live, and all things must die.

There was nothing different with people. They were born, lived, and died. Shouldn't they, too, go back to the earth instead of some box?

It's the where, the when, and the how that no living thing has much control over. When it comes, it comes, wherever you are at the time.

Breakfast eaten, he poured another cup of coffee. He sure did like his eggs fried in bacon grease in an iron skillet over an open fire. The hell with what some dietician said about how bad it was for you.

The paper plate went into the fire. "Beats washing one," he said. He stood, holding the cup of coffee, and went to the truck. He rinsed off the fork and knife in the basin he refilled with clean water, poured the bacon grease into a container, and popped a lid on it. He wiped the residue of grease from the skillet with a paper towel that he tossed into the fire as well.

He got his backpack from the lean-to and laid it on the front seat of the truck. Although he knew nothing had changed in it from the hike the day before, out of habit, he checked each pocket anyway. Two bottles of water, power bars, matches in a waterproof container, a small tin of dried pine pitch for fire starter, extra pants, shirt, and socks. Extra ammo for the rifle and handgun. A flashlight and extra batteries. He put in a small hatchet and a fold-blade bone saw. He added a long coil of cotton rope from under the seat of the truck. Not optimistic, just hopeful. This was opening morning, after all. He also had two sandwiches he'd made the night before, some chips in a Ziploc bag, and a couple of apples for lunch. Binoculars. And a roll of mountain money. The kids thought it funny when he first told them about taking some mountain money when you left camp. "'Cause if you are on that mountain and need just that thing before you pull your pants back up, you will pay all the money you have to get some," he'd told them with a smile. His sons smirked. His daughter blushed.

He loosened his belt and slid on his knife and handgun, then re-threaded the belt back into the belt loops. Pulling the rifle from its case, he inserted a magazine and chambered a round. Putting on the safety, he laid the rifle on the truck seat. As he walked back to the fire pit, he glanced at the sky one more time. There was no hint of daylight in the Eastern sky yet, but there were a few more stars visible. Maybe it would be a good day on the mountain. Most days were, for him. "This snow may be gone by noon," he said. Sitting on the log by the fire, he topped off the cup of coffee and watched the now low flames dance in the fire pit.

There was no need to look at his watch. It was in the glove box in the truck anyway. Time was more or less insignificant up here. His body told him when to go to bed, when to get up, and when to eat. If he listened to all that was around him and his instincts, he would do just fine. He nearly always had.

He knew where he was going this morning and about how long it would take to get there. And he wanted to be there just as it got light enough to see and shoot.

He'd made a few mistakes over the years. Usually, it was because he wasn't paying attention. Not listening to and watching the world around him and his own common sense.

One time a few years ago, it was the white-out storm on the top of Red Mountain. If that storm had lasted four days instead of four hours, he would have been in real big trouble. He'd had everything he needed except enough food for a long wait. And snowshoes. It would have been something serious getting back down that switchback trail buried in three or more feet of snow. It hadn't been all that easy anyway.

Another time was on the same ridge he would go up this morning. The first time he hunted here, he had waited too long in the evening to head back to camp and wouldn't make it until well past dark. In the darkness and his haste to get back, he stumbled into a large blow down of trees. Large and small trees scattered every which way. He had missed it going up the ridge and was surprised to stumble onto it coming down. In an attempt to get around the jumble of downed trees, he misjudged his direction and was actually walking away from camp rather than toward it. But he knew if he just kept walking downhill, he would cross the main trail, which paralleled the creek— *if I'm on the right side of the ridge,* he'd thought back then. That thought had flickered through his mind and tightened his gut just a little. Once he found the trail and the creek, he would follow that back to camp. If he missed the trail somehow or actually was on the wrong side of the ridge, he could stop, make a temporary camp, build a fire, and be fine until morning. The buddies who were with him that trip were probably back at camp. They would worry about him through the night but would not start looking for him until daylight. When it came down to it, he was just pissed off at himself for not paying attention like he should have.

As he had trudged down the hill in the dark, he heard a gunshot far behind him. That could only be his friends in camp at the end of the road giving him a directional shot. "Man, that sounded like a long ways," he'd said. Turning more down the hill toward the sound of the shot, he soon found the trail and the creek in less than half a mile and headed in the right direction. He would have found the trail eventually, but he would have been much farther from camp than he'd thought. In the end, it only meant a late supper and not a cold night on the mountain.

The next day, he had gone back to the same area to find out what he had done wrong. Along the ridge top, he found the large area of blown down trees. Probably from the high winds of a micro-burst. Several acres of trees were scattered like a dropped pile of toothpicks on the table. Disoriented in the dark by the blow down and trying to skirt the tangle of fallen trees, he realized he had been walking a finger ridge the night before and not the main ridge as he'd thought. He had been more than two miles from camp and headed in the wrong direction.

No such thing would happen today. He knew the lay of the land and the hills far better now and had tagged his trail up the main ridge with white marking tape tied to tree branches. He could follow that trail no matter how dark it got.

"Time to head out, old son," he mumbled. He poured the remains in the coffee pot on the fire and stirred it. With his boot, he pushed a bit of snow into the fire pit. Retrieving the rifle, he put on his gloves, locked the truck, put the keys on the top of the right front tire, and turned toward the trail head. With another look at the sky, he shouldered the rifle. A good morning for the walk ahead of him in the dark.

CHAPTER 2

Near the head of the trail, he passed an old fire ring. It looked as if it hadn't been used in years, maybe not since the last time he'd hunted here when there had been a big camp around this fire ring. It wasn't a bad place for a camp. Not as level as he liked. For him, it was out in the open too much. Plenty of room for tents, but he didn't have a tent. Good parking if you had a camper or camp trailer, but he didn't have one of those either. He had tarps for a ground cloth and the lean-to. For the kind of camping he did, he needed trees for cover from rain or snow. And he needed to tie the roof of the lean-to to those trees. It sure would be nice to have a good camper or trailer, but the lean-to was all he could afford now. And it wasn't all that bad. It was what he had and how he'd had camped for years.

Passing the old fire ring, he thought of the big camp that had been there a few years ago. Opening day, he had been on the mountain since before first light. As he came down off the ridge to the meadow just after sunset, he smelled the smoke from their campfire before he saw them. He stopped in the gathering darkness beneath the trees and listened and watched.

Looking down through the trees to the end of the ridge, he had sagged at the thought of neighbors for the next week. With a sigh, he moved down the ridge to where the trees opened up and saw that it was a big camp. Three trucks with horse trailers. Five saddle horses and a pack mule. Two large tents, camp chairs scattered around the fire, and more coolers than any camp needed. *These guys aren't going to starve to death up here, that's for sure,* he thought. *Probably more beer in those coolers than they should be drinkin' with guns around.* Bales of hay and bags of oats for the stock were stacked under the trees. A rope corral around a stand of trees kept the stock fenced in. *They must have worked nonstop for weeks to get all that stuff ready.* As he walked past the camp, some of the men looked his way but said nothing. He just lifted a hand in greeting. None of them waved back.

He walked on to his camp and went about his own business of starting a fire and getting dinner.

In the evening and on into the night, he heard their voices and laughter. "Those boys will be a little too hung over to make it out on the trail at shooting light in the morning," he said.

So much for talking to the trees and listening to the creek's secrets. So long quiet nights. And there was no way to move his camp at this point. He laid his book in the back of the lean-to, turned out the lamp, and snuggled down into the sleeping bag. "It is what it is," he said aloud and rolled over to get some sleep. "I'll still have my time alone up that ridge."

For the next two days, he passed their camp morning and evening. Only one of them acknowledged him in passing by raising his hand in a wave. Two of them obviously turned their backs and ducked their heads when they saw him. Anger at the snub flared. *Why should I care? I'd be better off if they weren't here in the first place, but they are.* For some reason, it just galled him to be snubbed like that. By anyone. A simple "howdy" would be neighborly and sufficient.

On the third evening, after dinner, he wandered down to their camp, cup of coffee in hand. *Why the hell am I doing this?* he wondered as he approached the camp. *I should just leave this alone. If they're rude, so what?* But he kept walking. A conflict between wanting to be alone and being neighborly baffled him. At their camp, he stepped into the light of the fire and said, "Howdy." All talk stopped, and they stood or sat looking into the fire. After a minute or so of silence, he was ready to just turn and walk away. *To hell with them,* he thought. *I should just leave well enough alone. I wanted *to be alone anyway.* As he was about to walk away, one man, standing across the fire, pushed his hat back on his head and shifted his weight. The man looked up and said, "I see you're out every morning. Have you seen anything?"

"Just a few cows." he replied. "One spike bull quite a ways off. And a lot of deer." He paused. "I should have come here for a deer hunt. I've seen some mighty big bucks the last couple of days."

"You hunted here before?" the man asked.

"Yeah, a few times over the years. I stick to the ridges and draws to the East and North. You guys ridin' back to the river on the trail?"

"Yep."

"I've never gone back that far myself. Too far to packboard anything out on foot. You seen anything back there?"

"Nothing yet. Some tracks is all."

After another pause, he asked the man, "You guys hunt here before?"

"No. A friend told us it was pretty good back toward the river. So far, it hasn't been."

The other four men remained quiet, staring into the fire, sipping from glasses, beer cans, or coffee cups. None of them had even acknowledged his presence.

"You alone?"

"Yep. More often than not, I am. I'm alone this trip."

"You been here long?"

"Came in three days before season opened. Been scouting, checking game trails and the like. A lot more sign than animals so far."

And that was it. None of the other men even looked up at him or said a word. "Well, have a good hunt, fellas."

Unfriendly bastards, he thought. *I would have been better off to read my book.*

The next morning, as he drank his second cup of coffee after breakfast, he heard an alarm clock ringing again for more than a minute before it was shut off. They were finally getting the fire started as he walked past their camp in the dark. *Fools,* he thought. *By the time they get breakfast out of the way, the horses saddled, and on their way, it will be well past shooting light.*

Then a very long ride to the river. And the elk will be bedded down long before they get there.

That evening, as he passed their camp, he noticed the lathered horses, all still saddled but one, tied to a rope strung between two trees. Hay was scattered beneath their feet. He looked toward the camp and the man who had spoken to him waved. He waved back and went on to his camp. After supper, he sat by the fire with a cup of coffee. He couldn't figure, why his mind was drawn back to the five men in that camp. For some reason, they bugged him. Not just that he had planned on being alone this trip. They weren't really intruders. They had as much right to camp and hunt here as he did. This wasn't *his* mountain, after all.

After supper, he glanced toward their camp and noticed that four of the horses were still saddled. *I bet the one taken care of belongs to the guy that talked to me last night,* he thought. In his mind, he studied the man as he had seen him the evening he had visited their camp, standing across the fire. He wasn't all that tall. Around six feet or just below. But he seemed bigger somehow. And he looked strong, well-muscled. Dark, tanned face and forearms below rolled up sleeves. There was something about the man that said he didn't sit in an office all day. You could get shoulders and arms like that in a gym, but he didn't think that was the case with this guy. With a broad chest and narrow waist, he looked very comfortable in his body. He probably worked with his hands for his living. Maybe construction of some kind. With the tan he had on his arms, probably ranching or farming. But he was definitely a working man.

The others he had no real feel for. No sense of who, or what, they were. Nondescript. Just people in an office somewhere with a picture of the wife and kids on the desk maybe. File cabinets filled with busy work. But if they left their horses saddled all this time, they sure had no thought for taking care of their stock. Ride them where they wanted to go and give them as little attention as required. Nothing more. To him, that spoke volumes about their character.

He sat his coffee cup on the log, stood, and went to the truck. From under the seat, he pulled out a bottle of Jack Daniels. He put the bottle in his coat pocket, returned to the log and put more wood on the fire, refilled his coffee cup, and headed toward the other camp.

As he approached the camp, one man turned and looked at him and then looked back to the fire with his head down. The man who had spoken to him the other night was sitting on a log. He looked up and smiled. The lines in his face said smiling came easily to this man. "Hi," he said. "See anything today?"

"A nice herd of cows and calves," he replied. He paused, glancing around the fire at the others. None of them looked his way. "There was a bull down in the trees off the end of the next ridge over, but he wouldn't come out. He squealed a couple times, and I squealed back, but I never got a look at him. I cow-called him a few times, but he must be a cagey ole coot," he replied. "How about you guys?"

"A couple of cows is all," said the man. "By the way, my name's John," the man said, and held out his hand.

"Hi, John. My name's Bob," he replied as they shook hands. John did not introduce the other men around the fire. Later, in bed, he would wonder about that. Was it some kind of subtle statement? Distancing himself a bit from the others? *Curious,* he thought.

John scooted along the log and said, "Wanna sit?"

"Don't mind if I do, thanks." As he sat, he pulled the bottle from his coat pocket, uncapped it, and splashed some whiskey in his coffee. He held the bottle out to John. "Wanna warm your coffee a bit, John?"

Taking the bottle, John poured a touch of whiskey in his coffee. "Thanks," he said.

"Just pass it around for whoever wants some." he told John. John handed the bottle to the man on his left. Each man took some of the whiskey as the bottle went around the fire, and the last man handed it back to him. The two men with beer had taken a sip from the bottle before passing it along. The others sweetened their coffee with it. He sat the bottle on the ground at the end of the log. Each of the other men had looked up and said,

"Thanks" as they took the bottle. Nothing more. But the ice had cracked just a bit.

That's how to break the ice, he thought. *Pour a little Jack on it.*

As conversation gradually picked up, he watched each man around the campfire. None but John looked like they really belonged here. Two had on what looked like brand-new blue jeans. Most of their boots looked new as well. *These guys probably spent a few days a year in the mountains and called themselves hunters.*

John certainly was a different breed than the other four. *Where does he fit in with this group?* Bob wondered. *Maybe he's a relative to one of them. Brother-in-law to one of them I'd think.* His boots weren't just scuffed. They were well worn and comfortable looking. *A few miles in the dirt on those boots.* Blue jeans faded nearly white on the thighs and a wool shirt patched at the elbows. His hat was white and grimed with sweat rings. His clothes sat on him like they belonged there. Like they had been there many days in the past. Working days. Callused hands confirmed his first impression of John. A working man. But the most noticeable characteristic was his face. Open, honest, and relaxed. When he smiled, he smiled with his whole face. He looked comfortable with himself and where he was. Now and in life. A smile seemed to be his normal expression, with broad lines around his mouth and eyes. *John's a man to ride the ridge with,* he thought.

The bottle of Jack made its way around the fire again when John refilled his coffee cup, and the conversation, mostly about hunting, continued.

Finishing the last of his coffee, he turned to John and said, "Well, fellas I'm going to hit the sack. You guys have a good hunt tomorrow."

"You, too, Bob," John said, and held out his hand again and shook with a firm grip. He had a strong but not aggressive grip. He lifted his hand to the others, picked up the bottle, and walked into the dark. As he turned toward his camp, John said, "If you get something down and need help getting it back to camp, let me know. I have a good pack mule."

"Thanks, John. I'll keep that in mind."

Back in his own camp, he filled the coffee pot with fresh water from the creek, got out the coffee and filters, and readied the pot for breakfast. He replenished the firewood in the lean-to, took his whiz by the stream, and got ready for bed. When he climbed into the sleeping bag, he picked up his book and held it on his chest. The sounds from the other camp took his attention back to them.

How many times had he hunted with guys like those four around that campfire? *All too many,* he thought. Sometimes with men he really didn't know—friends of friends.

He lay looking across the space between the two camps. Hearing their chatter and laughter. *What do they come here for?* he wondered. *Just for the hunt? Not likely. They're not hunters. Spend some time with the boys? A chance to get away from the wife and kids for a spell? Time away from the boss and the job?* It was hard to say for sure. They would have to get pretty lucky to head back home with meat and horns from this trip.

But it wasn't fair to say he'd hunted all that often with men like those guys. There were some he knew well and had hunted with who would have understood his feeling about the voices of the earth and his need to listen to them.

That was one thing he liked about his close friend Frank. They could spend time in camp or sit side by side on a log overlooking an old brushy burn and not speak for hours. They could lie in their sleeping bags staring at the stars and say nothing more than, "See ya in the morning." Guys like Frank were good to hunt with. He and Frank had spent a lot of time on the mountain together.

It wasn't that they didn't want to talk to each other. They just didn't need to talk all the time. Listening was far better than chatter. They each understood the other's need to get off alone for a time each day.

The others, the ones who thought they had a right to brag and jabber all the time that you were obligated to listen to, he tried to tolerate. Some he could. Some he couldn't, no matter how hard he tried. A time or two, he or

Frank had to mention that the beer stayed in the cooler until the guns were put away.

There was that preacher who talked his way onto the hunt one year. He had brought walkie-talkies for everyone and was jabbering on the damn things continuously. Five minutes of that constant chatter, and he'd turned off the preacher in mid-sentence. When he'd arrived back in camp mid-afternoon, the preacher was there wanting to know why he couldn't raise him on the walkie-talkie. He shrugged and handed the walkie-talkie back to the preacher. "Not my thing," he'd said. The preacher's voice was not one of those he wanted to listen to up on that mountain anyway.

CHAPTER 3

There was no camp near him this morning. Just a dead fire ring in the dark. No smell of horses. No alarm clocks going off in the dark. He was alone this year. Just him, the mountains, and hopefully a nice bull elk. He walked on to the bottom of the ridge.

He had been on several hunts with horses in the past. What a joy it is to ride a good horse in the mountains. There was that tall jenny mule Dave brought for him to ride one year. She was so tall, he had to get on a stump in order get into the saddle. Her gait was smooth, and being in the saddle on her was like sitting in a rocking chair. Not like that hammer-headed mare Larry brought for him to ride one year. She was like riding a pogo stick with a broken spring. She bucked him off on the upside of the mountain one afternoon. He preferred walking for miles uphill than riding that hammer-headed mare. Larry was ready to shoot her when she wouldn't load in the trailer when they were ready to leave.

Of course, he wished he still had that high-spirited Appaloosa mare. She was a good horse to ride anywhere. But especially in the mountains. She made sure you paid attention. She knew who was boss on a mountain trail and wouldn't let you forget it. She knew more about walking a mountain trail than he did, and she was always right. Especially when it came to getting through any tricky spots. If she decided she wasn't going a certain way at a certain place in the trail, you might as well just forget it, let her have her head, and hang on. She was always right. Trying to make her do what she didn't want to do was just plain stupid.

But it sure would be nice to have her here now on this hunt. It would have been especially nice for the days he was scouting. He could have seen a lot more country. And maybe more game. And an easy ride to take him up this ridge line to the game trails he was headed to now.

*   *   *

He spotted the first white tag tied to a tree limb near the trail. This was his jump-off point from the main trail. Another marker was barely visible in the dark a little way up the slope. Following the line of markers, he would be just over the top of the ridge overlooking a game trail winding up the other side. He had found that trail two days ago and had scouted it from top to near the bottom of the draw. There was good sign all along the trail. Plenty of water and feed below in the draw and canyon and good tree and brush cover for game to travel through with some security. Bedding areas were throughout the trees along the south-facing top of the ridge. Hopefully, he would be there when the sun came up and find that the herd moved up the mountain after a night of feeding. The breeze moving up the slope from the warming of the ridge top would keep his scent away from the herd.

What he wanted was to get a good kill shot near the ridge top. Without a quick kill, complications were certain. An injured bull elk would charge back down hill and be gone in a twinkle. That could make for a long tracking of the blood trail to finish the kill or find him dead somewhere. A bull elk hit, even hit hard in the body, could travel for a long way before going down and bleeding out. When he was found, it made for a lot of hard work to get him back to camp. And that could mean several trips with a packboard loaded with chunks of elk meat. And there was always a chance, if he didn't make a good shot, that the bull could travel a long distance and escape completely to die in the brush somewhere far away. Food for the coyotes and birds. But that's why he spent time at the range sighting his rifle and practicing.

A heart shot meant an obvious and relatively short blood trail. A good lung shot meant collapsed lungs and a short trail. A good head shot ended it all immediately.

The climb up this side of the ridge was not too bad, even in the dark. The little snow in the trees was no problem. The trail he had marked in the trees was easy to follow, and he didn't need to use the flashlight to find the tags he'd tied to the branches. He maintained a steady but not too fast pace. He was in good shape from miles on miles of walking year-round just for these times. There would be no panting or breathing hard when the time came to take a shot. Actually, the way things were going this morning, he should be on point before the sun came over the far mountains. Hunker down, stay warm and wait. "Wish I'd brought a thermos of coffee," he said.

In his mind, he went over the configuration of the slope below where he would be, how the trail looked as it wound up from the small creek in the bottom of the ravine, and how he would like to take the shot near the top. The far side of the ridge was not too heavily timbered. There were places of chest-high brush along the trail as it came up the slope. As the sun warmed the ridge top, the breeze would blow up the slope, carrying his scent up and over the ridge, away from any game below him. His stand would be above the trail, and if game came up that trail this morning, they would never have a chance to wind him. The stand he had selected yesterday afternoon was a good one. If he were still and quiet, no animals would know he was there until it was too late.

The only unknown at this point was whether they would come up that trail this morning as tracks indicated they had in days past. When he had scouted the trails yesterday, the trail closest to him had the most tracks and droppings, going both up and down. A small herd had obviously used that trail earlier in the day.

While scouting, he hadn't walked directly on the main part of the trail to keep his tracks and scent to a minimum. And he didn't want to check it this morning. Tempting, but not smart. That would be too risky, and he would leave fresh scent behind. There were other ways for them to get to the top of the ridge; other trails both above and below his stand. But from what he had seen yesterday, this trail appeared to be the most used. The trail branched about halfway up the slope, but he had checked both branches yesterday, and the branch coming closest to his stand was the most likely.

During the scouting, as he climbed the ridge, he had deliberately walked directly up the other branch, leaving his scent as he climbed. Near the branching of the trails, he had stopped and peed on the farther trail. If the elk started up that branch, they would smell him along that trail and where he had peed. He hoped these measures would guide the elk up the correct trail to where he would be waiting.

When he reached the stand, he removed a heavy cloth game bag from his pack and laid it on the ground where he would wait. Sitting on the bag would offer extra protection against the cold of the snow and ground and keep his pants dry. Too many times, years ago, he had sat directly on the ground, and the cold seeped up through his butt to his whole body. Wet pants were not something you wanted to be wearing when the temperatures were below freezing.

The stand itself consisted of a large fallen tree that had toppled from the up slope of the ridge and dropped straight down the side of the slope. The trunk was about three feet thick. Few branches remained attached to the trunk. All bark had sloughed off long ago. Partly rotted, the log provided good cover and a good rest for his rifle. He had good visibility to the bottom of the canyon where he hoped the elk would be traveling. Sitting behind the tree, only his head and the tops of his shoulders would be visible above the top of the log. A broken branch about five inches thick stuck out from the log and made a good back rest. His view of the draw below and nearly all the way down the deepening canyon was almost completely unobstructed. It was as if he had constructed the perfect stand.

He settled into place, back resting against the branch, and looked to the east. The sky over the farthest mountains showed some signs of sunrise. It would be more than half an hour before it was light enough to shoot. "Perfect," he said. "All I have to do now is wait." He was warm and comfortable. Only one thing would make it better. "Man, I wish I had that thermos of coffee."

As the surrounding area began to lighten enough to see, he surveyed the bottom of the draw and the trail as it wound up through the brush and small trees. There was no movement. Not even the birds were up yet. The only sound was a squirrel in the trees up on the ridge. No bugle or grunt of a bull elk. No squeal of a lead cow calling to her sisters.

He continued to scan the trail with binoculars from top to bottom, looking for places he could take a good safe shot if he had to before they reached the top. Options must always be considered. And you need to know what each looks like and feels like. He scoped every possible shot he may have to take, finding the right body position and how to hold the gun for that shot.

As the trail reached the top of the ridge and disappeared into the trees, the brush thinned out and was shorter. The best place for the shot he wanted was just before the trail entered the trees.

It was nearer the top of the ridge and would be less work to pack from. Not far to go uphill and then down the ridge the rest of the way to camp. It would have to be a drop him in his tracks shot. A wounded animal would run back down the slope when hit and then up into the trees on the opposite ridge and be gone, maybe for good. A solid head shot would be best. It would be a lot easier to make a short climb up the ridge and down off the point. No brush and good footing. The small creek to the meadow near his camp offers a gentler climb, but that path is cluttered with brush, thick willows to fight through, and a rocky, ankle twisting base.

Was it likely that it would happen the way he wanted? Probably not. It seldom did. You just took what you were given and made the best of it. He'd had it easier than what he was hoping for now in times past. But it was not a thing you could count on. Most often, it was long walks, mostly up and downhill, or hard rides on a horse, and a hell of a lot of hard work to get the game back to camp.

He brought the rifle to the top of the log, sighted on a small tree at the top of the trail, no more than seventy-five yards away, and adjusted his position so the area he wanted to shoot into would be easily reached with little movement. A comfortable, solid rifle rest and not a long shot. "It should be easy," he said. "If they come this way, that is." He brought the rifle back to his lap and looked over the top of the log to where he had chosen to shoot. Holding the rifle parallel to the log, he slipped it up over the edge, keeping it as close to the log as he could, practicing the movements he might need to use. In the same motion, he raised the stock to his shoulder and brought his cheek to the shooting position on the stock. With that minimum movement, he had the gun where he needed it. "Yep, easy," he said. And he would not give away his position.

Scanning the area again, he saw no movement in the trees below or in the brush along the trail. Nothing moved in the canyon as far as he could see. For such a large animal, a seven- or eight-hundred-pound bull elk sure could move quietly. And quick. Not there one second, and there the next. Too many times, that is what most hunters had seen, not there one second, there the next, and then poof, gone again. A few seconds of thundering hooves, crashing brush, and then . . . nothing. No sight. No sound. Just gone.

Glancing at the sky, he saw the clouds were continuing to scatter. "This is gonna be a good day on the mountain," he whispered as he smiled. But then, every day on the mountain is. The skiff of snow would melt when the sun was full up and the day warmed.

For more than an hour, he sat behind the dead fallen tree scanning the draw and the trail. He'd thought the elk would have been along by this time. But their day is not timed for him or any man. If they come this way, they will. If not, that's just the way it is sometimes—actually, most times.

And then. . . what was that farther down the draw? A cow squeal? Definitely a cow squeal. Or could that have been higher up, an echo from the ridge? It was hard to tell the exact direction sound came from in places like this. Trees, rocks, and just plain space can distort sound. Movement, that's what he needed. Movement. A few minutes later, he heard the sound again—definitely a cow talking to her sisters in the trees, in the lower part of the draw. They were on the move down there, but he couldn't tell which side of the canyon the cow was on.

Edgy now, he continued to glass the timber below him. "Come on, girls. Bring daddy to me." Glassing the timber and the sides of the small canyon, he controlled his emotions and breathing. "Stay calm. Take it easy." Movement out of the corner of his eye drew his attention. Eyes moved to pinpoint what he'd seen. "There it is." A squirrel running up a tree. He moved the binoculars back along the tree line at the bottom. Carefully looking from one place to another, slow and easy, he watched for any other movement. He stayed alert for more cow talk, or hopefully, the grunt of a bull. That would be nice. And then another cow squealed to his right. Had it been on the same side of the draw that he was on? Hard to tell. His excitement ratcheted up a notch.

With the binoculars still at his eyes, he reached into his coat pocket and brought out his cow call. Every movement he made now was slow and deliberate—hand movements, head movements, even his eyes. Placing the wedge of plastic and rubber in his mouth, he blew the two-toned short squeal of a cow elk calling to the herd. "I sure hope that sounds like a cow up here on the ridge." Watching. Watching. No movement in the trees. No more sound. "Where the hell are they?" he whispered. "Patience, boy." That's what he tried to teach the kids. But this is the heat of it. The crux. Short of actually taking the shot, the real excitement was in the final minutes of waiting, glassing, the anticipation. The pivotal thrill.

After the shot? That's when the real work began.

Hoof beats. Close. Real close. *Where the hell are they coming from?* he wondered. Slowly cocking his head this way and that, he tried to pick up the sound more clearly and get a fix on the direction of the sounds.

And then the sound stopped. Just plain stopped. No sound at all. Anywhere. *How could it just stop like that?* he wondered. With slow movement, he cocked his head to the right and saw slight movement out of the corner of his eye. The image of the flicker of an ear flashed through his mind. Turning his head further to the right with the slowest motion, there she was. A big cow elk was straight behind him, not more than ten yards away. His own cow call had brought her right to him. And he froze, gun in his lap.

She just stood there looking right at him, her head hanging low. From the corner of his eye, he watched her. Obviously, she had not winded him yet or she would be gone. How could she not smell him that close? He watched her without looking directly at her and scanned the trees behind and around her. She was alone. No calves, no other cows visible through the trees. And she stood there looking right at him. Could the camo clothes he wore make him that inconspicuous? *How can she not see me?* he thought.

Heart pounding, he gradually turned his back to her and slowly raised the gun chest high and brought the stock to his right shoulder, listening for any movement. He could feel her there, behind him. Watching him. And he thought, *What the hell can I do?*

No chance at all to turn to his right to get the gun into position. *That's the shortest way. But too awkward. I'll never get there and keep the gun in play.* He had to turn back to the left, against the lay of the log. It was a longer turn, but he could keep the gun in position all the way around. Was there any way he could turn slowly enough to get the gun into play? Not likely. Did he want a cow? *Hell yes!* he thought. *Meat is meat. You can't eat horns. And a cow is legal here.*

Gun still in position, he turned his head as slowly as he could back to the left until he was looking over his left shoulder. At the same time, he shifted his body to the left. The gun barrel swung over the top of the log. And he froze. Ninety degrees until he could get the gun on target. Tension built in his back and shoulders as he continued to turn into position, his legs pressing against the log, restricting a full-body turn.

Two things he could not believe—that he could move this slowly and that she was still there, head down, staring right at him. Watching him. *Almost there. Almost. Keep it slow.* Seeing her with his peripheral vision, he wanted so much to look right at her. Study her. But eye contact would spook her just as surely as too quick of a movement would.

Because she was uphill from where he sat, he needed to raise the gun higher, gradually making more tension in his back and shoulders. He needed to get the barrel past the bole of the roots where the tree had been ripped from the ground. If he got there, it would be a straight on, into the front of the chest shot. Hopefully, a heart shot. All these thoughts went through his mind as he continued to turn slowly.

With just a few inches to go, he came against the limits of his turn. His body was against the wall. There was no more turning without a complete change of his body position. The gun would have to come tight against his chest with no chance for sighting it. He would never take a snapshot without sighting. It might kill her, but she would die somewhere far away. He would never find her, wounded. And it just wasn't possible that she was going to stay where she was. He had turned as far as he could go. He knew it was over. She would get away. There was nothing he could do about that. So close. Ten degrees too short. But it was over.

And it happened. A jerk of her head to her right on that thick neck, pushing off on powerful front feet with explosive movement, she was on her way up the ridge farther to his left. He snapped his body to his right, spinning to lay prone on the ground, rifle thrust in front of him. Too late. He was only in time to see her disappear into the thicker trees. Nothing now but a brown body and a yellow butt charging away through the trees up the ridge. No chance at all for a shot. And then, as always, no sound at all. No hooves pounding on solid ground. No brush snapping. It was as if she had come to a dead stop or vanished in a breath of wind. Gone.

The only thing to do now was track her, try to come on her along the ridge. Or perhaps there were others with her that he hadn't seen. He walked to where she had stood and looked at the tracks, earth scarred by hooves where she had bounded away. With his rifle in the crook of his arm, he began the tracking with not much hope or effort.

Following her tracks, he saw where she had come down from the far end of the ridge on a well-used game trail. Her tracks were the only ones fresh this morning. When she bolted, she followed the same trail up the ridge for only a short distance. Then she had angled over the top of the ridge to the right and down the other side toward the creek that bordered the main trail. There was no catching her now. She was spooked and gone. Standing over her tracks, he said, "By golly, I called her to me though. How about that?"

He sat on the crumbling stump of a tree logged years ago. He could see partially down both sides of the ridge and both up and down the trail she had used in coming to him. He wanted a cigarette real bad but knew that would not be a wise thing to do at this point. If she had been here, there certainly could be others nearby, even though he had seen no sign of them. Smoke would warn them from a long way off. If they had been here, close, they would have gone with her, and he would have seen their tracks. All that he saw told him she was alone. A cow alone at this time of year was certainly unexpected. She should be with a herd, large or small. But she had been alone.

He lay the rifle in his lap, inhaled a deep breath, and let out a long sigh. So close, yet so far. "Man, that was something," he said with a deep sigh. And he smiled to himself as in his mind he saw her again, standing there behind him, looking right at him, trying to figure out what in the hell he was. A jarring encounter for both of them, no doubt. And a thrill. A real thrill. At least for him. More than likely frightening for her. He would never forget her. To be that close to a wild, on the hoof elk was something he never could have dreamed would happen. To him or anyone else.

For several minutes he sat, rethinking how it had gone, collecting himself, all the time scanning the trees on all sides. He turned to look over his right shoulder and mentally slapped himself in the head. "Not again, you dummy." he said with a smile. He would never again look over his right shoulder while hunting. That was a lesson he had just learned the hard way. He stopped the turn of his body and only turned his head a short way to the right. Then he turned to the left, nearly all the way around, until he could see the entire area behind him and down the ridge. At least his gun would be in position if there was something there. Of course, now, there wasn't.

The sun was higher in the sky now. It felt as if it might be somewhere around nine or ten in the morning. It was getting late for further movement by the herds. They would most likely be in bed by now. "What do I do now?" he said. That was the question. He slipped off the pack and got out an apple, a power bar, and a bottle of water. "Have a bite and think it over."

Finishing the food, he drank more of the water and put the bottle and the power bar wrapper back in the pack. Slipping his arms through the pack straps, he threw the apple core into the brush and stood. "Might as well back track that trail she came down and see where she came from," he said. He wanted to learn as much as he could about her movement and file it away for future use. He walked to the side of the ridge he had been watching from, looking for the trail. When he saw it in the near distance, he began to parallel it up the ridge, a gentle climb.

From time to time, he swung closer to the trail to check for tracks and droppings. There were several old tracks going both directions, but hers were the only fresh tracks in the dirt and pine needles. There were also old tracks wandering through the trees. Elk, and a few deer, had moved through this area on a regular basis in the past few days. Maybe she was the cow that had been calling earlier looking for her herd. Maybe. It was unusual to find a cow all alone this time of year. Or any time for that matter. In less than a quarter of a mile, the trail veered to the left and down the ridge to the draw he had been watching.

He walked to the head of the trail where it dropped off to the canyon below. This trail, unlike the one he had been watching, wound through heavy brush and trees. It was a steep trail, twisting along a rocky ledge near the top, no doubt easy travel for deer and elk. Not so for a man. Up or down this trail would demand your full attention. And it would be very noisy through all that brush. There were no indications the cow had come up that trail.

He walked back to the right to the other side of the ridge. Among the trees, he found obvious bedding areas on the south-facing slope. Round places with pine needles showed elk had lain here to sleep the day away. They usually bedded on the south side of the ridges for more warmth from the sun during the day, in the trees for cover and quiet. A great place to rest after a night of feeding. These bedding sites were like the ones he had found on the south side of the ridge adjacent to his stand and in many other places he had hunted.

Like he'd always told the kids, "Find their dining room, find their bedroom, and wait for them in the hallway."

He walked back to the trail and turned up the ridge to see where the cow had come up from the bottom. For the next half mile, he followed the trail, and somewhere he lost her tracks. "Not really paying attention," he chided himself. He stopped, looking up toward the end of the ridge at least another half mile or more away. He knew that from there, the ridge dropped off sharply to the bottom and was heavily timbered. "No need to go there," he said.

Ahead, a bit lower along the ridge, a large outcrop of rocks jutted out into space. He had seen the rocks before but had not checked them out. Now he headed for them to view the bottom of the canyon and see where he was in relation to landmarks he had memorized. From there, it would probably just turn into another day of scouting trails, trying to figure out game movements, trails used, and directions of travel. The more you know, the better the opportunity to get some meat.

Then again, there is always that stream by the camp. It looked as if there might be some good fishing holes close to camp. He'd brought his pole and some bait. He could even grub for some bugs to use as bait as well. Maybe an afternoon of fishing would be a relaxing way to while away some time and catch some dinner.

Moving across the rock outcrop, he came to a boulder about the size of a car that overlooked the canyon. The canyon side was much steeper this far up the ridge. From the top of the boulder, it was a drop of about seventy-five feet to the slope below him into rocks and brush. He lifted the binoculars, sat on the edge of the rock, and scanned the canyon bottom and the slope across from him. In the sun the rock beneath him was warm. Clouds in the sky had broken down to scattered white balls drifting lazily across the blue sky. Cloud shadows skimmed across the roof of the forest. He took out a water bottle and sipped from it.

To his right, the canyon continued downhill between the two ridges, which widened to where they ended. He could see that both ridges dropped off sharply not far above where he now sat. Over the past mile or so, the stream had collected more water, and he could hear it gurgling through the bottom of the canyon. A large bowl of heavy timber spread for maybe a mile or more beyond the end of the ridges. From that point the terrain dipped out of sight, or almost seemed to. It was difficult to tell even with the binoculars.

Tightly packed pines stood shoulder to shoulder all along the ridges, where they dropped sharply to the bowl, then spread tightly packed across that shallow bowl and beyond. Here and there, pockets of Aspen groves, now red and gold, flared color like spot fires among the dark green. Yellow-needled Tamarack dotted the dark green of the pines. The small creek that flowed through the bottom of the canyon disappeared into a small marsh of tall, light green reeds and scrub willow at the edge of the trees and the head of the bowl. No stream bed was visible through the forest of trees. From the bottom of the ridges and the start of the bowl, it was a long distance to dark mountains rising in a line of peaks stretching north and south. How far that might be he could only guess. Miles away, no doubt. "That must be the big river way over there against those mountains," he said.

For several minutes, he gazed into that far space, wondering how it would be to just roam over there for no other reason than to see what it's like, not on that Forest Service maintained trail, but right down the ridge and overland through the trees. How would it be to walk through that thick timber, shaded by massive old pines? A thick bed of dropped needles and cones soft beneath his feet. Maybe camp beside the big river for a time. Just to be there. Carrying in only what he needed and bringing out nothing but his trash and memories—mind pictures of all the things he would see and touch and hold close to his mind and heart forever.

"Yeah, that would be nice, but it sure isn't the time of year to take that walk," he sighed. Overnight, snow and sub-zero temperatures would lock him in along that river for six months. The game would leave for winter grazing areas, and he would really be left alone. Forever.

Raising the binoculars to his eyes again, he glassed the bottom of the canyon where he could see the streambed winding down through the brush. "A lot of water must rush down that wrinkle in the world when the snow melts in the spring."

CHAPTER 4

Warm sun caressed his back. Leaning back on his hands, he looked to the bottom of the shallow canyon and the creek that flowed through it. Directly across from him, a buck stepped into his field of vision and stopped inside the edge of the trees just above the level of the stream. Ears perked, the deer looked from left to right and back again. His tail raised and flicked back and forth. Some three hundred or more yards away, the deer was indistinct through the binoculars. It stood well back in the shadows of the trees, wary of coming into the clear until he was convinced there was no danger.

Laying the binoculars on the rocks beside him, he picked up his rifle and shouldered it, elbows resting on his knees. He adjusted the scope to twelve power and sighted on the buck. The head and front quarters were now clear. The main body was behind a large pine. "Mule deer," he said. "Good solid body. Big. Wide horns. Sure wish it was deer season."

Slowly he pivoted on his butt and pushed his legs out behind him. Prone now, he anchored his elbows on the rocks and sighted on the deer again with a more solid rest for the gun and scope.

Yes, it was a large mule deer. Its horns were in the shade of the pine, and he couldn't tell how large they were or how they branched. Where the horns protruded from the head, the beams appeared very thick at the base. The eye guards were tall and curved slightly to the outside. "Man, what a beauty," he whispered.

The deer stepped one front foot forward and froze. Nose twitching, tail flicking, he tested the wind. Large ears turning left and right, he listened for anything out of the ordinary, nose touching the breeze for any foreign scent.

For what seemed like long minutes, the deer remained as he was. Then he stepped forward with the other front foot and his head came into the sunlight. "Holy shit. That's one big deer." Right front foot, left back foot. Pause. Left front foot, right back foot. Tiptoeing slowly forward, the deer moved toward the flow of water in the stream bed, head held high, alert. He moved so cautiously, it was as if he knew he was being watched.

When the deer reached the stream, he again scented the air, looked down the canyon and then up. His horns were broad and thick. Four widespread branches on each side. "No, wait a second, there's another point on the longest branch of the right side." A four by five. Must go thirty inches wide or better. And he could go two hundred and fifty pounds on the hoof. "Wow! Now that's one monster of a deer!"

He watched the buck through the scope as it lowered its head to the stream and drank. He had no thought of pulling the trigger. Hunting season or not, this was just too sweet. To see a deer like this, here on the mountain, and watch him as he went about his normal activity was just breathtaking. "I'll bet this old boy has populated these mountains with a good many sons and daughters over his lifetime," he whispered.

The deer raised his head, water dripping from his chin. Always alert, he nibbled leaves from the brush growing close to the stream. He dipped his head and drank again. Head up, he turned broadside in the scope. The deer turned his head back over his shoulder to look back down the canyon. He wasn't really on high alert now but certainly wary. "He didn't get to the age he is by being stupid," he whispered. A few more bites from the brush and the deer turned away from him. The horns, now compared to the width of the front shoulders, were wider than what had first appeared. *That's a real trophy mule deer.* he thought. *Maybe those horns are way wider than thirty inches. That deer would make the 'Boone and Crockett' book for sure.* How special to have seen such an animal like this, here, in his own backyard.

Slowly, the buck walked back up the slope to the trees from where he had come. Before he entered the trees, the deer turned his head back over his left shoulder and looked across the canyon as if to say, "I know you're there." And then he was gone. With confidence, he bounded up into the trees and no doubt off to bed for the rest of the day.

And he let out a long sigh, releasing breath he didn't realize he had been holding, and raised his head from the scope. "Amazing." he said aloud. "Just absolutely amazing. Pure beauty." The entire trip up here, the long treks over the ridges each day, the sore muscles, all had just been validated. He was stunned with awe.

Rolling back to a sitting position on the rocks, he laid the rifle across his lap, stared into the canyon, and took his pack off. He removed the sandwich, chips, another apple, and a bottle of water from the pack. He watched and listened to all that was around him as he ate his lunch and watched the shadows change as the day moved on. Silent clouds pulled their shadows across the forest roof. No sound but the breeze in the pines. Even the squirrels were quiet now. And he sensed the life all around him. Trees, animals, the breeze, the rocks. The trickle of water far below. All alive. All speaking to him. All touching him with their magic. "There's no better place in this world right now than right here on this rock."

When he finished the apple, he threw the core into the canyon below him, mapping out the game trails in his mind. He put the sandwich and chips bags back into the pack and took another long drink from the water bottle. Shouldering the pack, he picked up the rifle, turned on his butt, and slid off the back side of the rocks. Standing, he looked around him through the trees on the ridge top. "A whole herd of elk could have walked right up to me like that cow did while I watched that deer, and I wouldn't have seen or heard them," he said. And then he snorted a laugh at himself for the rapture he had felt watching that deer. What an amazing and beautiful animal. Not many people in this world had ever seen such a thing.

Without thinking or making a conscious decision, he turned down the ridge spine, through the trees, and headed back to camp. He was in no hurry now. But then, up here, he seldom was in a hurry. Oh, there were things that needed to be done right away, at the right time. But hurry? There was no real need for hurry. Not up here.

He walked downhill, no brush under the trees to fight through, and it was a nice, sunny day. He didn't have to think about what he was doing, wandering in and out of the shade of the pines and aspen. His mind floated back and forth between the two events of this morning—the cow elk sneaking up behind him and that magnificent mule deer buck. With both, it was easy for him to relive the excitement he had experienced. Every second of both events was locked in his memory forever. They would be good stories to tell the kids.

With the cow elk, he went over how it had happened and what he did. Could he have done something different? Could he have done it better? Ultimately, it was what it was. The situation dictated what he could do. He'd never expected an elk to come from that direction. *That's another lesson learned,* he thought. And to get that close to a man was unheard of. His position had been such that there was just no way to get the gun into play without spooking her. Even if he had looked back sooner and seen her coming, changing his position to get the gun into play would have alerted her to where and what he was. As soon as she saw him move so he could aim the rifle, she would have spooked and been gone. He had never in his life been that close to a live elk on the hoof, and he had been transfixed by her sheer size. He had taken several elk and was always awed by their size. But standing that close to him on the hoof seemed to magnify her.

The buck was something different. He could not have taken a shot because it was not deer season. Would he have taken the shot if it were in season? Despite how he had been awed by the sight of such a magnificent animal, he knew now that he would have taken the shot. Admitted that to himself. That is what the hunt is all about, after all. It would have been a risky shot, well over two hundred yards or more, downhill. But the rock would have been a good rest for the rifle, and he was confident of a clean kill.

And then he would have spent two or three days getting him out of that canyon on a packboard.

"I sure wish I'd had my 35 mm camera with me with the telephoto lens to get a shot of him as he fed on the brush, or the one where he looked back over his shoulder before he went back into the trees. Those pictures would look as good on my wall as the horns would."

During scouting trips or other times on the mountain, he had taken many more shots of deer and elk with that camera than with a rifle. Eagles in flight or sitting high in a tree. Red Tail hawks on the wing, circling in a blue sky. The Great Horned owl warming in the mid-morning sun. Those were not just memories. He had them to look at any time he wanted and remember all the circumstances of each picture. "I sure wish I'd had that camera with me out there on that rock this morning."

On his way down the ridge, he stopped at the stand, folded the ground cloth, and stuffed it in the backpack. "Just getting' on back to camp," he said.

CHAPTER 5

When he reached camp, he unloaded the rifle and laid it on the seat of the truck. From his cooler, he took out a Pepsi, popped the tab, and took a long drink. He sat on the log by the fire ring and lit a cigarette. The entire afternoon was his to do with as he pleased. He wasn't sure what that was. That was the issue. When he finished the Pepsi and the cigarette, he went to the truck and removed his spinning rod from behind the seat. From the cooler, he got a container of worms and headed toward the creek. Not a thought-out decision, just a subconscious act. He followed the bank of the stream to the big pool downstream from camp. The stream made a wide turn at a high cut- bank where the water was clear and deep. "There should be some trout in that hole," he said.

For him, fishing was a lazy sport, just sitting on the bank, cool grass under his butt, his back against a log or tree trunk, and the breeze in his face. Cast upstream, let the worm swim down the current and through the deep water. If trout were in there, and hungry, he might catch something. If not, it made no difference to him. If he dozed off and took a nap, line still in the water, no big deal. To catch or not to catch was all the same to him. The ease of the task was just how he liked it. The shade of an aspen with its fidgety leaves and the sound of the stream were all he really needed.

He didn't even take his book with him. Just he and the stream and the aspens, and they would get along just fine. The reflection of white clouds in the blue sky drifting upstream smoothed some of the wrinkles in his soul. If he caught something big enough for dinner, that would be a plus. Two hours on that bank took nothing away from him, catch or not. It was just another piece of the pleasure of being up here. Another piece of the tapestry of this mountain, this stream, this time spent up here.

Back in camp, no fish on the stringer, he put the pole in the gun rack behind the truck seat, the worms went back in the cooler, and he got out a can of Dinty Moore's Stew. The sun was low in the sky. Shadows were sneaking across the meadow. A good dinner and maybe a short evening hunt across the meadow where the land was more or less flat. He started the fire, put the grill across the rocks, and got out the deep cast-iron pot from the container in the bed of the truck. He poured the stew into the pot and sat it on the grill over the fire. Two pieces of buttered bread and a glass of milk would complete dinner, with a Hershey Bar with almonds for dessert. While the stew was heating, he got his book from the lean-to to read a few pages.

Reading for him was not a hobby. It was a passion. Almost any type of book. Often, he had two or three books going at the same time. Up here, the book was an accessory. Something to do to fill some time. It was the total experience of being here that counted. Reading was a part of his life, and that included here.

Occasionally, he stirred the stew until it began to boil, then he sat it off the fire to let it cool while he buttered the pieces of bread, poured a glass of milk, and got out a bowl and spoon. Yeah, the stew would be greasy, but he loved it. Who knows how many cans of Dinty Moore Stew he had eaten over the years. Especially up here. It was easy, nutritious, and tasty.

When he'd finished eating, he sat by the fire that was now nearly dead with just a tendril of smoke curling up through the trees. Looking around, he felt a bit edgy. He had been up and down the ridge nearly every morning and evening since he had been here.

He went over the game trails in his mind. But he hadn't been around the country all that much. At least not on this trip. He was familiar with most of the surrounding country to some degree because he had scouted and hunted it in years past. So far, he had confined himself on this trip to the ridge he had been on this morning because he had seen so much sign there the first day out. *Maybe I should have looked around more. Checked for other game movement,* he thought.

He sat looking across the creek. He had never crossed the creek and knew nothing about that part of the country. There was just no good place to cross the stream without getting wet. Sitting on the log, he took a deep breath. His body odor caught his attention. "You're getting' kind of rank, old boy. You need a bit of a washin' and some clean clothes. Later, if I get back from my walk in time. Or tomorrow afternoon, for sure."

It didn't seem odd how he talked to himself out loud up here. That's just the way he was, had always been, and he didn't think much of it. Alone, talking was just thinking out loud. And it was good to hear a voice, even if it was just his own.

He washed the bowl and spoon at the creek. What was left of the stew went in a plastic container with a lid snapped on it. He wiped out the cooking pot with a paper towel and tossed it in the fire pit. The bowl and spoon along with the leftover stew went on the floor inside the truck. There was no need to attract critters, big or small, to the smell of the stew. He had seen no bear sign, but that didn't mean they weren't here somewhere. The last thing he needed was a bear grubbing around the camp while he was gone or here in bed.

He put on his coat and hat, slung the pack on his back, and picked up and loaded the rifle. He slid a Hershey bar with almonds into his shirt pocket. Turning away from the camp, he walked around the back of the truck and toward the long meadow to the north. He had only explored the far side of this area and the ridges beyond some five years ago on his first trip here. At that time, it didn't seem promising. Not much sign of game movement, so he had ignored it.

The ground was covered with low-growing plants and grass. When dry, these plants were like walking on Rice Krispies on the kitchen floor. They were wet and soft now after the snow had melted. He made little noise as he walked through the meadow. The ground would be boggy toward the far end where the ground water formed the small stream that ran down the canyon where he had seen the buck this morning. From there, even into the trees, the ground stayed relatively level for most of a quarter of a mile.

With no actual plan in mind, he moved toward the trees to the left to avoid any swampy ground. A large grove of aspen lined the west side of the meadow between the bog and the pines. Looking at the sky, he estimated he had a bit more than an hour of good shooting light left. "This isn't really a hunt," he said. "Just a walk through the country." He had taken the gun just in case. You never knew when you might come on to game.

He moved through the aspen grove that grew along the edge of the meadow, red and gold leaves scattered on the ground, and stopped to peer into the pines up the slope beyond. Lodgepole pine and a few tamaracks grew thick up the ridge to the west. It would get dark in there pretty quick once the sun sank below the ridge tops. He remembered that the area ahead of him formed a shallow bowl before rising sharply around the edges. No actual stream was in the meadow, but ground water collected on the east side of the meadow where it formed the stream that emptied into the canyon. The ground at the far end of the meadow was wet and boggy.

He had only been up on the higher ground years ago and didn't have time for that now. He decided he would follow the rim of the meadow and the bowl as much as the lay of the land and the trees would allow. "No sense in gettin' your boots all muddy, old son," he said. This would be a nice late afternoon walk and circle back to the camp. He pulled the Hershey bar from his shirt pocket, ripped open the wrapper and took a bite. Winding through the trees, he started up a slight slope angling to his right and then stopped dead still.

Elk tracks going the same direction he was going were everywhere. Lots of elk tracks. And a few deer tracks as well. There was no actual game trail, but there were enough prints to indicate that several elk had been through this area in the last day or two while he was camped right over there. Musing, he thought, "How would it be to get a nice elk here, so close to camp? Now that would be just too easy, loading it into the truck right here." A smile formed on his lips and a chuckle rose in his throat. He swiveled the rifle from his shoulder and held it in the crook of his arm. "Might as well be ready, old son. You never know."

He moved up the slope to where it began to rise more steeply up the mountain. He continued to follow the arc of the bowl, circling back toward the head of the canyon and the camp. The trees were thicker, and he moved slow, stopping often to listen and watch and check the tracks. As he neared the mouth of the canyon, the elk and deer tracks increased. Elk tracks were everywhere. He found numerous piles of droppings for both deer and elk. A glossy sheen on some of the droppings indicated they were fresh enough to have been left this morning.

A trail came out of the near side of the canyon, near the head of the stream, and then scattered through the trees up the slope. Both deer and elk had used that canyon to funnel into these trees and then probably up the south-facing slope of the mountain to bed during the day.

Once past the canyon mouth and back toward his camp, there were virtually no tracks. "No surprise there," he said. "Day or night, they aren't going to walk into my camp." And, of course, they knew he was here. "No surprise there either. They could have stood right over here in the trees and watched me have breakfast or dinner."

He sat on a decaying log, rifle across his lap to think. He needed to put together all that he had seen here and tie it in with what he had learned this morning and what he knew about the trails over there. Had he been in the wrong place the past few days? Did the game know he was on that specific ridge? Did they then change their pattern to avoid him? That's possible. Or were there more herds in this area than he'd thought? One group bedding on the ridge where he had seen the cow this morning? Another coming along the opposite ridge, following the canyon to its end, and moving through these trees? That was possible, too. From what he had just seen, there were obviously two, maybe three small groups in the area.

Or were they just on the move? No question they would have to move to lower winter range when the snow got serious. "Was that it? Did they sense the snows coming soon?"

What do I do now? Where do I hunt? he thought. There was a lot to ponder. A lot to mesh together. The trail he had watched this morning had frequent travel. There was at least one elk in that area. He had seen her up close and personal. And where there was one, there were usually more. On the other hand, there had definitely been elk and deer moving through this area as well. Some of it probably this morning. "So, what do I do in the morning?" he wondered.

He lit a cigarette and tried to let his mind settle. When the cigarette was finished, he ground it out on the log, put the butt in his pocket, and stretched his legs in front of him. "Hell, old son, just do what you're gonna do and don't worry about it. Don't overthink it. Just let it happen as long as the weather holds, or the week runs out, whichever comes first." In the morning he would just do what came to him. No second-guessing. The way he had always done it.

Rising from the log, he put the rifle in the crook of his arm and headed back to camp. It would be dark by the time he got there now. What was he going to do? He just wasn't going to think about it now. He'd sleep on it and see what choice came with the morning.

Back at camp, he unloaded the rifle and put it in the gun rack above the fishing pole. He fixed tomorrow's lunch, put the pack in the back of the lean-to, got his book, and climbed into the truck. He started the engine to make sure the battery would stay fully charged and read from the book for a while by the roof light. Thoughts and questions of tomorrow's hunt were put away for now. The container of leftover stew was on the truck floor. He took off the lid and spooned out bites to nibble on as he read.

Before he went to bed, he rinsed and filled the coffee pot at the creek and sat it by the fire, ready for the morning. He replenished the firewood in the back of the lean-to for the morning fire. As he undressed, he thought, "Bath and clean clothes tomorrow afternoon, boy. Definitely. Getting a little gamey your own self." He smiled. Rolling his pants and shirt, he stuffed them to the bottom of the sleeping bag, slid in, zipped it up, and pulled the lamp close. He read until his eyes drooped, stowed the book in the backpack, turned off the lamp and slid down into the sleeping bag.

The questions about where he would hunt would be answered in the morning. Tomorrow would be another good day on the mountain. A brief look to the stars through the trees and he was asleep within minutes.

CHAPTER 6

When he woke in the morning, his first thought was, *Damn, it's cold*. His ears burned. Even his cheeks seemed stiff. His body was warm in the bag, but from the shoulders up, he was really cold. In the dark, he could see little. "No snow. That's good. But damn, it's cold." Looking up through the trees, he saw no stars. The dark sky was nondescript. He quickly got a fire going and turtled back into the bag.

When he got out of the bag several minutes later, the cold hit him hard. "It's gotta be well below zero this morning," he said. After throwing a couple of logs on the fire, he put the coffee pot over the flames, went to the truck, and got in on the driver's side. He started the truck and cranked the heater up to maximum. From the clothes bag, he got out thermal underwear, fresh blue jeans, a clean flannel shirt, and heavy wool socks. Shivering, he stripped down to his boxers and wriggled into the clean clothes. A few minutes later, the heater was blowing warm air. "Didn't count on this cold this morning." he said.

He knew he should not find the conditions odd. Not up here. He was over seven thousand feet in elevation. Weather can change in a heartbeat at this altitude. A little something growled in the back of his mind and tightened his stomach just a pinch. "Hey, no big deal." he said. "Just another day on the mountain. Don't get stupid. Keep an eye on the sky."

The fire was going well and would keep him warm while he ate. He broke out breakfast and went to the fire. The coffee was ready. As the bacon sizzled in the skillet, he rolled the sleeping bag. Instead of leaving it in the lean-to, he took it to the truck. Mentally, he noted the change in his routine but didn't dwell on it. The rule he lived by up here was just do what your mind and body tell you to do. Everything is for a reason.

The log under his butt by the fire was cold. Real cold. It seeped up through his body into his lower back. Eggs, bacon, and hot coffee. Always a good start for the day on the mountain. "When the sun gets up, it'll be warmer."

Pulling a cigarette from his shirt pocket, he lit it and stared into the fire, thinking now about what he would do today for a hunt. He weighed the options based on what he had found on the other side of the meadow last evening. That would be the easiest hunt by far. Walking there and back was just minutes instead of an hour or more up the ridge. He could find a spot to sit in that aspen grove and watch the area in the trees where he had found all the tracks and the head of the canyon. If he got something down there and dropped it in its tracks, he could drive the truck to the left of the meadow and probably get all the way to the end of the aspen grove while avoiding the bog. That would be good. No need for the packboard. Skin it out, quarter it, and put it in the bed of the truck. He had been able to drive right to a downed elk a couple times. And with an elk, that sure made the job a lot easier.

On the other hand, he had seen just as many tracks on the ridge and the trails that ran up its side. And there was that cow, the only elk on the hoof he had seen so far. Where there was one, there were likely to be others. This time of year, they certainly would be herding up, gathering for the rut and the move to winter range. The cow on her own yesterday was an anomaly. In weeks, maybe days, the herds would be much larger. Dominant bulls would establish their herds. And soon they would all be moving to winter range.

The two options faded in and out of his mind. He wasn't confused, just juggling the choices. "Almost time to head out," he said. "Get going and what will be will be."

Preparing his pack for the day, he added a thermos of hot coffee. That would help against the cold. The thermal underwear made a difference against the cold as well. The heavy gloves were a must today. From the clothes bag, he put a camouflaged ski mask in the backpack.

The pack on his back, rifle on his shoulder, he locked the truck, pulled on the gloves, and placed the keys on top of the right front tire. Turning to his right, he headed for the main trail and the ridge. He didn't look back at the meadow and gave it no more thought. He just did what he did and lived with it. It would be the ridge again today. Tomorrow? Who knows? A glance at the sky told him nothing. Dark, distant, and starless. There were no clues what the weather held for the day. "We'll find out when the sun comes up," he said.

When he reached the area of his stand from yesterday, he continued on up the ridge at a slow pace. It was still dark with no wind. But as he climbed, he felt the air getting colder. Not much, but noticeable.

He passed the log on the left side of the slope where his stand would be and went a short distance further up the ridge and then doubled back. As he sat on a stump, he laid the rifle across his lap and removed the pack. His body was warm from the exertion of climbing the ridge, and the thermal underwear held his body heat in. But his nose was running, and his ears burned from the cold. He removed a ski mask from the pack and put his baseball cap in a side pocket. The ski mask would keep his ears and his entire face warm even if the cold continued or got worse. He took out the thermos and drank hot coffee directly from it, setting the cup on the ground beside him. "Now that's good," he said with a sigh.

He needed light to see what was what. There was no way he could see tracks or determine if they were fresh if he couldn't see them in the dark. In the meantime, he might as well just sit and wait. The stand was about one hundred yards back down the ridge. He could get to it quickly if need be.

The meadow and the aspen grove came to mind, but he didn't question his decision, if decision it was. He was here and that was that. Whatever happened today and from this point on would be the result of coming back to this ridge instead of the meadow. If he got skunked here today, he could try the meadow tomorrow. Or maybe even the next ridge over. The coffee was good, hot and warming. From the pack he took a power bar, unwrapped it and took a bite.

As he put the wrapper from the power bar in a pocket of the pack, his head snapped up. The long, challenging squeal and grunt of a bull elk echoed through the trees. It sounded as if it came from down in the bottom of the canyon, between the head of the two ridges. Maybe! Definitely a bull elk. Definitely to his right and below him. And absolutely down toward the end of the canyon. Exactly where it had come from was hard to tell. He turned his body on the stump to face the draw, alert now, ears perked for any sound. The sound of a bull elk bugling in the wild was no doubt the most thrilling, nerve tingling sound he had ever heard. It covered him with goose bumps and shortened his breathing every time he heard it. "Come on, big fella. Let me hear it again. Talk to me," he whispered.

He was probably close to a half mile below the rocks he had sat on where he saw the buck yesterday. "Should I go up there? No! Just sit tight. Wait and see." His voice now a whisper. He didn't want to have to shoot to the bottom of that canyon to get the bull. A risky shot to take. And a long, hard walk to get back out, loaded with meat.

If that bull was where he thought, he was sure there were several ways it could go. It could go up the other ridge, in which case it would be gone and he would never see it. He would hear it again if it bugled, but he would never see it.

It could go straight up the draw to the area he had been last evening. In that case, from the stand, he would have a shot at him down in the draw. Not a hard shot, but not the one he wanted.

It could come up the ridge he was on now, above him, and bed up there. That would make it difficult to move on him. But possible.

Or, fingers crossed, it could come up the draw to the trails he had watched yesterday morning. For him that would be perfect. He could move to his stand and wait.

Excited now, he felt no cold. He took another drink of coffee, replaced the cap, and screwed the cup on. With the thermos back in the pack, he slipped it on and stood with the rifle in both hands. The sky was getting a little lighter, but not light enough to shoot yet. The question was, how quick would the elk move, and where would they go.

As he moved across the ridge, closer to the slope that led down into the draw, a cow squealed down in the bottom. "That was definitely down toward the head of the canyon. They're not moving very fast," he said. "Probably a small herd." After a pause, "I gotta quit talking out loud to myself."

He pulled his cow call from his pocket and put the twine it was attached to around his neck. "Don't talk to her now. Wait. See where they're going. Patient! Be patient!"

Fifteen minutes later, there was another cow call. He wasn't sure if it was closer, but they were still down in the canyon. "Sounds like they could be going right up the creek," he murmured. With cautious steps, he turned and walked as quietly as possible back to the top of the ridge. There, he turned downhill toward the stand. A guess, but one he hoped was right.

When he reached the area adjacent to the stand, he removed the pack and leaned it against a tree trunk. He took out the thermos and binoculars and hung the binoculars around his neck. While he stood there, the bull grunted again. Just a grunt. Not a full bugle. It seemed closer and still down in the canyon. "They're coming. But what are they gonna do?" Taking a deep breath, he consciously controlled his breathing and excitement. He took the ground cloth from the pack and tucked it under his left arm. *This might be it. This just might be it.* These thoughts went through his mind as he crept down the slope toward the stand.

The elk were down in that draw, moving up. It was light enough to see now, mostly. Light enough to shoot if he had to. A little more light would be better. He wanted as much light as possible and the right shot. A knock-down shot. "Not down in that draw if I can help it," he said.

When he reached the stand, he stood behind a tree, keeping it between him and the draw. Around the edges of the tree, he glassed the bottom of the draw from the deepest that he could see and back toward where it branched out into the meadow. Nothing. No movement. *Did they head up the ridge above me? Are they still coming?*

Staying alert, he alternately scanned the draw and up through the trees above him on the ridge where the cow had come from yesterday. He turned to his left and scanned the trees on the ridge across from him. He saw nothing. The monologue continued in his head. *Slow and careful,* he thought to himself. *Slow and careful.* With his present position, he could watch the bottom of the draw and the ridge with only slight movements of his head and eyes.

Without thought, he stepped quietly to the stand, laid out the ground cloth, and slid to the ground, sitting as he had yesterday. He turned slightly more to the right in order to keep an eye on the ridge behind him. "Don't let them go slipping up behind you again," he whispered.

Scanning the canyon, he saw nothing. No movement. No elk herd. He unscrewed the thermos and took a drink of coffee. Still hot.

Waiting. That's all he had now. Wait and hope.

A long, full bugle brought his head up with a jerk, and he almost dropped the thermos. The bugle came rolling down through the trees on the opposite side of the canyon, echoing down toward the draw and toward the big river beyond. "Damn!" he growled. "Way up on that ridge? They went up that ridge? Damn!" He sat staring through the trees of the other ridge as far as he could see. "Another chance missed?" he asked dejectedly. More often than not, that's the way it went. Wrong place at the wrong time. "Have another cup of..."

Another long, full-throated bugle. This one was definitely down in the canyon, deep in the hollow. "Now that sounded like an answer to a challenge. Holy smokes. That means there are two bulls. One on the other ridge and one in the canyon. The ones in the canyon are still coming." The last of the bugle bounced from canyon wall to canyon wall. "You're back in the saddle, old son."

Bringing the binoculars back to his eyes, he glassed the draw again. Far down in the bottom toward the bowl, he saw movement. A cow walked slowly along the far side of the creek near a tangle of brush. *Definitely on the far side of the creek,* he thought. Through the glasses he watched her as she moved through the willows and brush along the creek. To her right, a calf stepped out of the brush on the far slope and walked toward her. "Good. They're still down there. And they're still coming." He slowly lowered the binoculars to his chest. He couldn't see her in the dim light without them.

Waiting for what seemed a long time, he finally raised the binoculars again. She was no longer where he had seen her. He slowly swept the glasses along the creek bed. And there she was a little further up the canyon. Three other cows and the calf were with her. "Will that bull come with them?" he whispered. He continued to sweep the area with the glasses. *Yeah! He'll come. Those are his cows.*

On the upper edge of his field of vision in the binoculars, he saw movement up in the trees on the opposite side of the canyon. He raised the glasses slightly, and there he was. *Horns. Definitely horns.* The bull moved just inside the tree line parallel to the cows.

Four more cows came up the creek about a hundred feet behind the first group. *That makes seven cows, a yearling calf, and the bull. No, there's another calf. A nice little herd.*

They were moving slow up the draw, browsing as they moved. The cows were staying close to the creek and the bull in the trees. Just as he should. From where they were now, they could only go three ways. Straight up the draw to the bowl and the trees around the meadow. Up through the trees on the opposite ridge. Or up the ridge he was on by using one of the trails he had scouted. The odds had narrowed in his favor. If they went up the ridge on the far side, they would be gone. And it would be over. But there would be no sneaking up behind him today. With that thought, he turned his head and looked up through the trees along the ridge. Nothing. No movement.

When he turned back to the draw, he could see the lead group clearly without the binoculars. With nearly full light now, there was no need for the glasses. He removed his right glove, pulling it off with his teeth, stuck his index finger in his mouth and wetted it. When he held it above him, the front of his finger chilled slightly. There was definitely a detectable air current coming up the slope. He would not be winded this morning. He put the glove back on, raised the glasses to his eyes, and scanned the tree line on the other side of the canyon. There was the bull, still in the trees, slightly behind the first group of cows. *Good. He's doin' just what you would think he should be doin',* he thought. *Stayin' in the trees as much as possible, lettin' the cows take the lead and the risk. But he'll go where they go. I just need him out of those trees.*

In the past, he had seen a herd of more than twenty-five cows and calves with one bull moving across a clearing. The bull was in the middle of the herd and actually seemed to hide with his head down to minimize his exposure—a smart old bull making for a very tough shot.

Picking up the cow call hanging from his neck, he placed it in his mouth. "Time for a little talk," he whispered. He let out one squeal and watched the elk. The lead cow stopped dead in her tracks, looking up the slope. *Now is not the time to move or speak at all,* he thought.

Without looking directly at the elk, he watched them in his peripheral vision. And watched them. And watched them. The lead cow was definitely on alert after his call. They were now about one hundred yards away from the trail that had held so much hope for these past two days. A hundred and fifty yards away, downhill. The bull still in the trees.

This was the moment. What they did next, or better yet, what that lead cow did next, would decide where they would go. She would determine what they would do and what kind of shot he would have on the bull. All would be decided in the next few minutes. She would decide when they started to move again. And she would decide if he had any shot at all.

Shifting his eyes to the trees, he looked for the bull. At the same time, he kept the cows in his attention. No sign of the bull. *Where the hell did he go? He's not going to leave those cows. They're his cows.*

Now was just a waiting game. There was nothing more he could do. If he used the cow call again, that could spook them for sure. If he used it at all while that lead cow was looking to where he was, she would know. Just a waiting game. If he moved at all, the slightest movement, with the cow looking up the hill, they would spook and disappear up into the trees on the far side of the draw.

CHAPTER 7

And then she moved. Turned her head to the trees on the other side where the bull was hiding and squealed once. *Spoke to him?* Then she moved slowly forward. He was still watching the trees beyond her and the others. The lead cow continued up the draw until she was nearly adjacent to the bottom of the slanting trail. *What're ya goin' to do, girl? Go on up the canyon or come to me?* He held his breath, still not looking directly at her, waiting. *Come to me, sweetheart. Come to me"* His vision and attention were as wide as possible to keep track of the cows and watch for the bull in the trees. And she turned up the trail and stopped. His breath escaped in a long, quiet sigh. And the bull came out of the trees. How many times? The wrong place at the wrong time. How many times had the game he had stalked and trailed gone the wrong way? How many times had he been forced to take a long, awkward shot? Was this the time it all came together? Everything falling into place?

Exactly when he had done it, he didn't know. The rifle was in position on the top of the log, both hands on the stock, finger near the trigger guard. The bulky glove was still on his right hand. Getting his finger on the trigger would be awkward. With the butt of the stock still against his shoulder, he brought his hand slowly along the stock to his mouth. Eyes and attention still on the elk, he pulled each finger of the glove loose with his teeth and slid his hand out of the glove. Slowly he took the glove out of his teeth, laid it on the top of his right shoulder, and moved his hand back to the rifle. Moving his finger behind the trigger guard, he pressed gently on the safety button and found that at some point he had already released the safety. All of his movements were in auto mode now. He was nearly in position to take the shot he wanted.

Still, he watched them above the scope. In single file, they came up the trail, seven cows and two yearling calves. And the bull followed. *I can't feel the breeze. Will they scent me? No way. Not now.* And there was nothing to do but wait, see how it played out, and hope.

When the lead cow headed up the trail, the bull moved out of the last of the trees quickly, at a trot, and caught up with the trailing cow as she, too, turned up the trail. At any time now, he could take the shot. If he had to.

Finger on the trigger, he waited. Watching them but not looking at them. As slowly as he could, he laid his cheek to the rifle's stock. With both eyes open, not looking through the scope yet, he watched them. Now in the open, only the brush around them, they began to move a little faster, bunching just a little. The bull moved up to the middle of the small herd, cows beside him, in front of him, and behind him. But he couldn't hide. No place to hide on that trail. All that bull wanted to do now was get up that trail and back into the trees. Under cover and out of sight. That was what his nature told him to do. Stay as hidden as possible for as long as possible.

Because he hid behind the log, the only thing visible to the elk would be the rifle and a small portion of his head. Movement, any perceived movement at all, would spook them. And it would be over. Only a quick shot at best. They were sharp. Sight. Smell. Sound. Instincts. That's what they lived by. That's how they stayed alive.

Eye to the scope, he watched the lead cow top the trail and move into the trees. The next three animals came through his sight. A fractional shift of the scope to the right got the bull in the scope. He put the crosshairs just behind and below the bull's left ear at the base of the skull, timing the head movement with each stride the bull took. He had a good rest and held the rifle steady, right on the target he needed and wanted. Following the bull with the scope, he counted to five, pressed his finger on the trigger, and took up the slack. He took in a shallow breath, let it out, held it, and squeezed the trigger slowly until the butt of the rifle bucked against his shoulder.

The bull disappeared from the scope. As the sound of the shot ratcheted down the canyon, echoing between the ridges, the cows and calves panicked into the trees and disappeared with a thunder of hooves. Within seconds, they were gone, and it was quiet again. All but the ringing in his ears. And still he held his position, watching through the scope where the bull had been. No sign of him. No movement.

Lifting his head from the stock, he looked to the top of the trail and the tree line. Nothing. No movement. No sound. But he knew. It was done. The bull had not charged into the trees. No real need to chamber a new round, but he did anyway, then picked up and pocketed the empty casing. Still, five minutes he waited and watched. A very long five minutes. But he knew. The shot was good. A clean, quick kill. He took a deep breath and relaxed as he let it out in a long sigh, his shoulders slumping. The glove on his shoulder dropped to the ground, and he picked it up and put it on. He knew it was done. Just as he had hoped. For once, it had all come together.

At least this part of it. Now the real work began.

CHAPTER 8

As he stood up behind the log, he realized how cramped his legs were, how tense his back and shoulders were—partly from his seated position and partly from the tension of the moment. The wait. The long minutes of no movement. He stretched his back and moved up and around the root bole of the log and walked toward the head of the trail. As he reached the tree line where the trail went through the trees, he stopped and looked down the trail. There he was. The bull. Just off the trail. Lying on his left side, brush crushed beneath him. He had fallen to his right and rolled completely over to his left side when hit. "He didn't know what hit him. Didn't feel a thing. As good a shot as I have ever made," he said aloud. He looked back to the log and the stand, some seventy-five yards away, and smiled.

And then, from deep inside him, an old familiar feeling swelled. He had it felt it before. Several times. As far as he knew, it came to him every time he made a kill, a harvest, some called it. He knew he had felt it with the very first deer he had taken. He didn't know where the feeling came from. It was just there. Each time just like this. Perhaps it came from somewhere deep in his DNA. Maybe from that place deep inside him where the voices spoke and where he listened. He'd wondered if there really was such a thing as collective consciousness. And if this could be a manifestation of that.

He'd often tried to define this feeling to himself. But only to himself. He had never spoken of it in depth with any other person. The feeling was his and his alone. Oh, the boys knew about it. They had seen him go through it, briefly anyway. But he had not actually talked about it with them or with anyone. If anyone might see him in this state, he would be embarrassed and exposed. In some way at least.

The feeling itself was hard to get a hold of. Even harder to understand. It was just there. Alone now, he let it overtake him. With someone else around, he suppressed it. Now, alone on this mountain, he let it come to him fully. Fill him with its mystery and wonder.

He knelt beside the elk, placed his hand on the heavy shoulder, and bowed his head. The words came unbidden. "Thank you . . . old boy," he finished. He almost said, "my brother." Those words were there, unbidden, below the surface. And then he let them come. "Thank you, my brother, for your gift." He was flooded with a mixture of emotions. Sadness for the death of this beautiful animal. And relief for his success on this hunt. And respect for this great and wondrous creature.

He heard the echo of some long-forgotten chant or song in a language no one now remembered. Like an itch that can't be found or scratched, in his mind, the rhythm of deep-throated drums grew. Tinkling bells rang. Voices sang and dancing feet pounded the earth. When he stood looking at the bull, his feet began to shuffle in time with the music in his head, almost of their own accord. The soles of his boots stamped the earth on the trail, raising a bit of dust. Dance steps no one had taught him.

Guttural, unintelligible sounds formed deep in his throat. Self-conscious, he glanced around, but continued to move his feet and let the sounds roll out of his throat. They were not words. Certainly not words that anyone knew. At least not sounds that made sense, even to himself. A low guttural chant. But in some subliminal way, he felt their meaning. A song of praise and gratitude. Praise for the spirit of this animal and gratitude for his sacrifice.

For several minutes, this song, for that is how he thought of it, continued to bubble out of him from some primordial root. And he felt their meaning at some level below conscious thought. These sounds came to him from somewhere unknown and continued until they were done. They started unbidden and flowed of their own volition until they gradually faded away. As did the 'dance.' The shuffling of his feet on the trail. Body swaying. As it faded away, he knelt by bull again, placed his hand on shoulder, and bowed his head. "Thank you, my brother. Go with my respect," he whispered.

And now it was time for the hard part. The real work.

He rose and walked back up through the trees to where he had left the backpack and took it back to where the elk lay by the trail. Examining the body, he found what he had hoped for. The shot had passed through the spinal column at the base of the skull, shattering bone and the brain stem. Instant death.

Looking at the bull now, as at other times at this point in a successful hunt, he was awed by the sheer size of this animal. He was daunted by the work he had ahead of him. He had to gut, dismember, and skin the body. Cut the body into quarters and then haul it all back to camp. On a packboard. One piece at a time. And he was over two miles from camp. True, most of it was downhill. But that didn't lessen the work that task would take. In some ways, with the weight of the meat on his back, going downhill would be harder on his legs than flat ground or even slightly up hill. He knew that from prior experience.

Just preparing the body for moving it was always tiring, hard labor with an elk. Not so much with deer. But elk were just big. Massive, actually. And he had to do this one all alone. But he had done it alone before and was certain he could do it again. No reason not to go for it. The work ahead didn't matter. It was what had to be done, and he would do it again. That, too, was ingrained within him. When a job needed doing, you just dug in and did it. All the way to the end.

The skinning and quartering would be a lot easier if the body were hanging from a tree limb. Or a rafter in his garage. That just wasn't possible here on the ridge, alone. No block and tackle. No heavy ropes. No way to hoist it. "It's the hard way or no way," he said.

He took the rope and bone saw from the pack and set the pack aside. He was lucky that the bull was lying butt downhill. Gravity would help with the gutting and cleaning. To prevent the body sliding further down the slope, he tied the end of the rope to a small tree just above the elk's head, knotted it around the antlers, and trimmed off the excess.

Funny, he hadn't paid much attention to the horns. A lot of men hunted for horns. The meat didn't matter so much to these guys. They wanted a big set of horns to brag about and would pass up good meat hoping to get what they wanted. Trophy hunters, they were called. But he was a meat hunter. *You can't eat the horns,* the saying goes.

More than that, it was the being here and the satisfaction of getting it all right. Or as close as you could get it. Working through the problems of the hunt, the tracking, and a good clean kill. And getting the meat out. That's what made a good hunt. He appreciated a good set of horns as much as anyone, and these horns were good ones. Not trophy horns, not heavily built or overly tall, but they were good horns. Maybe a three- or four-year-old bull. And he would be tasty.

But the hunt and the harvest were only a part of why he was here. If there was no hunt, he would still need to make his frequent trips to the high country. Usually alone.

Next, he tied the rope to the base of a bush near the body and secured it to the left rear leg just above the foot. The rest of the rope he tied to the right rear leg and walked to a tree some ten feet away. He walked once around the tree with the rope waist high and pulled it tight. From this point it was simply a matter of pulling the rope taut as much as possible to spread and hold the hind legs apart. When he'd pulled it as far as he could, he tied it off on the tree. Without the legs held far apart, the work to be done would be much harder. Anything to make the gutting, skinning, and quartering easier was just a plus.

He took his coat off and rolled his shirt sleeves above his elbows. Not that it mattered. He would be covered with blood before it was done. Before he began, he took plastic bags from the pack to put the heart, liver, and other pieces of meat into. He wasn't much for liver, but he really liked the heart with onions and mushrooms, mashed potatoes, and thick brown gravy made from the juices of the meat.

Knife in hand, he knelt between the hind legs and began.

.   .   .

When the elk was cleaned out, he moved the gut pile away down the slope. "That'll make a good meal for the coyotes and the birds. If they're still around." After a pause, he shrugged. "Still talkin' to yourself, I see." He smiled. "Time for a break."

He went to the pack, sat on the ground by the tree, and removed a bottle of water. He washed the blood from his hands and dried them on the extra shirt. Eating a sandwich and an apple for lunch, he leaned back against the tree and rested. He took a cigarette from the pack and lit it. A long, deep drag and a relaxing release.

Looking around, he took stock of the time of day and the sky. These he had paid no attention to since he had settled into the stand. "Must be movin' on toward noon or thereabouts," he said. The sky was still overcast with low-hanging clouds. *Storm clouds? Don't think about that now*, he thought. *But pay attention, old son. Just pay attention.*

When he went back to work, he began skinning the body from the hind legs up. Once he had the inside of the legs and the ribcage hide loose, he released the ropes holding the hind legs apart. He kept the hide spread beneath the body to prevent dirt getting on the meat. Skinning was hard work, turning the body from side to side until the hide was completely separated from the body except where it connected to the head.

Sweating heavily, he sat back and took a deep breath. He wanted to rest but knew that time was running away. He needed to quarter the body. Carry what he could back to camp and get the packboard. "Rest just a minute. Take a breather." Crawling to the pack, he drank from the water bottle until it was empty and put it back into the pack smeared with blood. While he leaned against the tree, he used a whetstone from the pack to re-sharpen the knife. Skinning, cutting through hair, dulled a knife faster than any part of this process.

Returning to the elk, he cut and sawed through the pelvis between the hind legs. Next, he cut and sawed through the spine just above the hind quarters. Each hind quarter now lay separated from the body, resting on the hide. He removed both front legs at the shoulders, leaving the muscles on the shoulder joints. These he laid on the ground cloth that he had sat on at the stand. He cut and sawed through the neck just below the head and separated the hide from the head at the top of the neck. Now he had all the body parts separated. "Tired. Man, I'm getting tired." He looked again at the sky. "No change there. I'll take another break."

Leaning against a log above the trail's end, he ate two power bars and drank another bottle of water. "Only one bottle left. Better save it." He took a taste of the coffee and found that it was cold. "I hate cold coffee," he grunted and poured it out.

Looking at the pieces of the elk, he knew this part of the hard work was done. The only hard part left was the getting each of those pieces down the mountain and back to camp.

He crawled to the torso, rolled it over to rest on the spread ribcage, and trimmed both sides of the back strap from the spine. "Good meat here. Gonna make a fine dinner tonight." He shaved off the flank meat from the rib cage and cut out the tenderloins. There wasn't much meat left on the ribs, and he decided to save time and leave it for the coyotes or bears. He trimmed as much meat from both sides of the neck as he could. This was intricate and tedious work, carving around the vertebra, but the two large pieces of meat would make a couple of real tasty roasts. These were the only part of an elk's meat that was marbled with fat.

The back strap, neck meat, and tenderloins he put in plastic bags and put them with the heart and liver in the pack. More than thirty pounds of meat, he guessed.

Looking at what was left on the hide, he said, "Do I take the horns? Yeah, if I can, I guess." He didn't need them to verify the sex of the animal. He had left the testicles attached to one of the hind quarters for that. "The horns could stay here if need be. I don't have to take them. But I gotta get the rest of this guy back to camp." He sat looking around at the pieces of the elk, thinking out how he would get this all back to camp. "What about the hide? Maybe. If I have time," he said. "I could get it tanned."

He stood, stretched his back, and put on his hat and coat. The gloves went back into the pack. He hoisted the pack to his shoulders. It was heavy with the meat. "Can I take one of the front quarters with me on this trip?" he mused. "At least part way, I guess." Glancing at the sky, he sensed he was running short on time for today. "Use what little time you have the best way you can, old son," he told himself.

He lifted a front leg by the foot and swung it over his shoulder. He collected the rifle from where it leaned against a tree and headed down through the trees, angling to cut across the top of the ridge lower down, and then on to camp. "Man, I'm getting' tired. That was just plain hard work."

CHAPTER 9

Tired as he was, he knew he needed to keep going until the work was done. He wanted to get as much of the elk to camp as he could today before dark. To get it all there meant at least three more trips. Four if he went back for the horns and hide. "No way I can make four trips today. Maybe not even three." He remembered a quote he read somewhere, "Keep behind the plow, boy, until the field is all done." That's how he lived. Do the work until it was all done. As much as he could get done today. Before darkness stopped him.

He walked on, the front quarter over his shoulder, pack on his back, rifle at his side, trying to block out the tiredness. And the pain. His legs were talking to him already. Loud and clear.

Sweat soaked his shirt when he walked into camp. He laid the rifle on the hood of the truck and lowered the front quarter to the ground. Shrugging out of the pack, he opened his coat but kept it on. The day hadn't warmed much, and he didn't want to expose himself to the cold as sweaty as he was. But he needed to cool down. "Sit down, old son." he said. His hands were cold, but starting a fire now would be a waste of time and firewood. Getting the truck keys from the tire, he unlocked the truck and took another length of rope from under the seat. He looped the rope over a lower tree branch, tied the rope to the front quarter at the ankle, and hauled it up nearly to the limb and tied it off on the trunk. "Now I can rest for a few minutes." He got in the truck, started it, turned on the heater, and leaned back against the seat. "Just a little rest, boy." Waiting for the heat to kick in, he ate two power bars and took a long drink of Gatorade.

"Ya gotta get in better shape if you're going to keep doing this, old son," he said.

When he was warm again, he zipped up his coat and turned the truck off. Removing the meat bags from the pack, he put them on the passenger's side floor. He unloaded the rifle, slipped it into the carry case, and laid it on the truck seat. From the containers in the bed of the truck, he got the packboard and more rope. As he headed back to the ridge, he put his gloves on.

When he reached the elk, everything was as he had left it. He leaned against the tree to rest a few minutes. "I'm going to be tired tonight, that's for sure."

Looking at what was left for him to do, he thought of the bull he had taken on Cottonwood Creek some years ago. The shot was one hundred yards up a steep slope above the Forest Service road. The elk dropped in his tracks and kicked a few feet down the slope. And that was all. He had cleaned him out where he had fallen but left the hide on and didn't quarter him. There was a skiff of snow on the ground, and it was easy to slide him down the steep slope to the cut bank above the road. The truck was only a quarter of a mile up the road. Driving back to the cut bank, he backed the truck against the hill with the tailgate down. Then it was a simple matter of rolling the elk off the cut bank right into the bed of the truck. An hour's work, tops. The rest of the work was made easier when he hung the carcass in his garage.

Now, hands on his knees, he pushed himself up and stretched his back. "Well, let's get 'er done, boy," he said. The horns and the head he placed under the tree beside the log. The other front quarter he hung on a branch from the same tree. Both hind quarters he lay on the hide. He hadn't put game bags on any of the meat. It was cold and there were no flies to get at the meat.

He knew all three of those pieces were not making it to camp today. It would be fine as it was until he could get it back to camp. No doubt it would be frozen solid when he came back to get the last of it.

Laying the packboard beside one of the hindquarters, he rolled it onto the board and secured it with rope. When he lifted the packboard, the meat shifted only slightly. "It'll do just fine," he said.

He needed a way to get it onto his back with as little effort as possible. A log would do. Looking around, the only log large enough close to him was up the hill about twenty-five yards away. "If I can't drag it to that log, I can't carry it back to camp. And carry it I gotta." Getting the packboard on his back and lifting it with the load of meat from a full squat would be really tough, but "It's what I gotta do." He dragged the packboard with the meat to the log and wrestled it up onto the log.

When he had the packboard on the log, he straddled the log and slipped his arms through the shoulder straps with the full weight of the meat on the log. He attached the cross strap to hold the shoulder straps in place. As he stood with the packboard on his back, he shrugged his shoulders, adjusting the weight. "Don't think about the weight, old son. Just get goin'," he said. He swung his leg over the log, ground his heels into the dirt, and pushed himself up. A moment's hesitation, and he headed down the ridge toward camp.

The trip down the ridge was exhausting. Legs struggling, back aching, he kept a steady pace. He believed that with the weight he had on his back, if he stopped to rest, he may not be able to stand again and continue on to camp. So he kept moving. Breathing heavily, sweating, he turned his mind off to all but the cadence of his steps and the end of this part of the work he needed to complete.

•   •   •

Back at camp, he lowered the tailgate of the pickup, turned, and lowered the meat and packboard into the truck. It was all he could do to stay on his feet. Thighs shaking, he slipped the shoulder straps off and let the meat fall back onto the bed of the truck.

Holding to the side walls of the truck, he walked toward the front fender. The truck keys were on the right front wheel, and he was on the left side of the truck. "Damn, you dummy," he grumbled at himself. Right hand on the hood for support, he circled to the right front of the truck. Back against the truck, he slid to the ground and leaned back against the tire. Legs stretched in front of him, he closed his eyes and rested. His thigh muscles were twitching, his feet were sore, and he had an ache in his back that wasn't going away any time soon. "Wow. That was one tough walk down that ridge." He needed more water or he was going to cramp hard. And still he sat, legs stretched out, eyes closed, head back against the fender.

After several minutes, he reached behind his head and took the truck keys from the tire. When he tried to stand, his legs buckled. Rolling onto his hands and knees and using the truck for support, he pulled himself erect and leaned against the fender. "Keep movin', boy," he said.

Walking to the creek, he lay face down on the bank with his head over the water. He laid his hat on the ground beside him, dipped his hands in the icy creek, and splashed water on his face. Then he poured water over his head. "Hot damn, that's cold." He continued to cup water with his hands and pour it over his head, sipping some from his cupped hands. The frigid water was a shock but refreshing.

Back at the truck, he dried his head and face, got a bottle of orange Gatorade out of the cooler, and drank half of it down without stopping. He slid the hind quarter further into the bed of the truck. "The hell with hanging it in the tree now. Maybe later."

It was time to make some decisions. He got in the truck, started the engine, and leaned back, sipping from the Gatorade, waiting for the heat to kick in. "Do I go back for more now?" Checking the sky, he saw no change in the low-hanging clouds. "God, I hope it doesn't snow." And he leaned his head back against the rear window.

"I need to get the rest of that elk back here as soon as I can. Can I do more today?" Still up on the ridge was one front shoulder and one hind quarter, with the hide and the horns. The hind quarter was the heaviest and would take a lot of effort. Each hind quarter weighed about two hundred pounds. The question was, did he have that much effort left in him today?

The decision was an easy one. "No way. I'm beat. I just can't do that today. That's final. Not today." He thought of the back strap on the floor of the truck. "I'm going to rest and have dinner. With fried potatoes and onion. So, I stay here, eat, and get a good night's sleep. Go back for the rest of it in the morning."

There was the risk that coyotes or a bear could get to the meat in the night. If it was a bear, he would lose a lot of meat. Maybe the entire hind quarter. But he had seen no bear sign in all the days he had been hiking around the ridges and the meadow. "I don't think there are bear in the area. I haven't seen coyote sign at all. I'll have to take the risk. I just can't make another trip today."

He shut off the truck and got out. His left leg nearly buckled when he put weight on it. "That settles it, then," he said. He started a fire and poured a can of Dinty Moore's stew in the pot and sat it near the fire to warm. "A late lunch and dinner later," he mumbled.

He filled a large pot with water from the creek and put it on the fire to heat. When the water was hot, he got out a towel, soap, and clean clothes, stripped down with just his boots on and took the only bath he had available. He was one big, shivering goose pimple in the cold air as he stood naked by the tailgate. Nothing on but his boots.

While soaping himself, he wondered, "How the hell am I going to rinse this soap off? Take a dip in the creek? No way. That water's too cold. I'll shrivel up right down to an ice cube." With the washcloth, he rinsed off as much of the soap as he could. Clean and definitely smelling better, he put on the fresh clothes. "Now I feel better."

He ate all the stew with a Pepsi for lunch. Feeling better, he rolled out the sleeping bag in the lean-to, lay down, and picked up the book. "Just a bit more rest," he said as he closed his eyes.

When he woke, it was nearly full dark. The book lay on the ground cloth beside him, unopened and completely ignored. "Time for some back strap, old son." he said.

He built up the fire that had nearly gone out. He got out the cast iron frying pan, a potato from the truck, and the back strap from the pack. Two thick pieces from the end of the meat, well-seasoned, should be just about right. All the bags of meat were on the floor of the truck. The frying pan with bacon grease went on the grill over the fire to heat. He sliced up the potato, diced half of an onion, and put them with the meat in the hot frying pan and sat on the log while they cooked.

"Am I gettin' too old for this?" he wondered. "That work just plain beat me up today." It didn't used to do this to him. But he loved it. He loved it all. It was satisfying to know that he could still do the hard part. Even the way he felt now. "Pride goeth before a fall, Ma always quoted," he said. But being here, the scouting, the tracking, the hunt, the excitement of the animals coming up the trail, "I love it all. Even the work." And he did. He really did.

Some day he wouldn't be able to do it all. Especially the packing. Some day he would either need a pack animal or hunt only with younger men to help him get meat back to camp. Of course, there was always the option of boning it out on the mountain and packing smaller amounts of just meat. More work at one end and less work at the other. Until that day came, he would do it as he wanted. And as he needed. As long as he could. Alone on the mountain. Just him and the stream, the pines, the ridges, and the earth to listen to. All the voices whispering to him.

What about the day when he couldn't do it anymore? "I'll jump that creek when I get to it. Not now."

During these minutes, he had turned the potatoes and the meat until they were done. With no hard plates to eat from, he straddled the log, the frying pan almost in his lap, and ate straight from the pan. This was definitely the finest meal he had eaten in a long time. Far better than a beef steak bought in some store.

When the meal was over, he cleaned up the frying pan and put another log on the fire. "Time to sit and ponder?" he wondered. But there really wasn't much thinking to do. No decisions to be made. He had work to do tomorrow, and that was all there was to it. He lit a cigarette, watched the logs burn, and relaxed. It was a cold night but warm by the fire. The only voice in the dark was the crackling of the fire eating the logs.

Later, he walked toward the stream in the dark, did his business by the tree, and sat on a rotting stump near the stream. He lit a cigarette and alternated holding it with one hand while he kept the other in his coat pocket for warmth. It was cold away from the fire and would get colder later in the night. But he couldn't hear the whispers of the stream over the fire's chatter. So he sat with his back to the tree, tired legs stretched in front of him, staring into the dark of the trees across the stream and listened. He let his mind clear and just listened.

Before going to bed, he filled the coffee pot with water from the creek, added coffee grounds and a filter, and sat it by the fire ring. Sitting by the fire now, he watched the flames dance as the log burned down. A glance at the sky told him nothing. Still dark with low clouds and no stars. Before he crawled into the sleeping bag, he took his pants and shirt off, rolled them, and shoved them to the bottom of the sleeping bag. He massaged his upper legs with Deep Heat rub and wiped the excess from his hands with paper towels. "I hope that stops any leg cramps in the night." He crawled into the bag and settled in for sleep.

"No book tonight, old son." He turned out the lamp and slid deep into the bag. Sleep came quickly, as he knew it would.

He woke once during the night, but he didn't know what time it was. It didn't really matter. His watch was still in the truck glove box. He knew it was the wee small hours, so he drifted back toward sleep, smiling in the dark and humming, with the words of a good song in his mind. *In the wee small hours of the morning while the whole wide world is fast asleep. You lie awake and you think about the girl, you never ever think of counting sheep. When your lonely heart has learned its lesson, you'd be hers if only she would call. In the wee small hours of the morning, that's the time you'll miss her most of all."*
"And I do," he whispered.

CHAPTER 10

He drifted in and out of sleep through the night. When morning finally came, he lay deep in the sleeping bag, warm against the cold. He dug a cigarette out of the pack and lit it, turned, and looked out of the lean-to toward the fire ring. "Oh shit. Snow!" A lot of snow. And it was still snowing. Not heavy, but it was coming down pretty good. He turned on the flashlight and looked across the open ground covered with about four inches of snow. And a lot of flakes falling through the light beam. "Get your ass out of bed, boy. Ya got some work ahead of you today." He pulled his pants and shirt from the bottom of the sleeping bag, wiggled deeper into the bag, and pulled his clothes on.

Once he got the fire started, he set the coffee pot on the grill. At the truck, he poured milk on a bowl of cereal. While eating, the things he needed to do to get the meat off of the mountain stacked up in his mind. Frequent glances at the falling snow filled his mind with what his day was going to be like. This snow was not heavy and not deep. At least not yet. But any snow at all blanketing the world around him put knots in his stomach. Up here, any snow was a problem. A lot of snow was a big problem. Four inches of snow wasn't a big deal yet, but it could complicate getting meat off the ridge and getting the old truck off the mountain. *Stick with what you know you need to do and how to do it and you will be okay.* Thoughts kept running through his mind, rehearsing what he needed to do and how to do it. The hindquarter would be heavy.

Thoughts of the drive out of here and how the roads would be with the snow trickled through his mind, but he shoved them aside to deal with later.

He filled the thermos with hot coffee, shrugged into the packboard, put on his gloves and ski mask, pulling the mask down over his ears. The handgun was in its holster on his belt, but the rifle would be left behind today. No need for it now. This was a working day, not a hunting day.

It was still dark when he passed the old fire ring, turned off the main trail, and followed his flag trail up the ridge. Under the trees, there was much less snow. "Walk careful, boy." With the low heavy clouds, it was darker under the trees. He turned on the flashlight to see his trail and the footing. Flashlight in one hand, thermos of coffee in the other, he moved carefully but quickly up the ridge. Light snow filtered to the ground between the trees. He felt better, more relaxed now that he was moving. Getting on with the job at hand settled him down.

When he reached the elk, it was light enough to see. The meat on the ground was covered with snow. Otherwise, it was as he had left it yesterday. No animals had gotten to it. "Wish I'd taken it up into the trees near that log, dummy," he said. "But I didn't expect this snow." At a gut level, he knew that if he had paid more attention to the sky, he might have known the snow was coming and be better prepared for it. But he wasn't going to say that to himself, aloud or in his head. There was nothing to do about it now. Deal with it and get the job done.

The hindquarter was frozen to the hide, and the hide was frozen to the ground. *That takes care of the hide. It ain't goin' down the mountain today. Or any day.* Light snow was still falling, and there were four or five inches on the ground. With gloved hands, he swept the snow away from the meat. He lifted the hindquarter by the foot and ripped it loose from the hide. When he squatted to lift it in his arms, he grunted and dropped it. Heavy, slippery, and frozen solid.

"Not much you can do but do it. Either pack it out or walk away and leave it here. And *that* ain't gonna happen." He dragged it up the slope and hoisted it onto the log. It slid off the back side to the ground like the block of ice that it was. He left it where it was and went back after the front shoulder that hung in the tree.

When he had both pieces of meat by the log, he returned to the head, pulled it loose from the ground by lifting the horns, and carried it back to the log. "I ain't carrying that head down the trail." It would be cumbersome, bulky, and unnecessary. "Maybe just the horns. When I get the other front quarter."

He had tied the bone saw to the packboard to trim the lower legs off. That would take off a little of the weight. Not much, but some. Sitting on the log, he looked out over the draw and the head of the trail, blanketed now with snow. He went over yesterday in his mind, watching the elk move, seeing the bull in the trees and all of them coming up the trail as if he had told them what to do. A smile spread across his face. He opened the thermos and drank a long swallow of the still hot coffee. "Good. Real good. All of it," he said. The hunt and the coffee. He took another drink of coffee. "Now, stop daydreamin' and get your ass back to work."

After another drink of coffee, he capped the thermos and sat it on the ground. Slipping off the packboard, he untied the bone saw and pulled the hindquarter back over the log and between his feet, the hoof in the air. Frozen as it was, trimming the hide around the knee joint with the knife would be impossible. The bone saw cut easily through the hide, sinew, and bone. He repeated this process with the front shoulder and tossed the legs behind the log. "What do I take first?" He wasn't anxious to load either of these hunks onto the packboard and head down the mountain. Especially the hindquarter. "Get a hold and hang on till it's done," he said. But there was no way he could take them both at once. Two trips was the only logical decision.

He laid the packboard on the ground and took hold of the closest hunk of meat, the hindquarter. He laid it on the packboard, took rope from his coat pocket, and tied the meat securely to the packboard.

Using his legs to lift, he hoisted the packboard and meat to the top of the log and balanced it while he slipped one strap over his shoulder. The second strap was more difficult, but he got it without dropping the whole thing off the back side of the log, taking him with it. Wriggling, tugging, and shrugging, he situated the pack where he wanted it and fastened the cross strap over his chest to secure the shoulder straps in position.

"Now, all I gotta do is stand up," he groaned. "Yeah, right!" He leaned forward at the waist, his butt and the weight of the meat still on the log, put his hands on his knees, and pushed up with his legs and arms. He easily made it to a standing position. The packboard felt settled and comfortable on his back. All but the weight. It was heavy. Real heavy. "I've done it before. I did it yesterday. I can do it again," he said.

"About two miles to camp, all downhill. Don't stand here thinkin' about it, boy. Move your ass. It's snowin'." He picked up the flashlight and the thermos, turned downhill with a short step, and was on his way. *Get this one done and there's one more load to go*

As he walked, head down, he considered briefly leaving that front shoulder up here, packing up the truck and getting out now. And rejected the idea. It was illegal to waste wild game. But that made no difference. It just wasn't in him to leave meat on the mountain. Getting it out was part of the job. You kill it, you clean it, you get it off the mountain. All part of the hunt. Top to bottom. *If you can't do the whole job, don't start at the beginning.*

The weight carried easily on his back without shifting back and forth with each step. Still, it was heavy, and the steady pace he kept downhill did nothing to relieve that. Twice he found a log large enough that he could rest on with the weight off his body. Each time, however, it was more difficult to stand back up. His legs were more tired than he had thought they would be. The work from the day before had taxed them a lot. But he was doing it because it had to be done.

When he reached camp, it was before mid-morning. With relief, he lowered the load onto the tailgate of the pickup and slipped out of the packboard. Without the weight on him, he felt light and walked about the camp shaking his legs to loosen the muscles. After he untied the meat from the packboard, he got a power bar and a bottle of Gatorade from the truck. "It's time for a bit of rest," he said.

He swept snow from the log beside the fire pit and sat with his legs outstretched. He realized he wasn't nearly as tired as he had been yesterday. No muscle twitches in the legs. No real ache in the back. He chewed on the power bar and sipped from the Gatorade as he looked around the camp.

There was now about six inches of snow on the ground here in the open. It had stopped snowing as he came down the ridge. "I can get out of here now if I want to. The old truck can make it now with the chains on." More snow would make it much harder. Maybe a lot harder, if at all.

The hardest part of the work was over. Both hindquarters were in the truck. Leaving the hide and the head up there, he had only one more trip to make. And the load would be a lot lighter. *When I get that front shoulder back here, I'll pack up the lean-to and get out of here before it snows again.*

The thought of leaving held a bit of sadness, as it always did when it was time to go back down below. All of his time here had been as good as it gets. The snow changed his need and ability to get out. And there was no question. He had to get out. Today. With the dark, layered, low-hanging clouds, he knew this storm was not going away. In a matter of hours, or even minutes, it was going to let loose that load of snow and bury everything on this mountain. For months.

Scanning the area around the camp, he saw how the world here had been muted by the snow. And in some ways it was more beautiful. Softened. *Like a pretty woman with just the right amount of make-up*, he thought. All the best of this world was accented by the snow. The bows on the pines were hanging low, heavy with layers of white. The open area to the creek bank was covered with snow all the way to the water's edge. The water still flowed, noiselessly, hushed now. And before long, it would be coated with ice. Completely voiceless all winter. His face, and his soul, spread in a curious grin. He couldn't help but wonder how it would be here in the dead of winter. "You really don't want to find out, old son," he said.

He flushed with warmth—of the spirit, not the body. It was the same feeling he had sitting in a theater after a very good movie, one that ended with wonder and love. Everyone else in the theater was standing, leaving, chatting, while he sat watching the credits roll. Reliving the emotions of the love he had watched on the screen. He didn't want to get up and leave.

And so, he sat on the log, reliving the events and the emotions he had created here. And he didn't want to climb that ridge again, bring that front shoulder back to camp, one more large step toward leaving. He didn't want to dismantle all that he had made here. Physically and emotionally. He didn't want all that he had shared with what was here to end. The totality of his experience this time, on this mountain, flooded his mind and his heart with awe and reverence. "It's been a good one," he said, "that's for sure. All of it."

And then with a jolt, it came to him. Here, right now, where he had come to listen to all the voices he reveled in, there was no sound. All was complete, absolute quiet. Not just muted, as he had thought. But soundless. The silence pressed on him. No squirrel chattered in the trees. No wind sifted its voice through the pines. No crow scolded him as it fluttered across the sky, wings whistling with each stroke. The creek was voiceless. And he had heard no sound all day. Nothing but the squeak of his boots with each step in the snow, or his own voice muttering to no one but himself.

He cocked his head, straining for any sound, any whisper from the voices of the earth. And he heard nothing. The layer of snow on the ground and the clumps on the tree limbs were mute. And it had silenced all the other voices.

In this silence, the reality of his present situation smacked him like running into a door in the dark. However pleasant these past days had been, it was time to get out. There were things to do before he could crank up that old truck. But it was time to get out. His time here was done.

The lean-to was sagging a bit with snow on top, but there was not as much as there was on the ground. The canopy of trees had kept it partially cleared of snow. There was no snow inside the lean-to. A tent or a camper wouldn't have made any difference, either.

Rising from the log, he walked to the lean-to and shook the snow off the roof. Back at the truck, he removed the ropes that held the meat on the packboard and pushed the hindquarter into the bed beside the other one. Snow plowed into a pile between them. He loosened the rope that held the front shoulder hanging in the tree and lowered it to the ground. He lifted it and laid it in the bed of the truck as well.

That done, he got into the truck and started the motor. As the cab warmed, he made a peanut butter and jelly sandwich, got out an apple, a bag of chips and the last full bottle of water. Everything in the truck was nearly frozen. As he ate lunch, he thought about what needed to be done when he got back to camp with the last load.

All the while the silence tugged at him. Pressed in on him. Even the sound of the running truck motor seemed muted.

The clouds were still heavy and low. More snow was up there waiting to fall. Waiting to lock him in on this mountain. It was just a matter of time, little or long. He needed to get out. Soon.

His original plan was to spend a few more days here, assuming he had gotten an elk, lollygagging, reading, fishing, and walking in the meadows just for the beauty of it. The snow had changed that. The snow and the silence. If he couldn't get the truck out, he couldn't get the elk out. And he might not even get himself out. "It makes no sense takin' that risk," he said. Even staying one more night could put everything in jeopardy if it snowed more during the night. Having only two-wheel drive, he was going to have to chain up the tires as it was. *Get out, old son. Don't be stupid. Get it done and get out. The old girl will get me out and back home.*

With the six empty water bottles, he walked to the stream and filled them. He put one bottle in his coat pocket and the rest in the truck. He slung the packboard on his back, locked the truck, put the key back on the tire, and headed toward the trail. He took a long look at the sky as he passed where the old fire ring was now buried beneath the snow. The silent snow. "No more snow, damn it," he growled at the sky.

No trip up here ever went as anyone originally planned. Especially a hunting trip. Otherwise, it wouldn't be called a 'hunt.' And that was part of the mystique. At least to him, it was. Make your plans within a loose framework, and then adjust with what the world here gives you. Balance things as the days and nights roll out. The mountains and the weather were always in control. Up here, you were only a fragment of the world around you. With only a small measure of control. Even if there was a way to organize every minute, that was not his way. And never would be. Not up here. Push time and control aside and take what life here offers you. And meld with it all.

.   .   .

He had made this trip up the ridge so many times now, he didn't have to think about it. His mind wandered from the things up here to things down below. Knowing now that he was leaving soon, his thoughts returned to that other life. The one he came up here to get away from.

His life down there was necessary. He knew that. It was where he worked, earned a living. It was where his children and grandchildren were. And he needed them in his life. A working life, surrounded by those we love, was how we all make it from point A to point B. "From birth to a hole in the big backyard," he liked to say. But he knew he would always have this place, this trip, and others like it, in his memory forever. And he was richer for it. All of this, up here, this time, was his and his alone. It would always be a part of his spirit. Even the snow. He could come back here any time he wanted. Even if only in his memories.

One day, sitting in his recliner, he would turn off the TV or put down the book, tilt his head back, close his eyes, and return to this ridge. He would see that magnificent mule deer stag down in the draw eating leaves and drinking from the stream. He would feel the boulder, warm from the sun, under his butt. He would see the bull elk come out of the trees and head up the trail with his cows and the look of him through the scope as he came to make his sacrifice. He would hear the wind in the pines and the gurgle of the creek. In his mind, he would walk through the dappled shadows under the trees. He would sit by the fire at night and look to the sky spattered with stars. He would hear the whisper of the owl winging by in the night on his own hunt. All of this was his for the rest of his life.

And he would never forget the silence—the chill of the silence deeper than the early morning cold with the wind blowing.

"I should come back here in the summer some time. Take the main trail back to the big river. Or walk that bit of canyon clean to the bottom and wander through those trees until the river water stops me, just to see what it's like. Walk that country to see all that I can see. Live it all when it's warm. With no hunt to get in the way. No rifle to tote around. Just the camera, the land and me."

•   •   •

Back at the log on the ridge, he made short work of tying the front shoulder on the packboard. This would be a lighter load, but a load nonetheless. The head, with the horns still attached, was lying beside the log. "Might as well take the horns." He straddled the log and balanced the head between his legs. It was hard now, frozen solid. Using just the bone saw, he sawed from the base of the skull forward to the eyes and the upper area of the nose. When the horns were loose from the head and the skull cleaned out, he dropped the head to the ground on the back side of the log with the legs and sat looking at the horns.

"It's time I put a tag on this ole fella," he said. He removed the elk tag from his wallet and notched out the month and day of the kill with his knife. He wrapped the paper tag around the horn and secured it with the wire supplied with the tag. "Now he's legal," he said with a smile.

The horns weren't big. Four points on one side, five on the other. Like the buck. Unlike the buck, the beams weren't thick. But it was a decent rack. Just fine, and they would look nice mounted on a plaque. He tied them onto the packboard above the meat and wrestled into the shoulder straps. He stood for a minute looking to where the hide was stretched out on the frozen ground beneath the snow. It would be nice to take it, too, but that would mean staying overnight and coming back up here in the morning just for the hide. Not a good idea. Not worth the risk or the effort. Besides, it was frozen solid now. Rolling it up to carry it back to camp would be nearly impossible.

Ancestors of his, buried deep in the generations, would have saved everything this animal had to offer. The hide for shelter and clothing. The brains for tanning the hides. Even parts of the guts for water bags and food. Bones for tools and weapons. All would be kept and used. Unfortunately, that time had passed. Evaporated long ago.

"One more trip down the mountain, old son. Then get out right away."

He looked one more time to the head of the trail to recapture those moments. Instead, there was only the snow covering the ground. And the silence. A chill locked his mind, and he shivered. He turned and headed down the ridge through the trees with determined strides.

•   •   •

This trip down the ridge would be the last. At least for this hunt. The sadness rolled in on him again. But they all ended, these trips up here, sooner or later. He would have loved to stay the remaining three days. Just to be here with nothing to do but be here. The snow wasn't going to let that happen. When he got back to camp, he would have some back strap over the open fire. The last meal on the mountain. And then, he would put the chains on the truck, dismantle the lean-to, load up, and pull out. And that would be that. Until the next time, when the call slid down off the mountains on an evening breeze, beckoning him to the high places.

The kids would be glad and relieved to see him home again, and early too.

Coming down the ridge through the trees, he kept a close watch on the sky. The snow that was coming had held off. He did not feel optimistic but was glad to not see more snow. At openings in the trees, the snow on the ground had piled up to around four to six inches.

As he neared the end of the ridge, the trees thinned. Ahead he could see the camp, the truck hunkered down in the snow. What snow had been on the hood and cab roof was gone, melted from the heat generated when he warmed himself in the cab earlier. The blue tarp of the lean-to was clearly visible. Everything else was buried in snow. The wood pile, under its tarp, was a mound of white. The fire ring was buried, a slight depression in the snow.

Still, there was no sound. No squirrel. No crow. No soft breeze. As cold as it was, he was very glad there was no wind. Even a breeze would have made the conditions bitter. Wind, real wind, would have made them extreme. With the thermals, heavy coat, gloves, and ski cap, he had kept warm. The exertion of carrying the meat helped with that as well.

As he came out of the last line of trees, he stopped and scanned the camp area. "Beautiful," he said, "but deadly." And totally silent. The animals and birds had known something that it had taken him too long to catch on to. "A misjudgment, but not serious. Get out, old son, while you can." He had a little work to do. Not much, but some. Take down the lean-to. That would be easy. Stack the firewood for someone else to use next year and collect the tarps there. Make sure everything was in the truck. Get the chains on the back tires of the truck. He was certain that he would need those to get back up the logging road and probably on the Forest Service Road as well. "Maybe an hour, tops. Then down the mountain to home. I can eat later. Get out now."

CHAPTER 11

He angled to the left to take the trail he had always used to reach the main trail and walked slowly down the slope. Just above the main trail, he lifted his right foot to step down onto the flat. His left foot slid sideways in the snow, his knee buckled, and he knew he was going down. The weight of the meat and horns on the packboard threw him backwards slamming his back to the ground. Sharp pain shot up his left leg, and a blow in the back of the head stunned him. His breath was driven from his lungs, and he was immediately nauseous. A wave of blackness overtook him, and he slid beneath it.

When he came awake, he lay still, looking up through the branches of a tree to the leaden sky. *How long have I been out?* He had no way to answer that. He couldn't tell, and it didn't really matter. Cold had seeped through his clothes, now wet from the snow.

So, I must have been out for quite a while.

He knew he was hurt but made no immediate attempt to move or evaluate how bad it was. His right arm was straight to his side. His left arm was slightly under his body, his hand near the small of his back. There was pain in his left shoulder. The left hip ached as well. There was an ache in his left ribcage. *Must have landed on my left side,* he thought. His left leg was beneath his right leg, and the pain there was tremendous. The back of his head hurt. He raised his right hand to his head and found that the ski cap had been knocked off. He felt for the soreness on the back of his head and winced at the sharp pain when he found wet, matted hair. When he looked at his hand, the palm of the glove was covered with blood. He removed the glove and probed the injured spot. It stung when he touched it. *Pretty good gash back there*, he thought.

He remained flat on his back, meat and horns beneath him. His upper body was in a semi-raised slant, leaning on the packboard. His legs and feet pointed down the slope.

Lifting his head, he looked toward his feet but saw nothing that caused the extreme pain in his left leg. When he tried to lift the right leg to look at the left one, pain jammed him back against the packboard. His head banged against a sharp point on the horns. Eyes closed, he lay still for several minutes breathing deeply, trying to relax. Fighting against the pain. Pain in his head. Pain in the left shoulder and hip. Pain in his left ribs, left leg, and the small of his back. He hadn't noticed the pain in his back until he tried to move. And pain anywhere indicated some degree of injury. The pain in his left leg was overwhelming. "Gotta check that leg," he said. The ache in his back and shoulder didn't seem severe, but it still worried him. A broken or dislocated shoulder would immobilize his arm and hand. A broken back, and he would die right where he lay. He had been able to move his right leg, which was good. There was no pain in that leg.

He lifted his head slightly, rechecked the gash in his scalp, and looked at his hand. "A lot of blood back there." He knew head wounds bled a lot and often looked worse than they were. Feeling around behind his head, he found that a sharp point of the elk's skull was directly behind his head. "Shit," he said. "I should've left those damn horns up there with the hide." His head began to throb with his heartbeat. *Concussion* flitted through his mind. "Deal with that later," he said.

He took the glove he had removed from his right hand and held it against the back of his head over the injury. He lowered his head to rest on the glove that now padded the sharp point of the elk's skull. Eyes closed, he took long, deep breaths. With each exhale, he whispered, "Relax. Deep breath, exhale. Just relax. Deep breath, exhale. Just relax." Trying to control his response to the pain, he let his body sag against the ground and the packboard beneath him. Mentally relaxing his body, he was able to release some of the tension he felt.

For several minutes, he remained as he was. Breathing, controlling, relaxing. Focusing on the mantra he had used many times to deal with stress, he slowly pushed away as much of the world outside his mind as he could. The ground, the trees, the cold snow beneath him faded. Even the pain became somewhat muted. All but the pain in his left leg.

In this relaxed state, eyes closed, he mentally examined his body, head to foot, assessing, evaluating. The gash in his head and the pain there he skipped by. "Worry about that later," he whispered to himself. "Nothing wrong with the neck. The chest is okay. The arms are okay." He slid his left arm from under his body and brought it up to lay his hand on his chest. The pain in his shoulder and left ribs increased only slightly with the movement. He'd broken ribs before, and the pain there now was nowhere close to what he'd felt with broken ribs. "The back hurts but doesn't seem too bad either." Lifting each shoulder off the packboard, he twisted his back and felt a little increase in pain. "Hips seem ok." An ache in the left hip but not bad. Right leg? No pain. He moved his right foot from side to side and wiggled his toes. "Movement's a good thing. No increased pain."

Every movement, however, increased the pain in his left leg. *The left leg? That's a bad one*, he thought. *The left leg is gonna be real bad.*

Instinctively he made no attempt to move it. He didn't even want to think about it. He knew that any movement would increase the pain to a brutal level. But he needed to find out how bad that leg was and figure out what to do about it. But any more pain than he now had in that leg would take him out of this world again, and he needed to remain awake, alert.

He lay as he was, eyes closed, cold seeping into his body from the snow and the ground. He did not want to move. Wished it would just go away. *Put wishes in one hand and dog shit in the other and see which one fills up first,* he thought. There was nothing to do but grit his teeth and go for it. *Either that or lay right here and turn into a Popsicle by midnight, old son.*

He started to reach for the knife with his left hand, and sharp pain stabbed his shoulder. With his right hand he reached across his body and pulled the skinning knife from its sheath at his belt and laid it on his stomach. The handgun was slightly beneath his right side digging into his ribs, and he adjusted it. Pain in the leg and his back ratcheted up immediately. He unhooked the cross strap holding the shoulder straps of the packboard together across his chest. With the knife he cut both shoulder straps, freeing him from the packboard. Now he could move his body without the weight of the meat holding him down. "I don't want to move anything," he moaned. "I don't want to move anything at all." But he knew that was not an option.

He replaced the knife in the sheath. In the back of his mind, he continued the mantra, "Relax. Stay relaxed." His breathing was still slow, steady, and deep. Throughout the actions he had just taken, he had kept his eyes closed, using only touch to feel what he was doing and guide his actions. Sometimes things seemed easier with the eyes closed.

After several minutes of continued relaxation, he opened his eyes. The trees still rose above him. The dark, heavy sky still hung seemingly just above the treetops. All he saw drifted slowly to his left, bringing nausea, and he closed his eyes again.

He knew he couldn't remain like this much longer. He had to find out how badly he was injured and deal with it. If he could.

The packboard and the meat kept his upper body in a slightly raised position. Lifting his head, he pressed his chin to his chest so he could see his legs stretched out below him on the slope. The right leg lay on top of the left from mid-calf to the foot. He could only see the toe of his left boot on the outside of his right leg. The position of his left foot seemed canted at an odd angle.

Even the movement of his head intensified the pain in his leg. That pain was focused in the lower left leg but radiated all the way to his groin, hip, and stomach. Nausea was just below the surface of everything. He needed to see that left leg and foot before he tried to sit up. "I really don't want to see it. But I have to." He took a deep breath and closed his eyes again as he let it out. "It's gonna be bad. But you gotta know how bad it is."

Concentrating on his right leg, he tensed the thigh, shin, and foot muscles without moving the leg. That didn't increase the pain. He wasn't sure anything could make the pain worse. And knew how wrong he was. He relaxed the right leg completely and tilted his head back. The glove had dropped from the packboard to the ground near his neck, and he left it there. Blood ran down the back of his neck and soaked his shirt collar.

Closing his eyes, he concentrated on his right leg again. Tensing all the muscles, he slowly lifted it, locked from the hip to ankle, and swung it gradually to the right before lowering it gently to the ground. "Don't jar anything, old son. Keep it slow and easy." But even that movement uncovered a new level of pain. Several deep breaths later, he raised his head, opened his eyes, and looked at the uncovered left leg. "Oh shit. There's not supposed to be a joint right there."

At about mid-calf above his left boot, his lower leg took a sharp turn to the inside with the inside of his foot lying flat against the ground. "Broken for sure." He saw no blood on his pants or in the snow. "Not a compound fracture," he said. "But that's one hell of a bad break for sure." Moving it now, or at any time, was going to be brutal. And move it he must, sooner or later. "No, sooner *and* later." Looking at it made the nausea return. Lightheaded, he closed his eyes.

He padded the back of his head with the glove again and leaned back to rest and think. The world was still turning slowly left. Eyes closed, pushing the nausea away, he went over what he needed to do. "Forget about how it's going to be. Don't think about how much pain. That doesn't matter now." What needs to be done has just got to be done. No two ways about it.

He turned his head to the right and looked at the truck. It, too, coasted to his left in a slow, dizzying crawl. How to get from here to there was what he needed to think about. The objective? Get to the truck. One way or another, no matter how, get to the truck. And the pain would have control of him through all of it. Staying where he was would be certain death. He looked again at the truck. Maybe a hundred yards away. "Might as well be a mile," he said.

"Time?" The word echoed in his mind. Looking to the sky, he tried to estimate. Through the heavy clouds, he was not able to tell where the sun was. "Mid-afternoon? Probably." He didn't know. "Long enough for your clothes to get soaked and the cold to settle in your bones, boy." He should have been back at the camp no later than noon. "So, let's say, three, maybe four hours of daylight left. Gotta get to the truck before dark. That's a given."

Next? Cold! "It's damn cold now, and it'll be real cold when it gets dark." He knew it was below freezing now and would be well below zero in the night. The temperature would start dropping fast when the sun went down. All the elk meat had frozen solid last night. "You stay out here all night and you'll be frozen steaks by dawn."

And the big question? "How do I get that leg back to the truck?" He knew the pain was going to be bad. Could he take it? "I'll have to take it." Thinking of how to get to the truck, he said, "I sure as hell can't stand with that leg the way it is."

Any movement was going to increase the pain and could cause more damage. He could open an artery and bleed to death. A sharp piece of bone could do that with the slightest movement. He could damage nerves and lose the use of the foot.

Those two things could have already happened. But he didn't think so. Only time would give him the answer. If they had happened already, he was a dead man. If not, movement could force a bone through the skin and cause a hemorrhage or invite infection. In time, he might get an infection anyway. Could a clot form? Travel up the leg? Go through his heart or brain? Into his lungs? Heart attack. Stroke. Pulmonary embolism. All probably fatal here on the mountain.

"Stop worrying about what might happen. None of that matters," he said. "Ya have to get to the truck. And take the leg with you. It's that simple." He paused. "And that tough." He took a deep breath and let it out. "Get the leg to the truck or die right here, old son." He rested his body against the packboard and closed his eyes, trying to relax. "I sure as hell ain't gonna lay here and die," he said through gritted teeth.

"Ok. Don't think about the pain. Wipe it out. If you can. As much as you can. Concentrate on getting to the truck. Where you can take care of the leg. And just maybe stay alive."

What he needed was a splint to stabilize the break. And a crutch if he could find something to use for one. Looking around, everything except the ground directly under the trees was buried under snow. There was no way he could move around under the trees to locate something to use as a crutch or splints. Too much movement and too much pain. And from where he was, he could see nothing for either splints or a crutch close by. And no way to attach splints here on the ridge. That left crawling to the truck. Dragging the leg behind him.

"So, leave the packboard and the meat, drag yourself to the truck, and then figure out the next step."

Putting his hands on the ground near his upper body, he closed his eyes tight, gritted his teeth, and pushed himself into a partial sitting position. Pain gripped his shoulder. Pain cramped his lower back. Pain tore at the leg clear to his stomach. Nausea took control of him. His ears rang with it, and the world spun to his left. His head throbbed. Tears formed and flowed. He sat motionless, forcing the nausea to recede, willing himself to remain conscious. When he opened his eyes, he looked at the leg and growled. A mean, deep-throated growl. "You son-of-a-bitch," he snarled at the leg. "You rotten son-of-a-bitch."

With a deep breath, he tried to relax and regain composure. "This sure as hell isn't gonna be easy." For several minutes more, he just sat staring at his leg, jointed where there should be no joint. "You're in deep trouble now, boy. And this ain't as bad as it's gonna get. This is only the beginning." As always, he turned his mind to what needed to be done, solving the problem as best he could, getting through it, staying alive. Fighting for control, he said, "Move your ass, boy."

First, he needed to get onto flat ground. On a level with the truck where there would be no brush to get through or around. That flat ground was only a yard or so from his feet. And a drop of a foot and a half down the slope.

Feeling the area near his head, he found the ski cap and shook the snow from it, a movement that jarred his body, increasing his pain. He put it on his head. He rolled the mask down over his face, adjusting the eye and mouth holes. He pulled the knife from the sheath again and with just a touch, he cut the bone saw loose from the packboard. Why he might need that he refused to think about. He just needed it. He replaced the knife and slid the bone saw under his coat.

Shifting his body to the right on his butt, he moved sideways downhill toward the main trail, dragging his legs behind him. Using his arms put a strain on his shoulder, ribs, and back. That pain was nothing compared to the leg. But it was there and nagged at him. All movement increased the leg pain. And that was more than just nagging. "Don't think about the legs. Keep them straight and still. Just drag 'em."

His butt and the back of his legs were now soaking wet from the snow. The thermal underwear was wet as well, and he was feeling the cold deep inside him. "Just keep moving," he said. "Don't think about the snow. Don't think about the pain. Don't think about the leg. Just get back to the truck," he growled. "That's all that matters."

CHAPTER 12

As he moved sideways down the slope to the main trail, his gloved right hand slipped in the snow, causing him to lose his balance and tumble to the flat ground below. His body turned and rolled in the snow, legs and arms flopping loose. His left rib cage slammed against a large rock under the snow. The left leg pounded against the frozen ground. Agonizing pain overtook him. Nausea gripped him. Breathing was reduced to small gasps. Struggling for breath, he lay flat on the ground on his back. Pain filled the world. Pain so intense he couldn't tell where it came from and where it ended. Pain was global. Pain was everything. Clamping his jaw tight, growling deep in his throat, he opened his eyes. The sky and the trees spun rapidly above him. A solid blur of trees. And there was no way to stop it. The sky and the trees faded, spinning away into the darkness that covered him, and took him out of this world. Away from the snow, and the cold, and the pain.

•   •   •

Again, he had no way of knowing how long he had been out. As he drifted back to consciousness, the first thing he felt was the leg. The pain had knocked him out, and the pain had brought him back. Second, the cold.

Snow was piled around his head. His body was trembling, and he was not able to control the shaking. Eyes closed, he said, "Damn, I'm in big trouble." His entire body was shaking.

Something landed on his right eyelid through the hole in the ski mask. Something soft, wet, and cold. He knew instantly what it was and groaned. He opened his eyes, and the sky was right in his face. The clouds were down below the tops of the trees, a swirl of mist just out of reach. And it was snowing. Large, quiet flakes drifting onto his face, body, and the world all around him. Hard, heavy, wet snow. Huge flakes everywhere. It was difficult to distinguish between the falling snow and the clouds. But no wind. *Thank God, no wind*, he whispered. Face to face with the falling snow, he had the sense of floating upward to meet it.

All around him, there was silence. Profound, frightening quiet. And the snow kept falling. The cold still weighed on him. It might as well be snowing all over the globe. The entire world was covered with white, cold snow and silence. That was all there was in his world now. Cold, snow, and silence. And the pain.

Twisting his head around, he could barely make out the truck through the falling snow across the camping area. "You're in the deep end of the pool now, boy," he said. "You've gotta move." His head sagged back against the ground. "You've gotta get to the truck," he sighed.

Putting his hands to his sides, he pushed himself to a sitting position. Snow fell from his chest and head onto his lap. Inches of snow had piled on him as he lay unconscious.

Pain rolled through him. Shoulders, ribs, back, and leg. He tried to force it away but couldn't. The fight was between him and the pain. For now, the enemies were the pain and the cold. And the snow. "And you're not gonna win, you sons-of-bitches. You can't have me," he growled through gritted teeth.

"I've gotta get to the truck" echoed in his head.

He put his hands as far behind him as he could, raised his butt off the ground, and dragged his hips to his hands, keeping both legs as straight as possible. "That's one." he said. And he did it again. "That's two." One slide at a time, one foot at a time, he continued toward the truck, snow piling up behind him before sliding off to either side like a wake. Counting each move of his hands and hips. Focusing only on the movement, counting each motion and small piece of ground gained. Focused on getting to the truck, one foot at a time. Keeping the pain outside of himself. As much as possible.

The first time he rested, he turned his head to look at the truck. His first impression was that it was not closer. "How can I work that long, that hard, and it's not any closer?" He had counted every move to thirty-seven. Only thirty-seven? The truck was still a hazy image through the falling snow.

Facing back in front of him, he slumped forward. Eyes closed, chin on his chest. After a few moments, he raised his head, staring into the falling snow. The tree line was already dim behind a curtain of drifting snowflakes. "Hey, dummy, it is closer. The truck is closer. It just doesn't look like it, but it really is. So, move your ass, boy."

Hands behind his butt, he moved again, pushing through the snow. For a second, he thought that he had lost his count. Then, teeth gritted, he growled, "That's thirty-eight." He paused and thought, "Don't think about how far it is to the truck. Think about how far you've come. You're doin' good, old son. You're doin' real good." Face grim and determined, body trembling, he continued. Reach back, drag. Reach back, drag. The pain outside himself. "Doesn't matter. Keep moving. Get to the truck."

"That's forty-three." Snow piled up behind his back as he moved, one foot at a time, in the steadily drifting snow. Reach back, drag. Reach back, drag. He checked the truck now only for direction, not distance. He ignored the distance. Getting there, however long it took, no matter how far away it was, was the only thing he focused on now. He watched the trough he made in the snow in front of him fade into the distance. Disappearing as he pushed on to the truck. He could no longer see the trees on the ridge through the falling snow.

Stopping to rest, he sat in the snow, slumped forward. Head and arms hanging. "Tired. Man, I'm real tired." Arms aching, back cramping, mind foggy tired. Body shivering beyond control from fatigue and the cold. "My ass is going to freeze to the ground. Keep going or sit here and die, dummy."

He put his arms behind him again. "Three hundred eighty-two." And his arms bumped something, just above his elbows. He turned his head and looked straight into the grill of the truck. Leaning his shaking shoulders against the bumper, head back against the grill, he put his hands in his lap. "I made it. By damn, I made it. Gotta rest now. Just a minute," and he closed his eyes. Immediately they shot open again. "No! You haven't made it yet. Get the keys. Get in the truck! You've gotta get warm. Then you can rest."

The keys were on the right front truck tire. To slide sideways, he needed to reach his right hand farther from his body, lift his butt off the ground, and shift toward his right side. That movement brought the pain back to an alarming level. His left shoulder and ribs were numb with fatigue and pain. "So what!" he growled. "Get in the damn truck."

From the corner of the right front fender, he reached to the top of the tire and found the keys. Gripping them tightly in his right hand, he shifted in the snow, now more than a foot deep, and struggled the last few feet to the left side of the truck and the driver's door. With his right arm, he swept snow from the side of the door and the key hole. Snow cascaded onto his head, down his neck. Reaching up with his right hand, the key slid in, turned, and he heard the beautiful sound of the lock disengaging.

Now would come more pain. He knew it. And knew that he must get through it. Get past it. And stay conscious. "Get in the truck," he growled.

Above his head, the door handle stuck out from the door. He gripped it with his right hand. Pulled his right foot up to his butt, leg bent at the knee. For a moment he rested his chin on his knee. With gritted teeth he turned his back against the door of the truck. Cold. Stiff and weak. Every muscle in his body trembling. The left leg lay flat on the ground. "I can do this. I can do this," he whispered. With a snarl, he pushed up with his right leg as he pulled on the door handle. Back sliding up along the door, he slowly rose to a standing position, right leg trembling, ready to give out. His left leg, hanging loose, came up with him, dragging limp through the snow along the ground. Pressure against the ground bent his leg at the break, screaming with pain. Groaning deep in his chest, eyes crammed shut, he continued. Standing on his right leg, he turned his body to the right to get behind the trailing edge of the door.

Keys in his right hand, he gripped the wall of the truck bed. Thumbing the door handle, the door swung open easily. Snow from the roof dropped onto the truck seat and threshold, and he swiped at it with a shaking hand. It was dark in the cab, snow blocking the windshield and the door windows.

"The last step, boy," he said, as he shifted his body to back into the truck, weight on his right foot, leg, and arms. All of his body quaking. Shaking beyond control. His butt against the seat, he took hold of the steering wheel with his right hand and placed his left hand on the seat. "Now it's really gonna hurt," he said. Jaws clamped tight, eyes crammed shut, pushing and pulling, he lifted his butt onto the edge of the seat and slid into the truck. Holding his weight with his hands and arms, he lifted his right foot to the floor of the truck. When he pushed and pulled himself further into the truck his left leg swung free and bounced against the threshold. This time he screamed. Long and loud. There was no stopping it, and he let it come.

The darkness was coming, too. "Not now! Not now! Not now!" he growled through his hard-set jaws and grinding teeth. Through the fog overtaking him, he pushed back, body sliding into the truck. He sat forward and took hold of his left pant leg at the knee and lifted his foot to the truck floor. His heel rested on the floor, pushing against the lower leg and the broken bones. Screams filled his ears as he reached for the door handle, missed, groped again, pulled the door closed with a bang, and fell back across the seat.

His relief was like floating away into nothing.

And then he was gone. Deep into the darkness. Where there was no pain. No snow. No cold. For a time he would never be able to measure, he lay deep in the darkness.

CHAPTER 13

The world drifted back by small degrees. In and out. Here and gone again. On the fringe of consciousness, he tried to sit up, and the pain brought him all the way back with a vengeance. Broken bones ground against each other inside the leg. He screamed again. No holding it back this time. When he opened his eyes, all was dark. Completely dark. An 'eyes closed in the night' kind of dark. He was lying on his right side across the truck seat, head against the rolled sleeping bag, feet on the floor under the steering wheel. The truck door was closed. And it was cold. Very, very cold. A cold deeper than he had ever known. Far beyond shivering. His entire body rattled with the cold.

Trying to sit up, he shifted his legs on the floor. Pain flared in his left leg, and he flopped back onto the seat. Motionless, he lay against the rolled sleeping bag. He groaned with the pain, acknowledging it, accepting it. He could not ignore it. He got the box of matches from his coat pocket and lit one. In the light of the flame, he found the lamp on the floor near the gear shift. He turned it on and looked around. Cooler, sleeping bag, and bags of food were on the floor. The bags of meat were piled near the gearshift. His right glove was still on his hand. The left glove was on the floor under his right foot. Truck keys? Nowhere in sight. "They're here. They've gotta be here," he moaned. Feeling and searching along the seat, he found them under his right hip. He sighed with relief, glad he hadn't dropped them outside in the snow. His hands were shaking from the cold. His fingers were so numb, he could barely feel the keys as he gripped them. He fumbled to select the ignition key and tried to hold it steady to slide it into the ignition. On the first attempt, he missed. On the second try, he hit the slot, but his shaking hand pushed the key sideways, and he nearly dropped the keys on the floor. His hands and arms from his shoulders to fingers were flopping, disjointed. His entire body was shivering in a quivering, quaking mass. No form and no control.

Gripping his right wrist with his left hand, he finally managed to insert the key in the ignition. When he turned it, the truck started immediately. "Oh, you good old girl," he said, patting the dashboard lovingly. He pulled off the ski mask, wet with melted snow, lay back down along the seat, closed his eyes, and waited for the heat.

The bone saw was still under his coat. He unzipped the coat and laid the saw on the floor beside the meat. The handgun was beneath his right hip, digging into him. He shifted his body and pulled the holster from under him.

He scooted his back against the rolled sleeping bag. Gripping his left pants leg at the knee, he pulled his leg onto the seat, foot sagging to the inside. He leaned back and rested his head against the passenger side window and was instantly reminded of the gash in his scalp. Probing with his hand, he found his wet hair matted with sticky, nearly frozen blood. It didn't feel as if the cut was still actively bleeding, but he wasn't sure. Crusted, frozen blood stiffened his shirt collar. He was not able to tell how big the cut was, but touching it brought sharp pain. "Hurt's a hell of a lot better than painful," he said. "Big difference between real pain and just hurt."

Again, he wondered about a concussion. He didn't think he had obvious symptoms. No dizziness. No blurred or double vision. No nausea as had come with the pain in the leg. He leaned forward, twisted the rear-view mirror so he could look into it, and held the lamp up to see his eyes. The pupils were the same size and responsive to the light. "Good. That's good," he said.

The cut on his head was partially crusted over now with drying, matted blood. Later, he would need to wash it and put on some antibiotic. He still had a pounding headache. But he had more serious concerns now. Leaning forward, he reached under the driver's side of the seat for the first aid kit. Doing so put pressure on his legs and pain rammed up his left leg into his groin and stomach. There was no way to suppress the groan. "Groanin's good. Groanin's okay," he said through gritted teeth. The pain was going to take priority in his life from now on. At least until he got out of here. In time, it may recede some, but it was still going to be there for a long time.

Warm air was now blowing strong, filling the cab with heat. "Lord have mercy, it's good to feel warm air again."

Opening the first aid kit, he located a bottle of Advil, a full, unopened bottle of 250 tablets. From the cooler, he got a bottle of water and took two of the 200 milligram tablets. The water was partially frozen. "Four hundred milligrams won't kill the pain, but maybe it'll help. Don't mess with the leg until those pills kick in, old son."

He lay on the seat, back resting on the sleeping bag. He needed to think things through. Figure out where he stood for survival. The leg would take priority over everything. But he needed to think about how to stay alive. Until there was a way out. "Focus, boy. Focus. Clear the mind and think. If you're going to make it, you have to stay as focused as you can. And you have to think as clearly as you can.

In front of him, the passenger floor of the truck was piled with bags of food, and the cooler was full of food and drink. He had elk meat and small bags of clean clothing. "Where do I stand with food?" He went over it in his mind. He had packed for a total of ten days of meals, three meals per day. He had used five days of those meals, minus one dinner of back strap. He had nearly a full jar of peanut butter and jam and almost a full loaf of bread, a few power bars, and half a dozen apples left. He had enough food to last for a while. If needed, he could cut down to two meals a day, and he would be fine for another week with the food he had brought. "They'll come get me before I run out of that food."

In addition, he had the rest of the back strap, the tender loins, the roast meat, the flank meat, heart and liver in the cab of the truck. That would make several good meals. And there was around 350 pounds of meat in the truck's bed, frozen solid. There was still a half gallon of milk, five cans of Pepsi, five full bottles of water, and two full bottles of Gatorade. If need be, he could melt snow for water. "Way more food than I can eat in the time I have left, as it were. Most of it's going to stay here all winter anyway."

While the truck continued to warm, he checked the gas gauge. It read just below three-quarters of a tank in a thirty-five-gallon tank. Plus, he had a five-gallon can of gas in the bed of the truck. If he rationed the gas, it could last several days. "Not all winter, it won't," he said.

When the truck was warm, he turned it off and lay back again with his eyes closed.

A thought of the kids flickered through his mind, but he put that aside for later. Time to assess the leg. He could tell it had swollen quite a lot, and he needed to stabilize it soon. "Eat first, old son. Then tend to the leg. That's gonna to be real bad when you do it. You know that."

How long had it been since the fall? He retrieved his watch from the glove box, slipped it on his wrist, and checked the time. "Friday, 9:57 p.m." The fall had to have been around noon or a little before. "Wow! That's a long time. Ten hours or thereabouts. And I was out for a big part of it. Three times. Maybe for half of that time?" He was shocked at how much time had passed, with a large part of it out in the snow and cold. Ten hours, he assessed. Up there on the end of that ridge, down on the flat. Dragging through the snow and here in the truck. Part of the time, totally out of it.

He went over the fall in his mind. All he remembered was losing his footing and the heavy packboard with the load of meat throwing him backward, then nothing more until he woke up. And that initial pain. With his hands in his lap, his chin on his chest, he shook his head. "Doesn't matter now how it happened. It happened. And I have to live with it. Live through it. And make do until I get out of here, one way or the other."

From a grocery bag on the floor, he took a can of Dinty Moore stew, opened it with a can opener, found a spoon, and got a can of Pepsi from the cooler. With the spoon, he stirred the coagulated fat into the stew and ate it cold from the can, sipping the Pepsi. He looked out through the now defrosted windshield and saw only darkness. It was still snowing, large flakes landing and melting on the windshield. He switched on the headlights. It was a big snow. Wet, heavy flakes piled on everything. It was hard to tell how deep the snow was now. The world around him was blurred, closed in to just a few feet beyond the hood of the truck by the falling snow. All that he could see was drifting snowflakes. He was encased in a cocoon of snow. The trail made when he had dragged himself to the truck had disappeared under new-fallen snow. And the snow continued to pile up. In his world and in his mind.

Every movement he made hurt. The leg throbbed constantly. The slightest movement shocked it. His ribs hurt, and his left shoulder ached. His headache was subdued but still there. The hours in the deep cold with wet clothing had invaded his entire body. His arms, back and stomach muscles were sore from the exertion of dragging himself through the snow. He felt as if he had been beaten for hours.

And he felt something he hadn't noticed before—a burning, tingling in his skin and flesh. "Maybe that's an indication of how close I came to freezing to death." The tingling was recovery from the extreme and prolonged cold. "You dodged that one, old son."

And he was completely exhausted. He wanted to sleep for a very long time. But not now. There were things that needed to be done first.

He sat what was left of the stew on the floor with the spoon in the can, "Save it for another meal," he said. The last of the Pepsi was good.

"It's time to do something with the head, and then deal with the leg." He took a tube of antibiotic ointment from the first aid kit and laid it on the seat beside him. He filled the cooking pot with cold water, soaked a washcloth, and began washing the back of his head. A sharp sting flared with each touch, but he continued until the clotted blood mostly washed away. When he looked at the washcloth, there was some of his hair and what appeared to be a lot of elk hair on the cloth. A piece of white flesh stuck to the cloth as well. "Is that a piece of me or is that a piece of elk brains?" He must have hit his head on a sharp part of the elk's skull and not the horns.

He rinsed the washcloth in the water and wiped the cut area again. This time when he looked at the cloth, along with the blood, he also saw minute particles of bone, chips made when he removed the horns from the elk's skull with the bone saw. These particles had been embedded in the gash of his scalp along with elk hair.

When he applied a large glob of the ointment to the cut, he found fresh blood on his hand. "It had to be done. Let it bleed. It's okay. Doesn't seem too serious." At this point, there was no way to bandage the cut. Monitor it, treat it, and hope for the best. He sat the pot of blood-tinged water aside.

"Time for the leg." He adjusted the rolled-up sleeping bag to make a better back rest against the passenger door. This part he did not want to do. The leg hurt more than anything he had ever experienced before. He'd had broken fingers, a broken foot, a shattered cheekbone, and broken ribs more than once. The ribs had been the worst. Up to now anyway. You can't even breath without pain when the ribs are broken. With broken ribs, the world stopped with the slightest body movement. But this, now, was going to be bad. Real bad. More than likely worse than broken ribs. Perhaps even fatal without proper treatment. "You'll know the answer to that somewhere down the road, old son."

He knew he needed to stabilize the leg as much as possible. Without splints. It flopped around too much below the break. He wondered if he could stay conscious for what he needed to do. "We'll see," he said. "We'll see."

He found a dirty pair of blue jeans in the laundry bag and brought them to his lap. With the knife, he cut the material of the legs into two-inch-wide strips. Wrapped around the leg, he hoped these strips would make good binding to hold the shattered part of the leg in place. "I sure could use some splints." And he thought of the packboard, lying at the end of the ridge still tied to the elk's front shoulder, now buried under the still falling snow. "I could have cut the damn thing up and used the back slats for splints. And I left it up there with that meat tied to it." He shook his head, holding the strips of material in his lap. "Not too smart, old son. You started with a bad decision right from the top. But you were in no condition to be rational then." He pondered going back to get it and shook his head again, dejected. "That's one decision you're going to have to live with. Right now, that packboard might as well be in China."

His foot was definitely swollen inside the boot. No way could he just pull that boot off. He would have to cut it off. The pain had his full attention just resting on the floor. It would be pure hell once he started moving and manipulating it. "It's gotta be done. And I'm the only one here to do it." He turned on the overhead light. He moved the lamp from the dashboard to the top of the seat back where it leaned against the back window. "Plenty of light. Not that I want to look at the damn thing. Or even move it. I just gotta get that boot off."

By inches, he scooted his butt along the truck seat, lower back tight against the sleeping bag. At the same time, he raised the leg to lay it on the seat by gripping the pants leg, lifting it, and swinging it over the seat. The foot still canted sharply to the inside at mid-calf. "No way to set it by myself." When the nausea sucked at him, he stopped, leaned against the sleeping bag and rested, head back, chanting the mantra. "Relax," and he took a deep breath. "Just relax," he said again as he took another deep breath. "You can do this," he said. Gradually, he slid down inside himself and rested.

Leaning forward, trying to block the pain, he slit the pant leg and the leg of the thermal underwear from well above the knee to the bottom with the skinning knife. Spreading the material out, he looked at the leg. It was seriously swollen and dark to just above the knee. The skin was cool to the touch. Flesh bulged around the top of the boot. He cut the boot laces from top to bottom, pulled the pieces out, and dropped them on the floor. The tongue was sewn to the sidewalls of the boot, and he slit these from top to bottom and pulled the tongue out over the toe of the boot. The smallest movement caused pain. Lots of pain.

The swollen foot spread the boot open, and the bottom of his foot and his toes began to tingle. "Circulation's been cut off. I should have gotten the boot off sooner." He mentally slapped himself for another bad decision. "Doesn't matter now. What's done is done. Move on!"

Because of the tingling in his toes, he involuntarily started to flex them inside the boot. And the pain took hold of him and dragged him immediately down below the edge of darkness. As he slipped beneath the surface of the pain, he heard a scream and wondered where it came from.

CHAPTER 14

The scream still in his ears, he felt the cold and opened his eyes. The lamp still filled the floor of the cab with light. The overhead light was still on. Looking at his watch, he saw that it was 11:40. "You've been out for a quite a while, old son." He was foggy and confused, and it took several minutes to clear his head and grasp where he was and why. He closed his eyes and took a mental pause. When he opened them again, he knew he was fully back in the truck. Pain and all.

He closed his eyes again and started a slow assessment. The back of his head was on fire. He wished he could see it so he could take better care of it. *Maybe it's better if I don't see it.* His back was stiff, and his left ribs ached with every movement and breath. But neither concerned him now. They were painful but just part of the whole. The pain in his lower left leg and foot were pulsing with agony. Swollen inside the boot, his foot felt as if it were being crushed from every direction. "You've got to get that boot off, boy."

His leg was swollen from above the knee down through his ankle and his foot inside the boot. It was pressed tightly by the material of his pant leg. Releasing his leg would be the easiest.

The only way to relieve the foot and ankle was to remove the boot entirely. And that was going to be tricky. And no doubt very painful.

The only way to get the boot off was to cut it off one little piece at a time. And do it without so much as a nick to his foot.

His face was still stiff from the time out in the cold while getting back to the truck. His hands and fingers were tingling as they warmed. Without the ski mask and the gloves, his ears and hands would be a lot worse than they were.

He needed to start the truck to get warm again. Leaning forward, he turned the key. The engine started immediately. "That's a good ole' girl," he said, lovingly patting the dashboard. He leaned back against the seat, closed his eyes, and slid away into the darkness again.

When he woke, he slowly became aware of where he was. And how he had gotten there. He pushed up into a semi-sitting position and fumbled with the truck keys to turn off the motor. When he leaned forward to get a water bottle, his head swirled, and he thought he was going to go under again. He held still and waited for it to pass.

When he tried to move his toes, serious pain shot up his leg between his foot to above his knee. The pain slammed him against the truck seat and radiated to his hip and stomach. He leaned back against the seat and rested for several minutes, trying to regain control. He almost got there.

The truck was running, and the cab was hot. It felt as if his entire body was sweating. He took a deep breath and leaned back against the seat and rested. His eyes closed.

Sometime later, he opened his eyes and took another deep breath. With his eyes closed again, he said, " It's time. Ya gotta do what's gotta be done with that leg and foot. No matter how much it will hurt. And it's gonna hurt a lot."

Immediately he began trimming the outside part of the boot top, a small sliver at a time. Down the front of the flap, he maneuvered between the metal shoelace eyes, leaning forward as far as he could. To get to the foot and the boot was a strain on his back, arms, ribs, and shoulders. Breath pushed from his lungs as he manipulated the knife through the hard leather without cutting his fingers or his foot again in the process. The work and position he had to work in were difficult and taxing. Frequently, he needed to rest his back and arms and catch his breath. The pain tugged constantly at his consciousness, but he fought it. The fog in his mind was a block to push through as well.

"Damn good pair of boots there. I've had 'em a long time. They've kept my feet dry and warm for a lot of years." Those boots went through two or three sets of new soles and heels. They had taken him up many a mountain. A lot of game trails and high ridges. "Sure be a damn shame to cut one of 'em up." But he knew that boot had to come off, and cutting it off was the only way.

He leaned forward against his body. With the knife in hand, he gripped the side of the boot, continuing to trim and loosen the boot back toward the heel. There was no moving that foot to help get the boot off either.

Resting often, he continued trimming the hard leather around the top and side of the heel until he had cut it all away, except the outside of the upper part that was under his foot. The swollen foot alone was more relaxed without the boot tight around it. He knew turning his foot to remove the other side of the boot would be more pain than he could stand. And he doubted that could be done anyway. His foot simply wouldn't turn that way now. What he had removed lay in a jumble of small pieces on the floor and seat of the truck. "There goes a hundred and seventy-five bucks for new boots," he said. "And then I gotta break in new ones."

He lay the knife on the floor near the gear shift and rested against the sleeping bag, eyes closed, breathing deep.

"Tired," he sighed. "I need to get this done and then sleep. If I can."

He took the bottle of Advil from the dash and washed down two more tablets with water. Still, he rested. Taking slow deep breaths. Eyes closed. No sleep tempted him. His world was all pain now. Throbbing, searing pain. And a brain full of cotton.

He sat up, took a long deep breath, and let it out all the way as he immediately leaned forward and took hold of what was left of the boot with his left hand. He cupped the heel with his right hand. With slight pressure, he pushed the heel toward the floor, tilting the sole up and away from him. With equal pressure, he tried to guide the toe of the boot up and away from his foot. His right hand slipped off the heel, and the arch of his foot stamped down on the hump of the floorboard. Lightning bolts of pain shot up his leg. He re-gripped the heel and increased a steady, slow pressure with his right hand, pushing the boot off his heel until it came loose. Growling deep in his throat, he dropped what was left of the boot to the floor. He sagged back against the sleeping bag, eyes closed, fighting for control. Taking a deep, slow breath, he went through the mantra, trying to relax and maintain control but slid deep within himself into the darkness once again.

Gradually, he came back to himself. The swirling in his head calmed. The nausea receded. The darkness pushed away for now. Pain was still there, but he was managing it. *The Advil must be helping some*, he thought.

The sock on the foot was stretched tight. A little work with the knife removed it with little increase in the pain. He nicked the top of his foot again at nearly the same spot, and a slow trickle of blood crept down the side of the foot toward his heel.

"Now, that's one nasty lookin' son-of-a-bitch," he said, staring at the foot. "It looks like a hunk of raw meat that had been left out too long." The toes had swollen like black, puffy sausages. The skin from knee down to toenails was smooth, black, and shiny. "That's going to lay me up for a spell."

Staring at the foot, he thought of how things would go when he finally got to a hospital. It would have to be set. Certainly, surgery with pins to hold it in place. And a cast for weeks. Pain starting all over again right from the top. *I'm probably never gonna walk on that leg the same ever again*, he thought.

"Don't get ahead of yourself, boy. You ain't even off this mountain yet. You're still up here in deep shit and deeper snow that's still fallin.' And this old truck is going to stay here all winter, even if someone comes to get you out. The main thing now is don't panic. Hang in there."

These last words he said with jaw set and in as firm a voice as he could. It was a defining principle he had lived by for a very long time. Stay in control. Never panic. Hang in there. That's not the same as not being afraid. He knew what fear was. And he knew he was terrified now. He was in big trouble, and it scared the hell out of him. But panic was something entirely different. Panic keeps you from thinking clearly. Panic freezes you. Panic makes you do things irrationally. "Use the fear, old son. Use it to stay focused and make the best decisions you can. And stay alive until you get out of here. Until they come to get you."

And that brought the kids to mind again. He knew they were there, down below, thinking of him. Did they know about this storm? If they did, what would they do about it? What was the weather like down there right now? "Probably raining like hell," he said. He couldn't expect them to get to him sooner than the time he told them he'd return. "Don't count on that, boy. Count on yourself. Do what you have to do and rely on yourself. At least for the time that you're here. You'll make it if that's how you work it. They'll come when they can." There was no doubt they would come to get him, probably sometime between now and the middle of next week. "Before next April would be nice," he told himself. "Your part in this, old son, is to stay alive."

Still he wondered, if it came down to it, could he get out on his own? Walk out some thirty-five miles, give or take? *In this snow with this leg?* he thought. *Maybe. No, not maybe, iffy. Real iffy. Probably doubtful. That is the last option when that's all that's left for you, old son.* He looked out the window at the falling snow. *Get serious, dummy. Trying to walk out is suicide! You wouldn't even make it to the main Forest Service road.*

The food and water he had would sustain him for a quite a while. For reasons he hadn't known at the time, he had put the small propane camp stove in a plastic container in the bed of the truck with one used and one new gas bottle. He didn't think he would need it because he would rather cook over an open fire up here. But a cooking fire was out of the question now. Too much movement, and movement meant more pain, more risk. Too much snow and too much cold. "Somebody was lookin' out for you on that one, boy," he said.

Getting to the camp stove meant getting out of the truck. And that was a problem. He needed a crutch. There were things he needed to do outside, bodily functions that would require him to get out of the truck from time to time. An empty Gatorade bottle could serve for a while. He would need a crutch for the other and for getting supplies. Being one-legged would make what he needed to do very difficult. But he had no crutch.

Pondering that, he thought of the push broom he always kept in the back of the truck. "Yep, it's there. It's always there, and I saw it when I put the meat in. When I have to get out, I'll find the broom. See how that works for a crutch."

For now, he needed to bind the leg and foot. That would help stabilize it and keep the lower leg from moving around so freely. It wasn't the best thing for it, but it would have to do with nothing to use for splints, along with icing it to reduce the swelling. At least a little. Maybe.

Looking at the leg lying on the truck seat, he was thankful that it was not a compound fracture. He had no open wound and blood loss to deal with. It would be nice if all he had to do was lie in bed and rest. But that was not one of the options.

What about the cut on his head? "I'll just have to watch that, keep it as clean as I can, medicate it, and see how it goes." If there was going to be an infection, that is where it would start, especially with the crap he had cleaned out of it already. And there was no way to tell how bad it was. The main plan was to stay as immobile as possible, take the Advil, eat, and wait. "Don't focus on the time," he said. "Time will always take care of itself."

Starting the truck for more warmth, he turned on the radio and found a country station that faded in and out. He lit a cigarette, leaned back against the sleeping bag, and closed his eyes to let his mind go blank for a while. *You're putting off icing and wrapping that leg*, he thought. "Yeah, I know," he answered aloud. But he remained as he was, ashtray on his stomach, listening to Hank Williams, Jr. sing about a pool party with all his rowdy friends.

Just as he was drifting off to sleep, his body jumped, and he was instantly and fully awake. Pain shot up his leg to his hip and groin. "Oh God," he moaned. He sat still, leg extended on the seat, and waited for the pain to subside. It wasn't going to go away on its own. Breathing deeply, he forced himself to relax, controlling his breathing, trying to regain control. In time, a measure of control came to him. The nausea slid away, the pain receded to some degree. Lying still along the seat, he rested, but no sleep was coming to him.

•   •   •

Searching through one of the grocery bags on the floor, he found the box of large freezer bags and removed two of them. The next few steps he had in mind were not going to be easy. He needed to fill the bags with snow for ice packs to reduce the swelling. He didn't want to get out just to fill the freezer bags. He mentally shrank away from that much movement.

After some thought, he moved the sleeping bag to wedge it above the steering wheel. There was no question about swinging his legs to the right side of the truck to get the snow out of the driver's door. Again, too much movement, and all the food stuff and the cooler on the floor would be in the way. That left the passenger door. Movement that way would cause the least disturbance to the leg, which meant the least amount of pain.

Switching off the truck and twisting onto his right side, he opened the passenger door. Numbing cold rushed into the truck. Snowflakes drifted onto his head, shoulders, and the truck seat. As he pushed the door open, it plowed snow away from the truck. "That's at least two feet of snow out there." he said. "It's really piling up." Sliding closer to the opening, he leaned out with a freezer bag in his left hand. He scooped snow into each bag with his right hand and zipped them closed. Sliding back into the truck, he closed the door, put the sleeping bag behind him again, and leaned against it, breathing heavily. This little bit of this movement had intensified the pain. Really stirred it. But did not bring nausea or threaten with the darkness.

He started the truck. As he waited for the warmth, he wrapped the leg as best he could with a shirt and placed the snow-filled bags on either side of the leg at the points of the fracture. Gritting his teeth against the pain, he continued to lean forward, placed a towel beneath the leg above the break and slid it down toward his foot. The edge of the towel caught on the snow-filled bags and pushed them away from him along the lower leg. One of the bags fell onto the floor. The other snagged against the driver's door before it could fall between the door and the seat. "You sure did that ass backwards," he said.

Retrieving the ice bags, he set them aside until he had the towel in place beneath the leg and re-draped the shirt on top. He laid a bag of snow on either side of the leg at the break and wrapped the towel around them. The ice bags were finally held firmly against his leg. He shut off the truck, adjusted the sleeping bag behind him, and leaned back to rest. Perhaps to sleep. "Ice it again in the morning, old son, then wrap it. You'll need to get out of this truck in the morning to take care of some business."

It was dark in the truck, snow slowly covering the windshield and side windows, closing him in. He drifted off to sleep. But sleep was fitful and intermittent. Sometime later, he turned on the truck and timed it for ten minutes. He lit a cigarette and ate what stew remained in the can. When the cigarette was done, he removed the bags from his leg. The snow had melted completely, and he set the bags of cold water on the floor. Sleep came again, off and on. Now, more on than off. And that was a good thing. He needed rest to restore and maintain his strength as best he could.

CHAPTER 15

When he woke for the day, he was cramped and stiff. His muscles ached. He was too tall to lie out completely in the truck to sleep. And it was cold again. Never-ending cold. He turned on the truck and checked the gas gauge. The needle had dropped a little more than he had expected, but it was still okay. "So far, so good."

Moving the rolled sleeping bag to the area above the steering wheel, he scooted his back against the passenger door. Lifting the t-shirt off of his leg, he looked at the swelling and color. There was no noticeable change. And it wasn't going to change until he got medical attention.

He lit a cigarette and stared at the snow on the windshield and side windows, waiting for the truck to warm and the windows to clear so he could at least see out. Dim light filtered through the snow. "Must be daytime out there." His watch told him it was 9:20 a.m. Saturday. "I should be sittin' by the fire with a cup of hot coffee reading my book in the morning sunlight. I sure could use a hot cup of coffee."

When he finished the cigarette, he turned on the windshield wipers to remove what snow remained. Snow on the side windows melted and slid down to the door frame. The day was not much different than yesterday. Low, heavy clouds still hung to the tops of the trees on the ridge in front of him. It was no longer snowing. All around him was white. The meadow out the driver's door window was an unbroken field of snow. The ridges in front of the truck and the surrounding camping area were all buried in snow. "You're stuck for sure, old son."

He settled back against the door, the armrest digging into his back, head against the door window, and closed his eyes. The cut on his head was stinging against the cold glass. Trying to not focus on the pain that was now a persistent dull ache from his toes to the back of his head, he started to go over in his mind things he needed to do today. He was startled by the obvious squeal of a cow elk. It sounded very close to the truck. His eyes flew open, and he sat up—much too quickly for the leg. His heart was instantly thundering in his chest, and he looked out through the windshield. Nothing but snow. Nothing out the driver's window. Turning his head, he looked through the passenger's window toward the creek. Again, nothing. Nothing out the back window. Had he imagined it? Was it real? Where had it come from?

For several minutes, he moved his head and eyes to look through each window and still saw nothing. No movement. No elk. And he began to question whether he had actually heard what he thought he had heard.

A second squeal brought him back to the driver's door window and the meadow to the north of the truck, the meadow that he had crossed on the evening of opening day where he had been surprised to find so much sign. And there they were, slogging through the knee-deep snow, coming right toward the front of the truck. From the trees to the left rear of the truck, in single file, a line of cows and calves had come out of the trees to cross the meadow.

As they moved toward him, the cow in the lead angled toward the end of the ridge where his packboard lay beneath the snow. On that track, they would pass in front of the truck by the old fire ring and the head of the main trail that led to the big river. He counted seventeen head of cows and calves, with one very large bull bringing up the rear. A nice small herd. The horns on the bull would have made a very good prize for any trophy hunter. Tall and wide, with thick beams, the horns jutted above the bull's head. Automatically he counted the points. Six on each side, symmetrically balanced and beautiful. Thick, dark beams at the base, and nearly all white points at the end of the tines. But none of the animals had yet looked in his direction. Heads bobbing, they plowed through the snow. How very odd that they didn't see the truck and did not realize how exposed they were to potential danger.

Then the bull stopped, raised his head, and looked directly at him through the window. The cows moved on as if he and the truck weren't there. How could they not see the truck? How could they not know he was there? Then he realized his truck was painted two-toned, brown on the bottom and top with a white stripe in the middle. The bottom brown stripe was no doubt below the snow level, making it nearly invisible. The top of the truck, the hood, and the bed were piled with snow. The only thing visible would be the white stripe along the side of the truck and maybe a small portion of brown. They simply hadn't seen it camouflaged against the snow. It apparently blended in perfectly with the surroundings. They didn't even know he was there watching them.

He sat frozen in the truck and watched as they moved by. For these few moments, the pain was no longer in control. It was obliterated by the sight of this herd of elk so close. He sat dumbfounded looking at the animals in front of him. Only the bull had looked his way. Only the bull had stopped to assess what he thought he was seeing. And then he, too, began moving again, following the cows and calves at a leisurely pace, but he continued to look toward the truck, wary and alert.

As the lead cow reached the old fire ring, she turned down the main trail. Each animal followed her lead, and they began to move away from him, yellowish butts swaying with each step. The bull followed the others. However, he stopped after several strides down the main trail and looked back over his shoulder at the truck. For several minutes, he remained looking back, while the cows moved on. And then he, too, continued down the trail toward the big river.

"Holy mackerel," he said, letting out his held breath. He continued watching them until they disappeared out of sight where the trail turned in the distance. Their trail through the snow was proof of what he had seen. They were real. They had walked right by him, and only one had even suspected he was there. Looking down the trail to where they had disappeared, he said, "You're late folks. You should have been well on your way to the winter range days ago."

After a few minutes, he picked up the freezer bags from the floor, shifted to his right and pushed open the passenger door. As the door swung open, he smiled and thought, "What the hell would that bunch of elk have done if I'd opened the door as they were passing by? They would have crapped and run all the way to the big river."

As he leaned out of the open door, snow cascaded from the edge of the roof onto the seat and his arm. He brushed the snow away, opened the freezer bags one at a time, and emptied the water. Lying on his side, he refilled both bags with snow. Looking past the open door, he couldn't see the lean-to between the trees. The ropes that had held it up disappeared into a bank of snow. The lean-to itself was buried out of sight. The open truck door had plowed through the top of the snow again in an arc nearly eight inches above the door bottom. "There has to be three feet of snow out there now. Only ten or fifteen feet to go this winter," he said. Staring at the snow, he thought, *Will I still be here then?* He shuddered and pulled himself back into the truck.

He closed the door and started the engine. Every time he opened the door, he lost all heat from the cab and had to warm it up again. He placed the bags of snow on the leg and wrapped it with the towel. A peanut butter and jelly sandwich would have to do for breakfast with Gatorade. "It ain't bacon, eggs, and coffee but it'll fill the hole. For now."

While he ate the sandwich, he looked at the disturbed snow where the elk had passed. Other than the cow that had snuck up on him on opening day, he had been close to a herd of elk on only one other occasion. But he couldn't really call it a herd. There were only five animals in that group. Three cows, a yearling calf, and a young spike bull. His horns hadn't even grown long enough to make him legal to harvest. The five elk had come down from the ridge above and behind him and stopped no more than twenty-five or thirty yards away. They were anxious and fidgety.

He watched them from the corner of his eye for maybe two minutes. Suddenly, one of the cows grunted, and they all turned sharply away from him and bolted along the side hill at a full run. The only explanation he could think of was they must have scented him.

He drifted back from his memories and looked again at the disturbed trail of the elk that had passed the truck. He smiled. "That's another great memory I can call on."

•   •   •

He began to list mentally the things he needed to do today outside the truck. Nature was calling, so he would have to get out of the truck soon. Get the camp stove and gas bottles from the container in the back of the truck. Locate the push broom and see how that might work as a crutch. Clear snow away from the exhaust pipe so he didn't get asphyxiated with carbon monoxide when he ran the motor. And not the least, see how he was able to maneuver in the snow—if at all.

Before any of that could happen, he needed to stabilize the leg by binding it. More movement, more pain. And increased pain was with him now. A deep throbbing ache. A constant companion, maybe for the rest of his life, however long or short that might be. Like it or not, that was his reality, the relentless enemy always stabbing at his consciousness. He took two more Advil and washed them down with Gatorade.

Then he checked his head. When he felt it, there was a bloody fluid on his hand. There was also warmth, not hot, but definitely warm. He washed it again with cold water and applied more antiseptic ointment. This process only brought a small amount of fresh blood to his hand.

Collecting the strips of cloth he had cut from the old blue jeans, he piled them on the seat beside him. "This ain't gonna be fun." A splint of some kind would be best, but he had no boards or anything else he could think of to make them. The slats of the packboard would have been perfect for splints. "What I need is over there on the end of the ridge buried under snow," he said. Binding would have to do. Wrap it to hold it in place as much as possible when he moved, and unwrap it to ice it. "That's a lot of movin' that leg. And it won't be fun. But if that's what I've got, that's what I've got."

Leaning forward, he began. Wrapping the strips of cloth around the leg above the break near the knee, he slowly worked them down toward the ankle, overlapping each strip. The foot was still canted toward the inside, and he didn't try to change that. "Both bones are broken for sure," he moaned. Lifting the leg to get the strips beneath it was agony. The lower leg and foot sagged when he lifted it. Leaning forward constantly strained his back, shoulders, and arms, but not as much as when he had cut the boot off.

Tying the strips off at the ankle was a struggle. Several times he leaned back against the door to rest and fight the creeping darkness and nausea. The last piece he ripped lengthwise, twisted it around his ankle, and tied it in place. When it was done, all he wanted to do was sit and remain still. "That ain't gonna happen," he said. "Nature's about to kick down the outhouse door."

He zipped his coat, put on his gloves and ski mask, and pushed open the driver's door. As he slid across the seat, he tried to keep his leg straight without bumping anything. When he reached the area where his knees hung over the side, his left heel bumped against the threshold again. Shocked with pain, he lay back on the seat, feet hanging outside, and chanted the mantra, breathing deep and slow. But he had to move. Pain or no pain, he had to get out now. He shoved a roll of mountain money in his coat pocket and pushed his body toward the door.

Standing in the snow on his right leg, he held his left as high as possible, bent at the knee and the hip. His right leg had sunk in snow to above his knee. The left foot was well below the surface of the snow. "This ain't gonna be easy at all," he said. *I can only do what I have to do and do it the best way I can.*

Holding to the side of the truck, he shuffled toward the back of the truck bed, leaving the door open. Pushing his right leg through the deep snow in one-legged hops while holding his left leg up was tiring and awkward. He had waded through deep snow on other hunts and on other mountains. Plowing snow one-legged was not something he thought he would ever have to do. He stopped halfway along the length of the truck bed to rest, already breathing heavily. "Doesn't matter, does it? There's no two ways around it. It has to be done." After a minute, he moved on.

Reaching the back of the truck bed, he found the tailgate was still down. He swept the snow off with his hands and rested his weight on his butt, partially sitting on the tailgate. He tried to ignore the hanging leg, the pain that threatened to overcome him, mind-numbing pain that slowed his thinking and clouded his mind. And he tried to ignore the cold that nipped at him hungrily, especially against his bare toes and foot. "Relax, boy. Let it go. You have to do this, and you can get through it."

Minutes later, when he'd caught his breath, he continued to the right rear corner of the truck. Once there, he moved as much snow from the area of the tailpipe as he could with his hands so that it wasn't buried in snow. Part of the snow was black from exhaust and sagged from melting when he'd run the motor. In the now shallower snow, he turned to face the truck and dropped his pants. Holding on to the tailgate support cable with both hands, gritting his teeth, he stretched his left leg in front of him under the truck bed and did a one-legged squat in the snow, his back toward the logging road. "This'd be a hell of a time for someone to come down that road on a snowmobile to get me out."

When he finished, he pulled himself up to stand in the snow, right leg trembling from the strain. The cold attacked his naked lower body and legs. "Now I gotta get my pants up one-handed and not fall down bare-assed in the snow." The pain was crushing him again. Lightheaded and dizzy, he fought to maintain control as he worked his pants and underwear back up and belted them in place. Shivering, he said, "And I have to do this every day?"

Redressed, he swept more snow from the tailgate, turned, and boosted himself with his arms to sit, legs dangling, resting. It was cold, but he needed to rest before going on. The way things were now, he tired quickly. The way he had to move, holding onto the truck bed, hopping one-legged through the snow, was a real struggle.

Sitting on the tailgate, cold from the metal numbing his butt and the backs of his legs, he looked up the slope to where the trees gapped for the logging road as it came down into the meadow. And he thought of how the road was going out. A slight rise at first. Mostly level for about the first mile. Then a steeper rise for a short distance that turned to the left and topped a low ridge. That turn was where the road had washed out in a few places. Once at the top of that rise, it was all downhill to the main Forest Service road some five miles or so away. "That'd be an easy walk without the snow," he said, "and the leg."

The Forest Service road was another thing altogether. As he recalled, it rose and fell frequently with a lot of turns generally working downhill. But there were no serious hills to climb or steep downgrades. The biggest problem was the distance. It was a very long walk on a good day, in good weather, and with no injury. Probably a two-day walk, going all day each day. As he was now? No way to tell what it would be like other than real hard. Or if he could even make that walk at all. That was one monster of a big if. Without a crutch, impossible. Even with the crutch, a long way past doubtful. "I'm here till they come to get me. Or forever. That's just the truth of it."

He sat until the cold told him it was time to get moving before his butt froze to the tailgate. His left foot and lower leg, with no protection from the cold, were getting numb. He lowered himself to the ground on his right leg and moved along the right side of the truck to the front of the bed. Snow was now piled above the top of the side walls. Two plastic storage containers were buried under the snow against the front wall of the bed. He swept the snow off with his right hand while he held onto the side wall with his left. In one of the containers, he found the camp stove and gas bottles along with a can of coffee and filters for the coffee pot.

The push broom and the shovel lay crosswise along the front of the bed under the snow. He pulled them out and tossed them to the back of the truck for easier access.

Opening the passenger door, he set the camp stove and gas bottles on the seat. The can of coffee and filters went into the truck as well. A pair of tennis shoes and a gym bag containing more clothes were all that was left in that container. He replaced the lid and moved it out of the way, pulling the second container closer. This container held only a tool box, a four-way lug wrench, some tie downs, and a wood bow saw. Nothing to use for splints. He replaced the lid on the second container and closed the truck door.

As he turned toward the back of the truck, dizziness swept over him. He leaned face forward against the truck, snow crushed beneath his chest, left leg held up, right leg trembling from the strain of holding his weight. Eyes closed, breathing deep, he fought the increasing pain and fatigue. The darkness was there, creeping toward him, threatening to overtake him. "Need to get back in the truck. I need to get back in the truck. Can't go down out here. Not now."

He was very cold. His entire body trembled from the cold and exertion. His mind was clouding, and it was hard to hold his thoughts. He was as physically tired and shaky now as he had been when he'd packed the first hind quarter down the mountain. *On the very edge of exhaustion*, he thought. Lifting his head, he looked at the world around him. All he saw was snow. All he heard was silence—cold, forbidding, and silent. And the silent darkness came at him, threatening to consume him, coming to take him away. Pounding his fist against the side of the truck cab, he growled, "Not now! Not now! Not now!" With a deep breath, he said, "Move your ass, boy."

At the back of the truck, he picked up the broom and shovel from his path and laid them on the tailgate. Leaning heavily on the truck bed, he moved on. Hopping, staggering, head down, his mind numbed by pain and fatigue, he anchored himself to the truck with his right arm. The darkness was coming. Mind slipping away. Each hop through the snow shocked his left leg, and the muscles of his right leg were quivering, nearly collapsing with fatigue.

And then he was back inside the truck, lying across the seat, head resting on the rolled sleeping bag, driver's door still open. His lower legs hung outside the truck. He had only a vague memory of how he got there. Cold. So cold. Pulling himself across the seat farther into the truck, he sat up, leaned forward, closed the door, started the motor, and turned the heater fan to high. "Too cold. Warm! Gotta get warm." His leg was throbbing from his toes to his hip. "Relax. You've got to relax, boy." Repeating it, over and over again. Pushing the smothering darkness away. Holding it off again. For now.

When he was finally warm and the shivering slowed, he turned off the truck, leaned against the sleeping bag, and closed his eyes, his body still trembling from the fatigue. And he drifted away. To sleep. A different darkness. Gentler. Not the enemy. Not the enemy - darkness.

CHAPTER 16

Hunger woke him this time. Hunger and, yes, the pain and the cold. Always the pain. Always the cold. He took two Advil with a drink of icy milk. It hadn't snowed again, and the windows were mostly clear, but partially foggy from his breath and body heat. He turned on the truck to get warm and clear the windows.

Staring out the windshield, he realized how important it had become for him to be able to see out and not be completely closed in. Separated from his surroundings. He hadn't thought of that before, being closed in and trapped when all around him there is so much space. And all that he saw now was snow. Everything blanketed in white. The trees were covered. Only small areas of dark green branches and brown trunks showed through. The brush and ground were completely buried. He turned his head to look out the passenger window to the creek. No water was visible. All was covered now with ice and snow. What he heard was nothing. Total, pressing silence. As insidious as the darkness that took him away. All the voices that he had come here to listen to were silenced by the mute snow.

Hungry, he fixed a sandwich, got out a Pepsi and chips, and stared out at the snow while he ate.

"It's Saturday afternoon." he said. His watch said 3:45 pm. He had slept for quite a while. "And that's A-OK," he said. "Two days and I'm supposed to be home. Three days and I'm late." How soon would they come? How long did he have to wait? How would they get to him? And what would it be like getting him out with the injured leg? These were all questions he had no definitive answers for. And that was okay, too. It wasn't even worth thinking about until it happened or until they were very late. "Take it a step at a time, old son," he whispered. "Get through it and go on from there." He paused. "Wherever *there* turns out to be."

And if they don't come right away? he thought. "Hey," he said out loud, "jump that crick when you get to it, old son."

Still, he realized he was glaring out through the windshield at the snow and the low-hanging clouds that would bring even more. And time was sliding away.

Eyes slitted. Jaw clamped. Face muscles taut, anger began to build in him. He wanted to scream his anger at the snow for what it had done to him. He admitted his anger. And in time, he would embrace it. He'd learned long ago that was the only way for him to deal with his anger. Anger was a natural emotion, as natural as any other emotion. Accepting that he was angry always calmed him. Accepting it didn't erase the anger but allowed him to deal with it. Many times in the past, when he became angry, mad enough that his anger demanded a physical response, he simply accepted the anger and calmed himself. He accepted the anger but didn't let it control him. So he held that anger inside himself and smiled. Smiling was a major factor in his control and acceptance. The more angry he became, the quieter he forced himself to be, and the more he smiled.

And now he was mad as hell. Angry at how the snow that had changed all that had been so good here. Until the fall. And yet, he knew that cussing the snow would change nothing.

Accomplish nothing. Snow was just snow. In reality, he had always thought it quite beautiful. Not an enemy. But right now, he was pissed off. Real pissed off. But even though the snow may kill him in the long run, up here on this mountain, there was nothing he could do to change what was. Snow was not his enemy. An adversary? Yes. But not his enemy. What had happened just happened. A part of life and nature. It was one of the risks of being where he was, doing what he liked to do, the way he liked to do it. Alone. Just him, the mountains, the pines, and the creek. And now the snow. He took a deep breath, slowly let it out, and smiled. A bit of a smile always made the difference.

This situation was what the kids worried about. And what he had thought about and dismissed out of hand. But here it was. Reality. His reality. For now, and until it was over, one way or the other. *Will it kill me up here?* he wondered. He paused to let that sink in more fully. "I guess it might," he said. "We'll just have to see how it plays out. But it's not going to get me without a good fight. As long as I have food, water, and gas in the truck, I can hang on a lot longer than most. And if I don't run out of mountain money," he chuckled. And there was no doubt in his mind that he would make it through this.

Then he sobered. *What if this is it? What if this really does kill me up here?* That certainly was a possibility, and he knew that too. "I'll never run out of food." He paused. "What I will run out of is heat." He knew there was a limited amount of gas in the truck, but he didn't dwell on it. When the gas was gone, his time would be limited.

If this is it, what will I miss the most? He knew he would miss the mountain tops and the view of far-off peaks. He would miss the pines and the whisper of the breeze. He would miss the creek and the crows, the squirrels' chatter in the morning, and the owl asking his question in the night. He would miss the earth and the rocks. And he would miss all the voices that spoke to him while he was here.

And he would miss the chance to see her, maybe just one more time.

And he would miss the kids. "Yeah, that's what I would miss the most. The kids." Their smiles and their laughter. Their hugs and their warmth. "God, how I would miss them all." Closing his eyes, brimmed with tears, he tried to block that thought out for now. He didn't want to deal with the pain of those thoughts. Not now. "If nothing else, they'll come get me out."

Head sagging, he turned on the radio. No reception anywhere on the dial this time, so he turned it off. Finally warm again, he turned off the truck, picked up the book from the back of the truck seat, and leaned against the sleeping bag to read for a while. The leg was stretched out across the seat. He was at rest as much as possible. The pain was there but subdued. If he could remain still, he knew the pain would subside to some degree over time. But remaining motionless all the time was not a real option. Movement from time to time was necessary. He took four more Advil, opened the book, and tried to read, pushing his thoughts away. "It's not going to get me. Not this time. I'll see the kids when they come to get me and take me home."

CHAPTER 17

He woke in darkness, his book on his chest. It was freezing in the truck. For a few minutes, he couldn't seem to clear his head of the sleep. Groggy and fuzzy headed. "I guess I drifted off again," he said. He knew sleep was good for him. Sleep would help him restore his strength and use up time in the process. But if he slept too long, or was unconscious too long, he would freeze to death and never even know it. They would find him when they came to get him this winter or next spring dead and frozen, his book on his chest. If he fell asleep with the truck running, he would drain the gas and lose his major source of heat. There was no question that would be fatal. *They'll sure have a hell of a time gettin' me out of this truck if I'm a 250-pound block of ice.* Not a good thought, but he smiled anyway.

He found and turned on the lamp. The windows were fogged over from his breathing and body heat. The book lay on his chest, closed. The bookmark was not between the pages. He found it on the floor and put it back in the book. He could find his place later. He didn't know how long he had read before he fell asleep. He didn't even remember getting sleepy. And he couldn't remember anything he read before drifting off. He'd held the book on his chest to read, but instead he went to sleep. And now he was awake again. No memory of anything in between. He rolled his head around, trying to shake off the grogginess. That movement brought on dizziness and aggravated the pain in the leg and other places in his body. When he checked his watch, it was 7:20 p.m. Still Saturday. "Gets real dark real early up here," he said. That was something he hadn't noticed when he wasn't keeping track of time with his watch.

He pulled himself to a sitting position, turned on the truck, and waited for it to warm. When the windows defrosted, he cursed loud and mean. "Goddamn snow." It was snowing heavily. Large, wet flakes obscured everything but the hood of the truck. There was no world outside of the truck. "Me, the truck, and the damn snow. That's all there is now." His heart pounded strong against his ribs and throbbed in the leg and in the gash on the back of his head. A light, dull pain remained in his head, and his body felt heavy.

"Damn the leg, too," he growled. He was suddenly angry again. Mostly angry about the snow. Angry with the pain, yes. And angry about being trapped in the truck. Except for the snow and one little slip, he would have spent the last three days of this trip relaxing, hiking, enjoying all that he had come here to be a part of. Maybe a little more fishing, reading his book, napping on the log under the tree by the stream, being awakened by the rustle of the wind through his hair. With the snow and no slip, he would have been home boning out the rest of the elk, having elk steaks for dinner, sitting in his recliner as he shared his time on the mountain with the kids. "One stupid little slip in the snow! Son-of-a-bitch!"

He wanted more of what the creek had to say. More of the warm breeze and what the trees had to tell him. He wanted more time to steep himself in the majesty and the mystery of this world, away from the hubbub of civilization. And now there was just the cold and the silence. No creek. No breeze through the pines. No voices of this world. They have all gone to sleep for the winter under the heavy blanket of snow. Isolated and trapped in the truck. Cold, pain, and snow, and the silence. His time away from civilization had been taken from him.

"Now, there's a misnomer," he grunted. "Civilization!" he sneered. "Civilization is not civilized." It is a world of hectic rush here and rush there.

"Move over or get run over," that other world said. The roar of civilization drowned out all the other voices.

And now, here, on this mountain? There were no voices either. There was just him and the truck. The snow, the cold, and the pain.

•   •   •

Without prompting, he remembered how it had been when he took her to that other high mountain. They sat quiet, bodies pressing against each other, looking across deep canyons into the fading distance at other mountains far, far away. His arm around her shoulders, he held her close. Her arm was tucked under the side of his coat along his rib cage. He reveled feeling the warmth of her body and the flutter of her breath on his neck. All else around them was quiet and peaceful. Absorbing each other and the world around them. He felt the slow rhythm of her heart beating against his ribs. No one else near. They gazed off to the faraway blue mountains with the breeze in their faces and the smell of the pines. Fluffy, white clouds drifted overhead in a soft blue sky. A fidgety chipmunk scurried through the rocks in front of them. She pulled him closer and leaned against him, the warmth of her body seeping into his. Her head on his shoulder, he could smell the fragrance of her hair as he breathed deep the scent of her. Her very essence. Tears in her eyes, she looked up at him, and with a quivering voice, she whispered, "Thank you." And she pulled herself tighter to his chest. That was all. And that was all that was needed. For each of them, that day on that mountain had been good. As good as it could ever get. With a finger, he lifted her chin, and leaning down to her, he kissed the tears from her cheeks.

•   •   •

With a sigh he willed these thoughts and memories to the recesses of his mind and his heart. In some ways now, alone on this mountain, those memories were more vivid and yet more painful than the leg.

Hands in his lap, the truck motor humming, he watched the snow melt as it landed on the windshield. All things around him now lay in darkness.

Darkness and snow and cold. All silent. How was it he had heard the voices of everything that was here? Even the earth had spoken to him. But the snow was mute. The snow had no voice of its own. It just kept coming and coming. Silent and insidious. Even in a blizzard, the snow never spoke. It was the wind that howled and snarled. The snow was voiceless. The silence of the snow had covered all the other voices. The silence of the snow, with her twin brother, cold, drowned out the murmur of the creek, the chatter of the squirrels, the hoot of the owl, and the whisper of the wind in the trees.

The silence and the pain now roared in his ears. His shoulders slumped, head hanging, chin near his chest. "Nothing you can do about it now, boy," he said. "Live with it. Live through it. And don't let it beat you down. Gut it out." But it wasn't that simple. Not simple at all. And it was getting to him. He knew that. A sadness, leaning toward depression, was invading his mind and his thoughts. He would fight it, wrestle with it, and try to stay positive. But his feelings of isolation and being trapped persisted. A dull, languid feeling was creeping over him. He was constantly aware of it, even when it lingered in the background. He tried to ignore it, but it was there.

He turned on the radio and found the same country station coming in loud and strong. Willie Nelson sang "On the Road Again." "Not me, Willie. I'm stuck in this damn snowbank and I ain't goin' nowhere soon." When the song ended, he sighed and took a deep breath, let it out and said, "Might as well have some dinner with my music."

The truck cab was getting crowded. A medium-sized cooler. The clothes bag. Grocery bags of food. The meat. Cooking pots, frying pan, and coffee pot. The backpack. The sleeping bag. And now the camp stove and gas bottles. The handgun in the holster lay on the dashboard, and the rifle hung in the gun rack across the back window with the fishing pole. "There's not going to be any room in here for me if this keeps up. At least I have a way to cook some dinner and make coffee. Whoo-eee, coffee." And he brightened with that thought.

Taking one of the bags of meat from the floor, he opened it and smelled deep into the bag. It smelled like fresh meat. Not stale or spoiled. When he took it out of the bag and set it on the top of the cooler, he found it was cold and partially frozen. "At least the cold is doing some good and keeping the meat fresh. I should cook up a bunch of it tomorrow morning just to have it ready."

Doing things in the limited space of the truck was difficult with his leg the way it was. Twisting his body this way and that to prepare the meal without moving the leg was a problem. Even the slightest movement increased the pain. Sometimes lightning-bolt strong. A big portion of his attention was always on the leg. The wrappings kept it more stationary, but it still sagged some and moved when he changed the leg's position. Any movement always increased the pain.

Using the cooler as a cutting board, he cut off two thick slabs of back strap for dinner and put the rest back in the bag. Paper towels cleaned up the blood left behind. He had eaten the only potato he'd brought but there was some onion left. Chopping what was left of it on a paper plate, the truck filled with the aroma of onion. He checked the gas gauge and turned off the truck. There was a bit less than half a tank left. "Gotta conserve more of that gas or it's gonna be gone too soon." He paused. "My gas mileage is gonna drop to about two miles to the gallon on this trip. And the truck ain't gettin' out of here 'til spring."

With the lamp on, he assembled the camp stove and screwed the used bottle of gas into it. "Now, you really need to be careful with this thing," he said. "Don't even get a little stupid with this stove on in here. Leave that stove on too long, you'll go to sleep and wake up dead." He rolled both windows down slightly for ventilation and fired up the stove. The two steaks with the chopped up onion on top went into the frying pan with cooking oil. The coffee pot filled with water from the water bottles went on the stove beside the frying pan.

Soon the cab of the truck was filled with the aroma of frying elk steaks, onions, and coffee perking. And heat. He took a deep breath. "Now that'll cheer a fella up real quick," he said. As the food cooked, he stared out through the windows into the dark, watching snowflakes melt on the windshield. Nothing but snowflakes beyond the glass. They were so thick he could barely see the front of the hood. "And that'll turn your mood upside down just as quick as anything," he grumbled.

When the meat was cooked, he turned off the stove and closed the windows. It was nice and warm in the truck. He ate the food directly from the frying pan with coffee in the tin cup. By the time he finished dinner, the snow had slowed quite a bit. The radio was fading in and out, and he turned it off. "Don't run the battery down, dummy."

Stiff and restless, he wanted to move. He felt bored and cramped in the truck, mentally and physically. He missed his previous activity each day since he had been here. He was always out of bed and moving around before sunup, climbing the ridges in the dark, watching the sun come over the far mountains and the day come awake. In the afternoon, he moved through the checkered shadows with the sun filtering through the trees, enjoying the beauty of all the surrounding country. He missed the chatty squirrels and the ragged call of the crows. He missed the murmur of the creek and the voice of the wind in the trees. He missed the crackle of the flames as he sat by the campfire in the evening. And the stars. Oh my, how he missed the stars. All of these things he had only in memory now. "And maybe forever," he whispered.

Getting out of the truck now would be cold and painful. "Maybe you should stay put, old son. You don't want to be movin' around anymore than you need to."

But he needed to. And soon.

Leaning forward, he looked at the leg. It had been wrapped all day and swelling was pressing against the wrappings. "I need to ice it again. Unwrap it and let some of the pressure off. And nature's callin'. Might as well get out, take care of some business, fill the ice bags with snow, and take a little care of myself."

He retrieved the two bags he had used for icing the leg before and took two additional bags from the box. Coat zipped and hat on, he lowered the leg off the seat, keeping his foot off the floor. He slid as far as he could across the seat and opened the driver's door. Cold slammed into the truck, forcing him back. The quick movement bounced his injured foot into the clutch pedal, and jarring pain gripped his leg. A deep growl rose in his throat. He closed his eyes and sat motionless until he regained a small amount of control.

Inside the warm truck, he had forgotten how frigid it would be outside. "I knew it was gonna be cold, but not like this." The temperature had dropped dramatically. Maybe below zero. It was immediately numbing to his bare hands, his face, and the uncovered flesh on the injured leg and foot.

Lifting the leg at the knee with his hands, he swung it out the door, careful not to bump it against anything else. The cold attacked every exposed inch of flesh. With his body weight on his hands and arms, he slid off the seat to the ground. His right foot sank through the snow to well above his knee and took all of his weight. Small granular snowflakes landed on his shoulders, head, and face.

As he leaned his left shoulder against the truck, he let the left foot sink slowly into the snow, the leg hanging loose. He'd thought it would feel good to let the leg hang relaxed for a few minutes and relieve some of the tension from hip to knee. He was wrong. His bare toes buried in the snow ached immediately. Even the slight pressure of the snow against the canted lower leg and foot sent shockwaves of pain up the leg to his hip. His instinct was to double over at the waist with the pain, but he forced himself to remain erect. Head up, back bowed. "I can't stay out here very long. It's too cold. Definitely well below zero."

He wanted to wiggle his freezing toes but knew what that would do. He remembered the agony when he tried to flex his toes after taking the boot off. There was no way he wanted to go through that again. Turning to face the truck, he hopped once to get nearer the bed of the truck. Pain slammed him again. Hopping was the only way he had to move around outside, and the movement jarred his injured leg with every step. He leaned his chest against the side wall of the truck bed, head drooping. For minutes, chest against the truck, he chanted the mantra, "Relax," Deep breath. "Just relax." Deep Breath. Gradually the pain receded slightly. Where the pain lessened, the cold took over with a vengeance. "You might be able to control the pain a bit, boy, but you can't control the cold at all. Not out here. Do what you need to do and get back in the damn truck."

He turned his body away from the truck, unzipped and took care of that part of the business. "Peein' in a water bottle ain't this easy, but it wouldn't be this cold either."

Finished, he took the freezer bags from his coat pocket with stiffening fingers. "And don't scoop up the yella snow, old son." Instead, he leaned his chest against the side of the truck again, taking part of his weight off of his right leg, and scooped handfuls of snow from the bed of the truck into the plastic bags. He sealed them and tossed them one at a time onto the floor of the truck.

With a hop and a groan, he turned his back to the door and pulled himself onto the seat. With the door closed, he sat with arms draped over the steering wheel, feet under the dashboard, the left heel on the floor, screaming at him. The foot and toes burned from the contact with the snow. No nausea, no darkness coming. Just the pain, consuming him. Mind and body. The back of his head throbbing.

He started the truck, cupped his hands, and blew on his cold fingers until the heat came through. His bare toes tingled when the heat from the vent blew directly on them. "A man could freeze to death out there in nothin' flat," he said. "You don't want to go down out there when it's like this, boy."

Scooting across the seat, he leaned against the sleeping bag and lifted his leg to the seat again. Eyes closed, head back, he rested. That small amount of movement had drained him far more than he thought it should have. Physically and mentally. The cold certainly had something to do with that. The pain certainly did. Each time he left the heat off for as long as he could stand it, the cold affected his body. Probably his mind as well. And cold was a real killer. His mind seemed as numb now as his fingers and toes had been a few minutes ago.

But he was back inside the truck now. safe, and warming up. *And still trapped*, he thought. His world had shrunken down to the cab of his truck. And he really was beginning to feel trapped. Closed in and isolated. If he got out of the truck, he needed to get back in as soon as possible. "Careful, old son. Don't start thinkin' negative. This is only temporary. They'll come and get you." But the feeling of isolation remained with him.

When he was warm again, he checked the coffee pot and found the coffee was lukewarm. A few minutes over a flame on the stove, and he poured a hot cup of coffee. Turning off the truck, he slid back against the sleeping bag.

After a sip of the hot coffee and a deep breath, he set the cup of coffee on the dashboard and began unwrapping the leg. Stopping to lean back to breathe and rest, it took longer than he thought it should. And it was not any less painful, not any less stressful. Groaning with each lifting of the leg to get the wrapping under it, he continued until it was done. The wrappings hadn't stabilized his leg as he thought they would. It was better than nothing but certainly not as good as splints would be.

Still swollen and very dark, the leg didn't look good at all. He laid his hand on the swelling just below the knee. The skin was tight with the swelling and smooth to the touch. And there was a slight warmth against his palm.

He slid the towel under the leg, draped it with the shirt on top, packed the snow-filled bags on either side, above and below the break, and wrapped the towel around it. Even that simple process seemed a struggle. Tiring. Very painful. "Always *the pain.*" He closed his eyes, leaned against the sleeping bag, and tried to clear his mind. Drive away the tiredness. Drive away the feeling of isolation. *I'm not gonna get any sleep any time soon*, he thought. *Not with this much pain.*

The coffee was good. Hot and warming in the stomach. He shook out two more Advil and washed them down with the coffee. Relaxing as much as possible, he lit a cigarette, turned off the lamp, and lay in the dark, eyes closed and smoking.

Later, after he had found his place in the book, he read by the light of the lamp. He could remember what he had read up to a point, but nothing of what he had tried to read the last time. The continuation of the story line was gone. Now, it was as if he was reading entirely new material. Paging back, he found familiar material several pages in front of where he had left the bookmark. Had he put the bookmark in the wrong place? He didn't think so. Had he read anything at all before he fell asleep? He was certain that he had but maybe not. And no luck this time either. He remembered nothing of the material that he believed he had read the last time. Nothing of what he read now fit with what he knew he had read before. He could not tie the two together, as if the new material was from a completely different story.

Frustration washed through his mind. It was like losing your glasses or your car keys, knowing that you had them in your hand just five minutes ago. And now you can't find them. Anywhere.

Unable to hold the story line in his head, he lay the book on his chest. The throbbing leg, wrapped in cold bags of snow, occupied his mind, and he couldn't focus on the words. Couldn't hold the concepts. Finally, irritated, he closed the book on the bookmark, laid it on the back of the seat and turned out the lamp.

The lamp was getting dim. He needed to replace the batteries. In the dark, he finished the coffee, smoked another cigarette, and rested. His mind was blank to all but the cold, the silence, and the pain. At some time without awareness, he drifted into sleep.

CHAPTER 18

He woke in the dark. It was freezing again. Always waking to the cold. And the pain. Groggy, he just wanted to go back to sleep.

Sitting up, he set the bags of snow from his leg, partially melted now, on the floor. He started the truck and fought off sleep while he timed the ten minutes he had decided to allot to warm the cab of the truck again. A partial bottle of water sat on the cooler. With it he washed down two more Advil. The water was very cold but not frozen. With the lamp off, it was very dark in the truck. Snow and frost had completely blocked the windows. When he next opened his eyes, he looked at his watch. The truck had been running for fifteen minutes. He had dozed off to sleep again, but not for too long this time. He turned off the truck and the lamp. The windows were partially clear now. He could see nothing but a wall of darkness outside. He lay against the rolled sleeping bag and closed his eyes. Sleep came off and on for the rest of the night, drifting in and out.

When he came all the way back to the world, he lay still, his body relaxed, his eyes closed. Wherever he was, that was how he often liked to wake and start his day. Eyes closed. Mind relaxed.

He had been doing it for a good many years.

Especially since she was no longer with him.

To know that he was awake, fully alert but keeping his eyes closed, he listened to the sounds around him. At other times, he just listened to the silence. Here, now, there was no sound.

At home, he heard the soft ticking of the clock. And he felt the beating of his heart, almost in time with the clock. *Time and life marching on. Ticking away"* That is how he often thought of these rhythmic sequences. How he felt at the start of a new day. The rhythmic sequence of his existence. Life and time moving on.

When he was younger, on summer mornings, he liked to listen to the singing of the birds and the cooing of the morning doves outside his window while he lay quiet, eyes closed. At other times, he listened to the wind in the trees out in the yard. Or the rain on the roof.

As he got older, some of the sounds he wanted to hear had diminished or completely faded away, leaving only the muted sounds of the morning traffic on the main street a block and a half away. He missed the birds singing in the morning, the cooing of the doves. He knew they were still there, but he could no longer hear them. Time and age had taken them away. And he missed them all.

And when she was there, he woke to the fragrance of her hair, the sound of her breathing, and the warmth of her skin.

Up here, he lay quiet in his lean-to or the truck and oriented himself to this world around him. A world he loved and connected with. Here he was a more sensory and tactile being. The smell of the pines, the sound of the creek, or an early-rising squirrel chattering at the sunrise.

And the feel of the earth and pine needles beneath his sleeping bag were the only alarm clock he needed. And there was no comparison to the fragrance of pine needles and the feel of the earth beneath his boots on the trail The jar of a cement sidewalk just didn't measure up.

But here on the mountain, there was more to it than that. There was a mysterious quality to his relationship with this world. A mystical 'something' he didn't understand. Nor did he expect anyone else to do so either.

In the early morning, he reached out to this world with more than his mind. With more than his arms. He reached out with the fingers of his soul and embraced it with the arms of his spirit. To do so in the city was to get your fingers grimed and your embrace rebuffed. You can't hold the hum of traffic, the scream of sirens, and the thumping of a car stereo close to you heart.

Some of the things he listened to up here weren't really "sounds," of course. He knew that.

Rocks and rotting logs, after all, don't really make noises, sounds you can hear with the physical ear. But to him, they spoke. And he understood them. The sky and the clouds have no audible voice. But there was an indescribable and subliminal connection between these objects and himself. And the only way he could characterize it, even to himself, was their voices. Here they told him all that was right in their world and with his soul. And so he listened to them whenever they spoke. And here on the mountain, they spoke often. He listened to them, and he understood them.

Down below, to him, the worst two sounds in the world were the telephone ringing in the night and the alarm clock going off in the morning. He always set the alarm clock down there. But he never really needed it. He wanted his eyes to open on their own. Not to the grating sound of an alarm clock telling him it was time to get up.

Now, in the snow and the cold, he heard nothing. The complete absence of any sound or any voice. The silence roared in his ears, weighing on him. Up here, the worst sound of all was the voice of silence. The voice of the snow. All the other voices had gone to sleep for the winter.

He felt the old truck seat beneath him. It had begun to break down in places where he'd sat for over two hundred thousand miles. It had gotten him back home more times than he could remember.

He could smell the acrid odor of his body. Gamey, sweaty, and sour with no chance for a bath until he got back home. Or at least to the hospital. No doubt that would be his first stop when they found him. If they came in time. And, of course, there was the voice of the pain. Always the pain throbbing in his leg. Pain in the back of his head, left ribcage, shoulder, and back.

The cold was all around him, stalking him, restricting him with its icy grip. The isolation squeezed him like a coat a size too small. Uncomfortable and restrictive. That caged-in feeling weighed on him and numbed his mind.

These, too, may have voices. Harsh and grating. Sinuous. Devious and destructive. Voices he did not want to listen to.

He opened his eyes and glanced at the watch. It was 10:17 in the morning. Sunday. He had slept late. Very late. And that was okay. He had nowhere to go today and no way to get there. "Sunday," he said. "Home on Monday. Late on Tuesday. That's the deadline." He cringed at that word *deadline.* But that's what it was. That's when they would really begin to wonder. If he wasn't home by Tuesday evening and hadn't checked in, their worry would ratchet up. The kids would call each other to see if anyone had heard from him. Wednesday they would mobilize to find him and get him out. Sunday. Monday. Tuesday. "Those are going to be three very long days for me. But out of here on Wednesday at the latest." He paused, looking out the windshield at the snow. *Wednesday might too late* trickled through his mind.

When he finally sat up, the motion put additional pressure on his bladder. "The good ole morning pee just ain't what it used to be," he smiled. "No trippin' off to the 'family room to make water noises." The empty Gatorade bottle he had intended to use in the night for that purpose, if needed, lay on the floor. He shunned it. "Not gonna happen that way." Turning on the truck, he slid across the seat and opened the driver's door. He lowered himself to the ground, took care of business, and got immediately back into the truck.

As the warmth filled the cab, he thought of breakfast. "Bacon and eggs this morning, you lucky bastard. And hot coffee." He turned off the truck, rolled both windows down about an inch, and lit the stove under the frying pan and a cigarette with the same match.

He got the eggs and bacon out of the cooler, ready to cook. Rolling the passenger window down all the way, he poured the last of yesterday's coffee into the snow and refilled it with water from the bottles. The old filter and coffee grounds went into a freezer bag. A new filter and grounds in place, he put the pot over the second burner of the stove. The truck cab blossomed with the fragrance of bacon and eggs frying and coffee perking.

As he cooked and ate breakfast, he thought about how his world had narrowed since the fall. His thoughts always seemed to come back to that.

His isolation. Shrunken to the cab of the truck and the area close around the truck outside. That's all there was now. Most everything he had within arm's reach. Everything he wanted far away or buried beneath three feet of snow.

He was running low on water bottles. The freezer bags he had used for icing his leg lay on the floor of the truck, the snow now completely melted. With the bags beside him on the seat, he punctured a small hole in a bottom corner of one of the bags with his knife and turned it upright with the hole positioned over the neck of an empty water bottle. Water slowly drained from the bag into the bottle. With shaking hands, some of the water dripped onto his lap and the floor. In this way, he filled three bottles with fresh water. The empty bags went into the trash. It didn't matter. He had nearly a full box of new bags.

Then with a mental slap on his forehead, he said, "Hey, dummy. All you have to do is fill the coffee pot with snow and melt it on the stove. Ya dingbat." Smiling, he shook his head. "That would be a hell of a lot easier way to fill those bottles. Like my old man always said, 'Work smarter, not harder.' There's more water out there on the ground than you can ever drink."

Through the windshield, he could see the snow-covered ridge where he had fallen. Not more than one hundred yards away. He wondered, "How long now? How long have I been stuck in this truck? How long has it been?"

Now, it seemed as if this ordeal had lasted forever. And an ordeal it definitely was. As much as he tried, he couldn't think of what day the fall had happened. Puzzled. Confused. Eyes narrowed, brow wrinkled, he searched his mind for that one piece of memory. "I should be able to remember that," he mumbled.

The act of the fall itself was always clear in his mind. The slip in the snow, the heavy packboard throwing him backwards. Into the dark. He even remembered coming to, lying on his back in the snow, looking up at the trees and the clouds. And that initial pain. Pain that lived with him still. All of that was clear. But he couldn't remember what day it had happened. The more he struggled to remember, the more confused he became. His watch said it was Sunday. Sunday morning. He tried to back track, day by day, but missed it somehow.

Frustrated, anger building, he went back over it again, mumbling to himself. "Wednesday was opening day. The cow elk snuck up on me, and I saw the big buck in the canyon. Thursday evening, fishing the stream, and the walk across the meadow? NO! That was Wednesday, too. Wednesday afternoon and evening. I found all those tracks over there in the trees. Thursday morning, there was the skiff of snow when I woke up. Back up the ridge, the elk coming up the trail. The bull, the shot, and the work skinning and quartering him. I brought part of the meat down in two trips that day. Thursday. Too tired to go back for more after carrying the hind quarter. Friday morning. More snow when I woke. Hurrying to get the work done and get out before it snowed again. Went back for the rest of the meat. Two trips. Bringing the shoulder and horns down on the last trip. And fell. That would make it Friday." Only at that moment, in a flashbulb of memory, did he realize what day it had been. "I fell on Friday. It was Friday, about noon."

He continued through the rest of it in his mind. Locking it all in his memory by rote. Tumbling down the slope. Falling into the darkness. Coming to again. Dragging himself through the snow to get to the truck. Exhausted, freezing, and delirious with pain. Now he had it all. Repeating the day, "Friday! Friday! Friday!" After a pause he said, "Two days ago."

"Oh no. Only two days? Is that all? It feels like such a long time." The two days had stretched out hour by hour, minute by minute, living with the pain every second. Fighting the cold hour by hour. It seemed to him now that he had lived with the pain and the cold for a very long, long time. Not just two days. It was so much a part of his every thought and moment now. The pain, and the cold, every moment of his day, awake or asleep. And the isolation.

"Why can't I remember what day it happened?" he grumbled. Anger at himself stacked inside his mind. An unease fluttered through his chest.

His head drooped, chin on his chest. After an unknown time, he raised his head to peer out the windshield at the place where it had happened, buried now under feet of snow.

"Let it go, old son. Just let it go." But he couldn't. Not completely. Fear crept through him. "This is not a good sign, boy. Not a good sign at all." Forehead creased, brooding as he stared out the window, he tried to think it through. Was it a sign of something more? Infection? Exhaustion? A blood clot that had moved from his leg? A symptom of his feelings of isolation? Or just a simple lapse in memory? He found no easy answer.

Could he let it go and not worry about it? That wasn't possible. And in reality, it shouldn't be. He knew he needed to be aware of any changes, physical or mental. He couldn't let it get to him. Not beat up on himself. Just be aware but not let it control him. No one was harder on him than he was or demanded more of him than he did. He knew that. But still, he couldn't afford to neglect anything.

Isolation is far different from being alone. And it has its own psychological effects. This is not the solitude he often sought and enjoyed. Being trapped is far different from choosing to be limited to a certain small space for an indefinite amount of time. Maybe to the end. His feeling of isolation was becoming a weight. A very heavy weight. Trapped in the truck was beginning to feel as restricting as being in a small box. As confining as a coffin. He cringed at this last thought.

Even knowing, intellectually at least, how isolation would affect his mental state didn't lessen its impact. It still gnawed at him like a cancer, eroding his confidence and understanding. And that is how it felt to him now. Erosion. A wearing away of something intangible in his mind.

"Maybe I need to get out of this truck and take care of some things. Cold or no cold. I have things to do outside. I need to move. Not just sit here and brood about it." Still, he sat, looking out the driver's door window at the snow-covered meadow. The trail in the snow where the elk had crossed was now nearly obliterated. "What I really need is to get out of here," he said. "All the way out. Down off this mountain. Out of this damn snow."

He had never had those thoughts before up on a mountain. Whenever it came time to leave, he had always resented it. He had never wanted to leave before. He only went back down below when he had to. Now, he *needed* to get out.

Although he had always thought of snow as beautiful, he had never been an outdoors person in the winter. He had never been a skier or snowmobile rider. He went outside in the winter only when he had to. One of his favorite sayings was, "My favorite winter sport? Putting another log on the fire." And now, the snow and the cold held him close in a tight embrace.

Determined, he shifted in the seat and put the ski mask on his head, well down over his forehead and neck. The rough cloth grated against the cut on his head, and he cringed at the pain of it. There was more pain there than before, but he pushed it aside.

He zipped his coat and picked up the gloves from the floor. Staring through the windshield, he did not want to go out in the cold again. But go out he must. He needed to move. Be at least semi-mobile. He looked down at his swollen foot and puffy toes. Bare. Black and bare flesh. Unprotected from the cold. "I've got to cover that foot," he said.

From the clothes bag he got a pair of heavy wool socks. He knew putting those socks on the foot would be painful, but his toes needed the protection outside. Rewrapping his leg was painful as well, but that didn't protect his toes and foot from the cold. He rolled the socks in a tight roll from the top to the toe. Stretching to reach his foot, he took a deep breath, let it out, and held the first sock against his toes, pain rippling up his leg at the first pressure. He rolled the sock up his foot and over the heel. It took five minutes of rest before he could talk himself into doing the second sock. And more time to rest and reclaim control once that one was in place.

The time it had taken to accomplish this task added to the pressure of his need to get out. Nature was really pushing him to move. Now!

With coat zipped, ski mask rolled down all the way covering his face, and gloves on, he slid across the seat and opened the door. "Yep. It's cold out there alright. But nothing like it was last night."

Standing in the snow, leaning against the truck, taking part of his weight on his left arm, he moved toward the back, hopping on his right foot, holding the truck bed side wall with his left hand. Moving the right foot and leg forward against the pressure of the deep snow was difficult. A normal step was impossible one-legged. The left foot dragging in the snow increased the pain. Every hop jarred his left leg and foot and taxed the strength of his right leg. Walking in snow this deep with two good legs would be very difficult, exhausting. One-legged, it was brutal. "Just keep moving. Get done what you need to do," he said.

When he reached the back of the truck, breathing heavily, he leaned back, partially sitting on the tailgate to rest. The broom and the shovel lay across the tailgate. The shovel he would use to clean up his mess. Leaning against the tail gate with his hands, he hopped to the right rear corner of the truck, dropped his pants, squatted, and did what needed doing. The cold grabbed his bare butt and legs. Literally. Redressed, he used the shovel to throw his waste out into the snow, away from the truck.

As he laid the shovel back in the truck bed, he stood looking down at the shovel handle. "Why in the hell didn't you think of that before, you idiot," he said. "Cut that handle off and use it for splints." Sitting on the tailgate, he tried to work out how he could use the shovel handle for the splints. *I can use the strips of blue jeans to tie them in place*, he thought. In his mind he went through the process of tying the splints to his leg. And the movements he would have to make for a few more days around the truck, inside and outside.

"Those rags won't be tight enough to hold the splints in place when I move around. And I have to move around. Even if it's just to come out here to take a dump. And tying the splints on won't immobilize the lower leg and foot like I need. It's not going to keep it from swinging loose." He needed something to hold the wood rigidly to his leg.

He eased off the tailgate. Using his left hand on the sidewall, he hopped along the right side of the truck, opened one of the containers in the front of the truck bed, removed a roll of duct tape from the toolbox and put it in his coat pocket. "Good ole duct tape. Never go anywhere without a roll."

Back around the truck to the driver's side, he moved the broom and shovel to the left side of the truck and leaned them just behind the driver's door. "Now you're thinkin', boy. Now you're thinkin'. Stay as warm as you can and keep workin' for yourself. That's all you can count on right now. Do what needs doin', Don't just sit there mopin', feelin' sorry for yourself. You can sit and whine about what's happened or you can do something about it,"

Vaguely, like something seen out of the corner of his eye, he realized he was having to concentrate to keep his thoughts on track. Like fade away spots in a movie, his concentration slipped away from time to time. A tickle of fear ran through him. But he pushed it aside, held it away from conscious thought. "You're okay, boy. Keep working for yourself. You're doin' just fine." At a deeper level, he questioned that resolve.

Back in the cab, he rolled the windows down an inch and turned on the stove. The stove warmed the truck and heated the coffee. He needed both. And he needed to rest. Every activity sapped his strength more and more quickly. And it seemed to have a deteriorating effect on his mind as well as his body when the cold shook him like a baby's rattle. He couldn't think clearly when the pain controlled him. The pain influenced everything. The rage of the pain covered everything. And, at whatever level, the pain was always there. The pain could be expected. But a pervasive weakness was taking hold of him as well, and that worried him.

The feeling he had now was similar to how he had felt the time he'd had serious pneumonia. He probably should have gone to the hospital back then like the doctor wanted him to. But he rejected that. Macho bull crap. He wanted to go home. Take care of himself more or less. It turned out to be less. At least in the beginning.

Back then, just getting out of bed to walk to the bathroom was exhausting. Sometimes he simply crawled because he wasn't strong enough to stand. Thinking had been a struggle. Most of his time had been spent sleeping. Awake, his mind was blank. The wife of a friend had come to his house twice a day to make sure he was okay, ate at least two good meals, and took his medications. By the time he was well enough to get around on his own, the house smelled like a gym locker. Sheets soaked through with sweat night after night. Wearing the same clothes for several days. Everything smelled like sweat. Much like the cab of the truck was getting now.

Because of his experience with pneumonia and the debilitating effects of that infection, he was concerned with getting an infection now. An infection that developed anywhere in his body now most certainly would find its way to the injured leg. At this point, he had only two open wounds on his body, the small nick on his foot when he had cut his sock off and, of course, the injury on the back of his head. He thought of the elk hair and the pieces of elk bone that he had washed out of the cut on his head.

Elk—any wild animal really—were dirty creatures. They lived in the wild and were covered with dirt and vermin. When dressing an animal after a kill, he had always been very careful with his knife. At all costs, he avoided cutting himself while cleaning and skinning, simply to avoid the possibility of infection. So far, he had been successful.

He had done what he could for the head cut now, or at least he thought he had, by washing it and applying an antibiotic ointment. But he wondered if it was enough. It certainly wasn't as much as he could have done down below. And definitely not near as much as would have been done in a hospital. But it was all that he could do here, under these conditions. And he hoped it was enough.

"Keep an eye on it, boy," he said. "Do the best you can and try to keep it under control."

The leg was screaming at him now. "This sure isn't getting any easier," he said. The toes of his foot were not warm, but they weren't freezing either. Putting the socks on was painful at the time but the right thing to do. "I should have done that before I ever went outside the first time. I just didn't think of it." Constantly fighting the pain, nausea and dizziness had consumed his thoughts. It was worming its way into his mind and kept him from thinking clearly. Pain in the body he knew he could deal with. At least somewhat. Pain in the mind could cripple him more that any pain of the body. "Don't let the pain take over. If the pain takes over your mind, you're dead. Plain and simple," he whispered.

Added to it all was the pervasive cold, and it was no wonder he was thinking slowly. "Maybe that's all it is. The pain, the cold, and I'm just plain tired."

When the coffee steamed, he filled his cup and set the pot aside, leaving the burner on for heat. Eyes closed, he leaned against the back of the seat, lit a cigarette, sipped the coffee until it was gone, and turned the stove off.

CHAPTER 19

Now for the crutch. The bone saw was under the seat, and he laid it on the seat beside him. Opening the driver's door, he brought the handle of the broom inside, laying it across his lap. Estimating how much to remove, he cut the handle off with the bone saw. Pressure against his left thigh was not good, but he ignored it until he was done. Even this minimal activity seemed to weaken him more than he thought it should. And that worry was just below the surface. *I need to think better and stay strong. I need to keep my head as clear as I can.* Over and over, these thoughts nagged at him and kept him going.

The broom went back outside the truck. He closed the door and rested against the sleeping bag, the leg along the seat, eyes closed. "I'll test my new 'crutch' later," he said. Taking slow, deep breaths, he relaxed and poured another cup of coffee. "Slow down. Think before you do anything. You have to get it right," he chided himself.

He thought through the process of making the splints, concentrating, holding hard to each thought. Fear of losing even one thought gripped his mind. He berated himself for not thinking of the shovel handle sooner. "Maybe I could have saved myself some pain. Maybe," he said. "Doesn't matter now. Get it done and see how it works out."

But he was badly shaken by the loss of memory of what day the fall had happened, the confusion with the story line on the book, and the fading periods in his mind. Were these things a manifestation of the head injury? If so, there wasn't anything he could do about it. Or was it just a part of his fatigue and isolation? "Probably both," he said.

He wondered if he was just worrying about it too much. Maybe obsessing about it. At the same time, he knew he needed to be aware of mental changes. He needed to have a clear mind to continue to function. He had to keep as sharp as possible to survive. Otherwise, he could make an irrational decision that could have serious, even fatal, consequences. And it was still his feeling that his mind was getting less and less clear by small degrees, and it was harder to stay focused. He needed focus.

"Today, tomorrow, and Tuesday," he said. "That's all you have to get through. They'll be here no later than Wednesday. Take care of yourself. Take care of the leg. And wait. That's all you have to do. They'll come and get you out."

Leaning against the sleeping bag, head against the cold door window, he closed his eyes. He had thought earlier of using the sleeping bag when he slept. It certainly would keep him warmer when it got cold in the truck. It was a very good bag and held his body heat well. The problem was getting into and out of the bag with his leg the way it was in the already crowded truck.

In addition, he was too tall to lie across the seat fully. Cramped sleeping wasn't the most restful under the best of conditions. In the truck, complete rest was nearly impossible. To unroll and re-roll the bag each day would be a lot of movement and work in a tight space. Movement was painful. And dangerous. Even a little effort now was tiring. To leave the bag unrolled all the time would take up too much room and get in the way of other movements he needed to make.

And he was very comfortable with things the way they were, at least as comfortable as circumstances would allow, except for the cold when the heat was off. Leaning against the rolled bag provided a very comfortable back rest, and it left room for him to stretch out his leg on the seat. "I need to do only what needs doin'," he said. "Nothin' more. Nothin' less."

Sleep came to him gradually, and he let it take hold of him, gently drifting away.

CHAPTER 20

As he had drifted into sleep, a dream formed in his mind and haunted his sleep. He was outside of a house in the weather. Darkness and cold gripped him. Snow, driven by the bitter wind, pelted his face. He stepped to the house near a window.

All the kids were there, inside of a house. A house he didn't know, didn't recognize. And she was there. With the kids. How strange that seemed to him, her being there with them. He was outside, in the cold and snow, wind driving against him. Through lighted windows, he saw them all with small plates of food and steaming mugs in their hands. They were all talking, laughing, together and warm.

Shivering, alone in the cold, he circled the house. Every window he looked through held the same scene. Window after window. Always the same perspective. He circled the house time after time, the cold wind pushing him. From window to window, he looked into the brightly lit room filled with those he loved. All them were there, warm, and happy.

Rapping on each of the windows drew no one's attention. He found no door. No way to get into the house. No way to be with them. No way to be warm and happy, like they were. Circling endlessly, getting weaker, colder, he was trapped outside. Separated from them. Bitter cold stinging his face, burning his lungs.

CHAPTER 21

A spasm jerked through his body, waking him. His leg banged against the side wall of the truck near the door. Pain slammed his back against the rolled sleeping bag, legs thrust beneath the steering wheel. His head banged against the passenger door window. Pain flared like a burst of light from the cut on his head.

Sitting up, eyes wide with fear, his head swung from side to side, eyes and mind searching for where he was. Dizziness spun the inside of the truck to his left, and he closed his eyes to control it. Caught between the dream and the reality of where he was, pain rippled up his leg in crashing waves. His injured foot pressed against the floor. The injury on his head was on fire.

Reality swept through him. He was in the truck. He was trapped and isolated. His leg was badly broken. Pain controlled every moment of his existence. Deep snow surrounded him, and there was no way for him to get off this mountain. He could only wait for them to come get him. Or the ultimate end. However it worked out.

Nausea and dizziness rolled over him again like a freezing wind in his face. Doubled over in the seat, elbows on his thighs, he moaned in the dark, the other darkness rushing at him, threatening to take him away.

"No. No. No," he growled. "No more. No more." Fear and cold crushed him as he fought for control of his mind and body. Sitting up in total darkness, he shivered uncontrollably. When he moved the leg, his foot and lower leg swung freely to the inside. "Oh God. Oh God!" he screamed. He fell back, shaking beyond control. "Cold, cold, cold," he moaned. "Gotta get warm. I've gotta get warm." By instinct, he reached for the ignition and the keys hanging there.

With the truck running, he sat as still as he could, breathing heavily, hands in his lap, head hanging, chin on his chest. His entire body trembled. The injured foot rested with the heel on the floor. He tried to lift it to relieve the pressure but was too weak and couldn't hold it up more than a few seconds at a time. And the lower leg and foot always sagged when he lifted it, causing more pain. He lay back against the sleeping bag and lifted his leg onto the seat.

Images of the dream swirled around him. Ate at him. Mixed in with the now and here.

Fumbling through the dark, it took him several minutes to find the lamp. With hands stiff and shaking from the cold, he held the lamp in his lap and thumbed the switch. Dim light illuminated his lap, chest, and face. The darkness was thrust to the deep corners of the truck cab. Staring at the lamp, he knew there was something he needed to do with it, but nothing would come to mind. He couldn't hold it in his thoughts. Cold and pain overwhelmed him, mind and body.

Gradually he warmed. The shivering slowed but never completely stopped. Shaking chills rippled through him every few minutes. The watch said 9:40 p.m. Sunday. "I've been out for hours," he whispered. And that scared the hell out of him. "Sleep I need. Freezing to death I don't need. Much longer, and I would have been a popsicle." He pushed himself back to a sitting position.

A movement of cold air drifted across his face. The truck was still running, the heater blowing warm air. Yet cold air was moving through the cab. He turned his head to the left and stared at the driver's door window, rolled down two inches or more. Looking to his right, that window was partly open as well. A low groan started deep in his guts, rolled up through his chest, and magnified to a loud, angry scream. "Are you tryin' to kill yourself? You fool! You dumb, brainless son-of-a-bitch!" he shouted. When he'd turned off the stove, he hadn't rolled up the windows before he fell asleep. "You're lucky you're not dead, you idiot."

He rolled up both windows and slumped against the sleeping bag, exhausted and dejected. The leg lay across the seat, exposed. Black, ugly, and twisted like a partially burned log in the fire pit. No splint. No wrapping. No ice bags. Uncared for all day. "Damn. You're not takin' care of business, boy. Not taking care of business at all." He paused. "Your brain just isn't working so good." And a flickering twinge came from somewhere, like a whisper in the dark. *You need to just let go. Give it up.* He was puzzled by that thought and instantly angry with himself. "Never!" he whispered. And then louder, "Never." And finally, he bellowed at the windshield, teeth gritted, "Never!" Breathing deep, he gradually calmed himself. His breathing relaxed and his heart rate slowed. He stared out the windshield at the dark, the snow, and the cold. "If you're gonna kill me, you're gonna have to work for it, you sons-of-bitches."

His head ached. The cut burned. The leg throbbed. Hunger rumbled in his stomach. He had not eaten since breakfast, and he was hungry. That woozy feeling kind of hungry.

He tilted his head forward and reached for the cut on his head. It was painful to the touch, his scalp swollen. What he felt shook him. The cut was partly crusted. Around the edges only. Down through the center of the cut it felt oozy. Slimy. When he looked at his hand, his fingers were covered with a slimy, red tinged fluid. *Infection?* he thought. "Oh, God I hope not," he breathed. "I hope that's just the ointment I put on it." He applied another generous gob of the ointment to his fingers and rubbed it into the cut, flinching at the pain. Touching it at all increased the pain. He pushed aside what he had seen. "Later. I'll deal with it later."

Wetting the washcloth with water from a bottle, he washed his hands. It was time to eat. Despite everything, he must eat.

Lightheaded, moving as if in slow motion, he got a bag of the meat from the floor and found it nearly frozen solid. "That could have been you, old son. That could have been you. Just 'cause you didn't roll up the fucking windows. You'd be another piece of frozen meat right now."

Unable to cut through the meat with the knife, he picked up the bone saw. With the washcloth, he wiped the blade of the saw clean. Using the saw, he cut two thick pieces of back strap for dinner. The saw blade left a long gash in the plastic top of the cooler. *So what?* he thought. *The damn thing's probably gonna be here all winter anyway.* He sat staring at the gash in the cooler lid, his mind floating, seemingly disconnected.

After minutes of lethargy, he fired up the stove, picked up the meat, put it in the frying pan, and said, "One steak for dinner. One for lunch. Both at the same time."

Meat cooking, a new pot of coffee perking, the truck cab warm again, he started to feel more normal. *Normal?* he thought. *What the hell is normal anymore?* The fog in his mind was clearing, but not completely. The fear remained. Like the smell of the old sweat in his clothes, the fear was there. A pervasive reminder of how things were and how they would remain for a while yet. Until they came to get him.

The bread was cold and stiff, the butter spread in little chunks. Milk came out of the plastic jug with ice crystals. The cold was getting into everything now. "And there isn't much I can do about it." He paused, head down, staring at the floor. "Except roll up the damn windows before you fall asleep, you idiot," he growled through gritted teeth. He turned off the stove, rolled up the windows, turned on the truck, and ate the meat and bread. The partial glass of milk he left on the floor by the heater vent to thaw out. A tin cup of coffee warmed his fingers and his stomach.

He knew the serious effects of long-term severe cold. He had seen it first-hand. Investigated it. And he suspected that the cold was causing his mental problems as well. At least some of them. Too much cold for too long, and his mind and body would start to slow down. Blood circulation would gradually be restricted to his major organs. The physical bodies attempt to maintain core heat and life. Sacrifice the extremities to frost bite to save the vital organs that kept the body alive. Frozen fingers and hands. Frozen toes and feet. Frozen ears and nose. Flesh turning to dark chunks of ice. In the extreme, the vital organs would begin to shut down as well. Eventually, near the end, delirium. Hallucinations. Unconsciousness. If he got to that point, he probably wouldn't even know it. And it would be over. Even before his heart stopped beating, the cold would have won.

What to do about the cold was a very real problem. Run the truck more, use more gas to stay warm, and he would run out sooner than he could afford. Using the camp stove more was dangerous. Used improperly, without ventilation, the stove would kill him more quickly than the cold. He had to maintain a balance between staying warm to survive for as long as he could and using his heat resources. And he had to make sure he ate regularly. "Just do what you can, boy. Just do what you can. And be careful. Think and be careful."

The lamp was getting dimmer. Without conscious thought, he searched the pockets of the backpack and found two new batteries and put them in the lamp. And the truck cab was bright with light again.

He needed to get out and take care of nature. He needed to make the splint. "Do I need to ice the leg with all this cold all around me? Maybe not, but I probably should." Four more Advil went down with warm coffee.

Holding four new freezer bags, he slid across the seat, opened the door, and lowered himself to the ground. All without a hitch and only a slight increase in pain. "Okay, you're gettin' better at this. At least you're getting' pretty good at gettin' out of the truck." He stood by the door and took care of nature's business.

Relieved of the bladder problem, literally, he held the sweeping end of the broom under his left armpit and leaned against it with his left foot held off the ground. The foot and leg still dangled in the deep snow, and that applied some pressure to it. He took two steps toward the back of the truck leaning on the broom. His motion was easier, more fluid, and did not jar his leg as much as the hopping had. Unable to take a normal step, pushing his legs through the snow was still difficult and probably would be for as long as he was here. But there was no jarring pain using the broom for a crutch as there was with hopping. His right leg wasn't taxed as hard as it had been since the broom took part of his weight. The brush end of the broom was bulky under his armpit but held steady. "Not perfect, but better." It took his weight well. "Tomorrow I'll sharpen the end of the handle so it won't slip in the snow. This'll be good for when I have to move around out here."

His mind seemed clearer now, too. A bit sluggish but clearing again. He filled the four freezer bags with snow and dropped them on the floor of the truck. "Man, it's cold out here. Glad I don't have to stay out in it tonight," he said.

•　　•　　•

There had been other hunts on other mountains when the temperature had dropped well below zero at night. Bone freezing cold. Those were nights spent in the truck cab with the sleeping bag and the warmth of a running motor when he needed it. These present nights were far different than simply seeking comfort. Those other times there had been no broken leg, no pain, and no deep snow. He had not been trapped in the truck. But he'd had no feeling of isolation. No dependence on others to come get him off the mountain.

•　　•　　•

Back in the truck, he reached back outside and pulled the shovel across his lap, handle first. With a strip of the pant leg he'd cut for wrapping his leg, he measured from his knee to just past the bottom of his foot. "I haven't tried touching my toes this much since I was in the army." Using the cloth measurement, he found he could get three pieces of the shovel handle for the splints. *I'll put one on each side and one in the back*, he thought. The bone saw cut through the wood quickly, aggravating the leg. He dropped the shovel blade outside and closed the door. He started to light a burner on the stove. "Don't do that, dummy, not while you're resting."

And he needed to rest. It seemed now that he always needed to rest. But he was worried he might fall asleep. "Can't sleep with that stove on," he said. He started the truck instead and leaned against the sleeping bag. "Rest now. But don't sleep. Just a little rest." Eyes closed, trying to relax, he said, "Still talking out loud to yourself, old son. It's a good thing there's no one around.

They'd think you're nuts talkin' to yourself like this. They would have you locked away in the cuckoo ward."

When the truck was fully warm, he turned it off and looked at the gas gage. There was a little over a quarter of a tank of gas left now. "I really need to put the gas I have in the can into the tank soon. I can't run out of gas." He took a deep breath and held it for a time. As he let it out, he said, "Now to splint the leg."

Examining the three pieces of shovel handle, he worked out in his mind how he should attach them to his leg, holding tightly to each thought.

Ignoring the pain, he turned the leg to the inside as it lay on the seat and put one of the pieces along the back of the leg, the top a few inches below the back of his knee, the bottom protruding below his heel. Another he held along the outside of his leg. There was about a four-inch gap between the two pieces of wood.

After a few minutes of pondering, he figured out how he thought it could work. Tape the three pieces together with a four-inch gap between each, forming a webbing of sorts that would go around his leg with a piece on each side of his leg and one in the back. Then it was a simple matter of setting his leg in this 'webbing' and taping it together around the leg. Most of this work wouldn't necessitate moving the leg much at all, at least not until the last phase. "That part is going to hurt. Probably about like when I wrapped it. But I'll just have to take it."

He'd left the tape on the floor in front of the heater vent beside the glass of milk to warm it. He took a long drink of milk and set it back down. From the roll of tape, he ripped three lengths of duct tape about a foot long and stuck two of them to the dashboard. He wrapped the ends of each piece of tape around two of the pieces of wood about eight inches apart. The third piece he stuck to the tape between the first two. Three more strips of tape he placed sticky side to sticky side on the first pieces to hold the three sections of wood together and firmly in place.

"Now comes the hard part," he said. Pulling his pant leg together along the top of his leg, he taped it loosely in place. With the swelling, the pant leg would not close all the way. When he touched it, the leg was still warm but didn't seem more so. "At least I don't have to look at the damn thing so much anymore. Only when I have to." Its appearance hadn't changed in the slightest from when he first cut open the pant leg. It was still swollen to more than twice its normal size and as black as fresh asphalt.

With the webbing laid on the seat, he lifted the leg with his hands and placed it on the top of the webbing. The lower part of the leg below the break and his foot sagged to the inside again. Pain shot through him and brought a deep groan in his throat, but he continued without hesitation.

With the leg in place on the splint, he leaned back against the sleeping bag until the pain lessened. "Relax. Let it go," he said, taking deep, controlling breaths. "You can take it and get through it." There was no question in his mind that the next step would be harder still.

The weight of his foot and lower leg rested on the piece of wood on the inside of his leg with the wood against his inside ankle bone. "That feels like somebody standing on it," he said. Slightly raising his leg, he shifted the wood forward of the ankle bone to rest more along the arch of his foot. He leaned back against the sleeping bag and chanted the mantra, forcing himself to relax. "Take baby steps, boy. Little bitty baby steps."

Everything he did, every movement, was exhausting. And that nagged at him more and more. With another strip of tape, he wrapped one end around the top of the bottom piece of wood on the inside of his leg. Pulling the two side pieces as close together as he could and tight against the leg, he drew the tape strip across the front of his leg and stuck it to the tape on either side, securing it around the leg. "That wasn't so bad." But the next two were. The second place he taped was right at the location of the break. Fiery pain ran from his toes up. *Not good planning*, he thought. *Should have put it just below the break.* He didn't remove it to start over but continued on instead.

Completing the process at the ankle, he had to lean far forward at the waist as he worked. Baby steps was all he had at this point. Weakness and nausea were taking hold of him. He attached the tape and leaned back to rest. Dizzy and nauseous, the darkness loomed over him. It took two attempts with a rest in between to pull the side pieces together before he managed to get the tape wrapped tight enough around his ankle to hold the wood firmly in place. As he pulled the bottom pieces tight, the foot's canted position changed slightly, closer to its natural position. He could feel the lower bone ends move inside his flesh. The pain and the darkness nearly took him away again.

When he finished, sweat ran down his face. Teeth gritted, moaning deep in his throat, tears blurred his vision. Sweat and tears combined to drip from his chin. He picked up the four snow-filled freezer bags and placed them along both sides of his leg above and below the break with the towel holding them in place. He leaned back with a long sigh. "Let the leg relax now, old son. Don't move it for a while." Breathing deep, he went down inside himself, seeking control, as much as the pain would allow. Eyes closed, tears on his cheeks, he dozed into a brief and fitful sleep.

CHAPTER 22

It was cold in the truck, but it didn't seem as cold as it had been the past two days. Still, he was shivering with chills, sweating and shivering at the same time.

It was dark now, but he didn't look at his watch. It didn't matter. Time didn't really matter now. The cold chilled the sweat on his face and hands. He trembled. Despite the cold, he'd been sweating again in his sleep. He pushed the thought aside. He didn't want to examine it or acknowledge its implications.

He was hungry, thirsty, and needed to pee. The leg was throbbing, pulsing with each heartbeat. He shook two Advil from the bottle and washed them down with a long drink of Gatorade. His body quiet for a time, he wiped sweat from his face and head with a napkin. He needed to get out or wet his pants.

When he opened the door and moved his leg to slide to the ground, he noticed the lower leg and foot didn't move within the splint, and his movements didn't aggravate the pain. The pain was still there as always but not exaggerated by movement. And that enabled him to relax more than he had been able to before. When he reached for the broom, he remembered he wanted to carve the broom handle to a point so it wouldn't slip in the snow and ice. Sitting with his legs hanging out of the truck, he slid the brush end of the broom into the truck behind him. With the skinning knife, he whittled the end of the broom handle to a point, letting the chips fall to the snow outside the truck. "That knife is gettin' dull," he said. "I'll need to sharpen it before I use it much more." He put the broom back outside and leaned it against the truck.

He lowered himself to the ground, and his right foot took his weight. Sliding the broom under his armpit, he leaned some of his weight on the broom and stepped forward, away from the truck. Turning to his left, he moved toward the back of the truck. He couldn't lift the broom completely out of the snow, and it moved awkwardly through the snow with each step. His left leg still dragged through the snow, hindering his movement more than he would have liked. He was not able to lift his right foot out of the deep snow either. Both the broom handle and the right leg plowed snow with each step—a laborious process that took his energy quickly.

The major difference was that the injured leg was not as jarred with each step as it had been when he was forced to hold the side of the truck and hop on his right foot.

"Trade-offs, old son. There's always trade-offs." His right leg was much less taxed with each step as well. "Man, oh man that's a lot better. Not real easy, but better."

At the back of the truck, he took care of the bladder problem as he looked longingly to the West where the logging road disappeared into the trees, a dark gash in the snow. At that moment, more than ever, he wished for them to come—perhaps as much as he had wished for anything before or ever would again. He could almost see them coming into the meadow. In a truck, on snowmobiles. most likely. Any way they could get to him would be fine. "Just let them come," he said. "Soon! I'm gonna need a doctor real soon, kids."

Leaning on the broom, he sighed deeply and hung his head. "Not coming yet. They probably won't come 'til Wednesday."

He slowly turned back to the truck, pivoting on his right heel. As he swung the broom handle through the snow, he looked toward the ridge and the tree line where he had fallen. *Friday* flashed in his mind. Now there was nothing visible to mark where it had happened. There was no obvious mound of snow where the packboard with the meat and horns now lay buried. No tines from the rack sticking out of the snow. All was completely hidden under the silent snow.

The dark sky was covered with broken clouds. The snow all around sparkled and glistened in the bright light of a full moon between the clouds. But in the thickest part of the trees, very little showed. Brush, tree branches, the ground. All buried. Snow covered everything. The silent snow.

"As long as it doesn't bury me," he said.

No sound reached him. No voices spoke to him. And his own voice died just beyond his lips.

To his right, he could make out the banks of the stream in the dark. Snow lay flat across the frozen surface of the water. "In a couple of months, you won't even be able to tell there's a stream over there. It'll be buried under ten or more feet of snow. Until late May or later, more than likely. And the truck won't be visible until then either. Just another hump in the snow, if that."

With each breath, a cloud vapor formed in front of his face and slowly drifted away. It condensed on his mustache and rimed there. He wiped it away with the back of his hand. With little cloud cover, it would be colder still. "And killing cold tonight," he said. "If you're out in it."

His left foot was getting cold, even with the socks. His stomach growled with hunger. He hobbled on the crutch to the still-open door of the truck and slid onto the seat. The broom remained outside. He closed the door against the cold, the killing cold. "Time to eat," he said. He turned on the burners of the stove and lowered the windows slightly. Opening the last can of Dinty Moore stew, he spooned it into the saucepan and put it on the stove. There was more than half a pot of coffee, now cold. He placed it over the second burner, sat back, and waited for dinner.

When he'd finished eating, he leaned forward and looked out the windshield. It was dark. All over dark, except the sky. The star-spangled sky and the silver full moon hung just above the ridge. The moon glowed as if from an inner luminescence. Shadows of sporadic clouds darkened the forest and meadow in places.

Resting against the sleeping bag, he sipped his coffee and smoked a cigarette. He knew he would have no problem sleeping tonight. It was late, and his eyes were drooping already. "I probably should pee again before I hit the sack."

Coat zipped, he slid across the seat, opened the door, and stepped into the snow. The cold was merciless and immediate tonight. He stared at the stars as he took care of his business. He wanted to just stand and stare at all those gorgeous stars and the slash of the Milky Way across the sky. But the cold denied him of even that, and he slid back into the truck, closed the door, and turned the motor on.

Smoking his last cigarette of the day, he watched what stars he could see through the windshield while the truck heated. When it was warm again, he turned off the truck, lay against the sleeping bag, and closed his eyes.

When he woke, sweaty body odor filled the cab of the truck. Sweat gathered on his forehead and face, in his hair, under his arms, in the hollow of his chest. The back of his shirt was damp with sweat. The glowing hands of his watch said 3:15 a.m. Monday. Dreams he couldn't remember floated just below the surface of his mind. He mentally reached for the leg and found it unaccountably relaxed and held firmly in the splint, though still painful with a slight burning tingle on the surface.

Without moving the leg, he sat up and reached for the ignition key. He turned on the truck and lay back against the sleeping bag, eyes closed. His eyes felt grainy and hot, eyelids drooping and heavy. He didn't want to go back to sleep right now. Not with the truck running. But he found he was nodding off again anyway. Drifting away. Half aware of the world around him, the truck running, and the need to sleep making its demands. When closer to the surface, he pulled himself back up and shut off the truck. He knew he had probably slept again but didn't know how long. It didn't really matter. Lying back down, he nestled deeper into sleep.

CHAPTER 23

As he noticed the world around him again, light flooded the truck cab, glimmering just beyond his eyelids. Lying against the sleeping bag, head turned toward the windshield, he opened his eyes. The cab was bright with sunlight. The windows were clouded with frost, and it was cold. Extremely cold. But there was sunlight. No longer was there the heavy dullness of a cloudy sky. He turned on the truck and looked at the gas gauge. "Less than a quarter of a tank. I must have slept longer than I thought with the truck still running last night," he said. "I need to put that gas into the tank today." Thinking what that would take daunted him. "And that ain't gonna be easy."

He sat up and shifted his weight to move his leg to the floor. It rested on the back piece of the splint instead of directly on the floor as it had been for all the time he'd been in the truck. The foot and leg were held steady in the splint. There was no pressure against the break, and the ache at this point seemed mentally manageable. He shook out four Advil and washed them down with a swallow of Gatorade. Nature needed attention. Again.

He slid out of the truck, left the door open, and took care of business. Looking at the snow near the truck door, he said, "Ya got a big hunk of yella ice out here, old son." Gazing around, he was relieved to see blue sky and took a deep breath, letting it out with a big sigh. No clouds anywhere in sight. He squinted into the glare of sunshine with a smile on his face. But he knew the warmth of the sun was deceptive. It was still very cold. Maybe as cold as last night. A bitter, penetrating cold, even in the sun. With no cloud cover to hold the earth's warmth, it would be much colder now, day and night. Especially at night. But to see blue sky and shadows again was a pleasant relief.

The snow glittered across the meadow. All the trees were still white with it. No brush was visible beneath the undulating snow cover. Facing to the east, where he knew the head of the trail and the start of the ridge to be, the sun glared brightly. Almost blinding. Squinting in the glare, he said with a smile, "You might need your sunglasses today, old son."

And all was still silent. No sound of any kind came to him. No crows. No squirrels. No breeze. No murmuring creek. No voices anywhere. "It doesn't matter," he said. "At least the sun is shining."

Back in the truck, he felt sticky from sweating in the night. That he had sweated at all, as cold as it was, nagged at him. He had no immediate answer and pushed the thought aside. *Work it out later if you want*, he thought. "For now, it's breakfast," he said. "Bacon and eggs and hot coffee. Yeehaw."

Rolling down the windows a little for ventilation, he started the stove and turned off the truck. He filled the coffee pot with fresh water, placed fresh grounds and a new filter in the coffee pot, and put it over a burner. Four strips of bacon were left in the package, stuck together and frozen. He dropped them into the frying pan in one lump. As the bacon warmed, he pulled the strips apart and watched them sizzle in their own grease. When they were nearly cooked, with grease covering the bottom of the pan, he picked up the egg carton. Four eggs left. "Save two for breakfast tomorrow, boy," he said.

And the burners flickered. They flickered again and went out with a pop. For a minute he sat staring at the stove and the unlit burners. "That's the end of that bottle of gas," he mumbled. He unscrewed the empty bottle, set it on the floor, and rolled it under the seat. The second bottle was there as well.

Moving his hand around as far as he could reach under the seat, he couldn't find the other bottle. Each time he thought he had it, he brought out the old one and finally laid it on the floor out of the way. He tried again and knew that he could never get his arm and hand far enough under the seat to find the new bottle. It had to be near the back of the seat against the gas tank. "How the hell am I goin' to get that damn bottle?"

The cooler was in the way. The clothes bag, backpack, and trash bags were all in the way. He couldn't reach very far under the seat with his left arm, and the right one didn't even come close. Even if he lay on his stomach on the seat, he probably couldn't reach far enough to find the new gas bottle. The leg was a problem as he moved around to get his upper body in a position to reach his arm under the seat. With the leg, lying face down on the seat would not be possible anyway.

"There's only one way you're gonna get that damn bottle, boy. Get out of the truck, go around, and get on your knees in the snow." With a disgusted sigh he turned onto his back and sat up. "There's just no easy way around it."

He turned the burner knobs off, zipped his coat, and opened the driver's door. When he slid out of the truck, his right foot came down on the shovel blade in the snow and slid off, tripping him to the right, throwing him off balance. He caught himself on the truck door and held on. When he righted himself, he picked up the shovel blade. The broom went under his left armpit. Holding the shovel blade in his right hand, the frigid metal stingingly cold against his bare fingers, he moved toward the back of the truck.

He left the shovel blade on the tailgate and moved around the truck to the passenger door. Moving through the snow with the broom under his arm was much easier than when he had made this trip to get the duct tape. The snow on the right side of the truck was much deeper than on the left. He had only walked once on this side of the truck, and the snow wasn't as packed down and disturbed as it was on the driver's side. This made walking with the crutch harder, pushing it through the deeper snow.

He opened the passenger door, moved the cooler as far as he could away from the seat, and bent over, holding himself with his left hand on the seat.

Leaning forward, he laid his chest and head on the seat with a sigh. When he reached under the seat with his right arm, he swept his hand from side to side and didn't find the bottle. "Damn," he swore. "Nothin's gonna be easy this morning." He remained lying with his chest on the seat for a few moments.

"Ya know what ya gotta do, boy. So just do it."

Hands on the seat, he slid his right foot away from the truck and bent the injured leg at the knee behind him. The part of the splint along the back of his leg dug into his flesh just below the back of the knee. Uncomfortable but not a real problem. With his hands flat on the floor just inside the threshold, he knelt on his right leg in the snow and pushed the left leg through the snow behind him. He leaned into the truck, wedged his head and body between the seat and the cooler with his head near the floor and his right arm above his head. As he looked under the seat, he saw the bottle right where he thought it would be. Clear at the back of the cab against the gas tank. "There you are, you little bastard." Lying on his right shoulder, stretching to the end of his right arm, he grasped the bottle, pulled it out, and set it on the seat.

With a deep breath, he laid his head on the floor. "Now all you gotta do is get back in the truck." Getting back upright was more of a struggle than he had thought it would be. Wiggling and twisting, pushing up with his right hand and arm and pulling with his left hand, gripping the back of the seat, it took several minutes just to get back to lying face down on the seat. He could put no weight at all on his left leg. When he bent it at the knee and brought it under his body, the pain nearly took control, and he waited for it to subside. He went over in his mind how he should be able to get back up. A reverse of how he had gotten down was the only way to manage it.

Putting his arms and hands on the seat again, he inched his body into the truck to lie face down on the seat. Pushing himself with his right foot was nearly futile. It continually slipped in the snow when he put weight on it and pushed. Inch by inch, with frequent periods for rest, he worked his way into the truck. When he finally managed to get his upper right leg back near the truck, his body still face down on the seat, he brought his right knee to the threshold where he rested it. His left leg was still straight out behind him in the snow.

Gasping for breath, heart pounding, he lay face down on the seat for several minutes, resting. "What in the hell have I done to myself?" he moaned.

His right pants leg was wet from kneeling in the snow. His quad muscle quivered with fatigue. A bit of rest was necessary despite the cold and wet pants legs. No matter that he had to stand up on one leg. He had to get back in the truck. No matter what it took.

With both hands on the seat near his sides, he tried to push himself up, taking his weight on his right knee, the metal threshold digging into his kneecap. He didn't make it the first time and lay back down. "Man, I'm weak," he said. He rested briefly. *I've got to get out of this cold.*

"Then give it another shot, old son. You can't just lay here. You can make it."

Arm muscles quivering, teeth gritted, he slowly made to an upright position, right knee on the threshold taking his weight, breath coming hard now.

"Holy smokes," he moaned. "That was like doing fifty pushups."

He took a deep breath and closed his eyes.

Minutes later, he took hold of the door frame and the side of the truck, tilted his right leg until his foot was on the ground, and pushed himself to a standing position. With slow, sluggish movements, still breathing heavily, he moved to his left, leaned his chest against the side of the truck, and closed the door.

Dizziness swam through his head, threatening to spin him into the snow again. He closed his eyes and waited for it to pass as he chanted the mantra. Eyes closed, he took deep breaths and exhaled slowly. And a measure of control came back to him.

When his breathing and heart slowed and the spinning stopped, he tucked the broom under his arm and made his way back around the truck and into the cab. He pushed things around in the cab to make more room for him. He put the new gas bottle in his lap and leaned against the rolled-up sleeping bag, head against the door window, and closed his eyes." I just need to rest a bit," he said. Under his clothes, his body was sweating. Cold chilled the sweat on his face and neck. His hands were cold and numb because he had not worn gloves. "That was a lot more work than I thought it was going to be," he said.

He leaned forward, turned on the truck, and lay back down.

While he rested, he mentally reached for the leg. It was never very far away. The pain was still in the forefront. The splint had done its job well. The leg was still firm in the webbing.

But somehow it felt different—something he couldn't identify, but different.

I'll have to check it later.

He sat up, screwed the new gas bottle into the stove, and relit the burners. The bacon grease congealed in the cold.

As the frying pan warmed, he cracked one egg on the side of the pan, held it over the hot grease, and pried the shell apart. Nothing came out. He tried to pry the shell farther apart, and it crumpled in his hands. The inside of the egg was a solid, jellied lump. He tried to shake egg from what was left of the shell, and it fell with plop, pieces of shell still attached. Unable to detach most of the shell fragments, he gave up and left them in the pan. "A few shells won't matter." The second egg was easier.

As the eggs cooked, they gradually thawed, spread out, and cooked just fine. Salt and pepper made them look just like fried eggs should look for breakfast. He inhaled the smell of perking coffee blended with the fragrance of eggs and bacon.

When the food was ready, he turned off the burner, rolled up the windows, and ate directly from the pan. When he finished, he leaned against the bag and lit a cigarette, shifting the leg onto the seat, and sipped coffee.

As he lifted the leg from the hip, the foot and the lower leg didn't sag or shift as they had done with every movement before he'd put on the splint.

His watch said just after nine a.m. Monday. "I'm late if I'm not home tonight, kids. Get me by tomorrow. Or no later than Wednesday. I've got a story to tell ya." When he tried to adjust his seating position, a bolt of pain shot up the inside of his left leg, flared at his knee, and exploded in his left hip. A deep groan rolled through his chest. Any movement was a hammer blow from his toes up through his hip.

He was still shaky from the ordeal getting the gas bottle. His arms were limp and tired, and his back ached. The leg ached, but there was not as much pressure on it as there had been before. The splint was doing its job more or less. Mentally, he felt drained and tired. His overall body seemed tied in a knot and achy. "There's no way I'm going to move today unless I have to," he said. As he shifted his body, rancid body odor repulsed him. "I really need to wash up, but that will have to wait until I get out of here. If they don't like the way I smell when they come to get me, I'll just walk out."

Looking out through the windshield, he smiled. "Hey, the sun is shining," he said. "And that's a bit of a good thing."

Sitting quietly, body at rest as much as possible, he closed his eyes and drifted to sleep.

CHAPTER 24

Awake to the cold again, he sat up and turned on the truck. That reminded him he needed to put gas in the truck today. He didn't think he had much more time on this mountain, but he couldn't afford to let the gas tank go completely empty just in case. He looked at the gas gauge and saw it was halfway between the quarter of a tank mark and empty. "I definitely have to put that gas in today." *When all I want to do is sit and rest.*

His body seemed more at ease. More relaxed. He sure didn't want to get out of the truck again. He wanted no more work and the fatigue it would bring. Not after what he had gone through this morning just getting the gas bottle. His breathing was shallow and too fast. Consciously, he slowed it to deeper, slower breaths. The coffee was still warm, and he poured a cup. Sipping the coffee, he focused on his surroundings.

All was silent. Snow still buried everything. The days of isolation, pain and cold had, no doubt, worn him down mentally. *Maybe that's what's wrong with me. Just plain worn down*, he thought. Since the snow had fallen, he had heard no sound but his own voice, the sound of the truck running, and the hiss of the stove burners. He hadn't been able to find the radio station again. "I might as well get out and put the gas in the tank," he said.

He pulled his coat together, zipped to his throat, put the ski cap on to cover his ears, and pulled on the gloves.

Outside the truck, the cold took hold of him immediately. Leaning on the side of the truck, he turned toward the truck bed. The gas can was buried in snow in the left front corner of the truck bed. Pushing and shoving the deep snow away, he uncovered the top of the red plastic gas can as much as he could. Pausing, he leaned against the truck and tried to relax. He didn't want to do this now after what he'd gone through a few hours earlier. But he had no choice. He needed that gas in the truck to stay warm until they came for him.

The simple movements of cleaning the snow from the gas can had tired his arms already and aggravated the leg, the pain level rising steadily. His toes were getting cold despite the socks on his foot. His right leg was already tired. *Man, I'm weak*, he thought. Even in the cold, sweat was already forming under his clothes and hat.

He needed to rest, but this job had to get done. The bitter cold was eating at him. "Sunshine or no sunshine, it's cold out here," he said. "Get this done and get back in the truck."

Leaning over the sidewall, he gripped the gas can handle with both hands and lifted. The first effort was not successful. The top of the can came up against the inside lip of the sidewall and thudded back into the truck bed. He nearly lost his balance on his tired right leg and grabbed the truck to keep from falling. Easy things that he had done all his life without thinking were not so easy now. Picking up a five-gallon can of gas was a monumental task now.

He repositioned his right foot, leaned his thigh and chest against the truck, closed his eyes, set his mind, and lifted. The gas can came up to the top of the sidewall where he balanced it and let it sit, hands still holding the handle. His breathing was deep and labored. After a minute of rest, he slid both arms under the bottom of the gas can, lifted it to cradle it against his chest, and realized he was ahead of himself again. There was no way he could move back to line up with the gas tank opening. The gas cap was still locked on the truck. And the drain spout for the gas can was still inside the can. "Way ahead of yourself, old son," he said. Dejected, he sat the gas can back on the side wall of the truck bed. "Think, stupid. You're wasting time and energy."

Again, he gripped the handle on the top of the can with both hands, turned on his right leg and swung the gas can to the ground with a barely controlled drop. He hopped around the can, reached into the truck, and pulled the keys from the ignition. Unlocking the gas cap, he laid the cap and the keys on the truck seat. With his gloved hands, he wiped the rest of the snow from the top of the can and filler neck and removed the nozzle from inside the can, mounting it on the outlet. "Now all I gotta do is lift the can back up, stick the nozzle in the hole, and hold the can up while I pour the gas in the tank. Piece of cake." He paused. "Yeah, right," he sneered.

He knew how heavy the can would be with five gallons of gas in it. He also knew how weak his arms and his right leg were now. And he knew how worn down his body was. But what had to be done he had to do. That's the way it always was, it seemed. No matter where you were or what you were doing in life, there was always something that had to be done. No matter how hard. "And you just take hold and get it done," he whispered with a sigh.

"And what I got to do now ain't gonna be anywhere near easy. But one way or another, I need that gas in the truck, and there's no one here to do it but me."

After a few minutes of rest, he leaned his left shoulder against the side of the truck, lifted the can with both hands, and held it against the side of the truck to take some of its weight. With the can trapped between his body and the truck, he slowly slid his right arm under the bottom of the can and turned to his right far enough to move the can away from the truck. Gradually tilting the can, he lined up the nozzle with the fill hole and slid it in on the first attempt. "Wow, that was easy. The first shot." He lifted his right arm, and gas gurgled into the tank, air whistling into the can through the vent hole.

His arms were immediately tired holding the can. Closing his eyes, he concentrated on holding it, cradled in his arms, and tried to ignore the tiredness of his arms and his right leg. The left leg was bent at the knee and hip with the left foot still in the snow, feeling the cold. The acrid smell of gas fumes blasted his face, stinging his nose and eyes. There was no way to avoid the fumes and hold the can where he needed it. He turned his head away from the can to minimize the effect of the fumes to his face. Arms shaking, he continued lifting the can little by little as the gas flowed into the tank. "Not fast enough. This may take longer than my arms have," he said. "Just hold on, boy. Don't drop the can. Hang on. Hang on. And get it done."

When he thought it should be near the end, he opened his eyes and looked at the side of the red plastic can. He could see that a little more than half of the gas had gone into the tank. He gritted his teeth, groaned, and kept pouring. Sweat was soaking his face. His arms were tired and shaking. His right leg nearly collapse. "Achin' and shakin' baby. Hang on a little longer, old son."

With gas still pouring into the tank, and the weight of the can getting lighter, he lifted his arms higher to let the last of the gas drain into the tank. And his arms gave out. There was no more strength in them. The can slipped away from him, and he dropped it. As the nozzle flipped out of the filler hole, he shoved the can away from his body and missed spilling gas on his clothes. At the same time, he grabbed for the truck bed sidewall and barely caught his weight to remain standing. The sharp smell of gas nearly overwhelmed him. Pivoting on his right leg, he leaned his chest against the truck and bent over the sidewall, gasping for breath. *I can't stay on my feet much longer*, he thought. "You're wrong on that count," he said. "It's foot. Not feet. You can't stay on your foot much longer."

The right leg was about to give out, his knee ready to buckle and collapse. He looked at the gas can lying on its side in the snow, a trickle of gas draining from the nozzle. He left it where it was. There was no thought of putting it back in the truck. And no need to right now. "Get in the truck before you fall on your ass, boy."

Two staggering hops and a shaky turn, and he leaned his butt against the truck seat. He wasn't sure he would be able to lift himself onto the seat and get into the truck. His arms and right leg quivered with fatigue, body ready to collapse. "Ya gotta get in. Can't stay out here." He reached behind him with his right hand and took hold of the steering wheel. He laid his left hand flat on the truck seat behind him. Pulling on the steering wheel with his right arm and pushing up with the left hand on the seat, he made it into the truck. As he dragged himself further across the seat, he felt the gas cap and keys dig into his butt. "Ah, shit," he grumbled. The gas tank filler neck was uncovered. "Don't stop now," he told himself.

When he sat up, he closed the truck door, lifted his left butt cheek, and got the keys and gas cap from under him. He dropped the gas cap on the floor. Key in the ignition, he started the truck and looked at the gas gauge. The needle had risen to a little below half a tank. "That's better," he said. "It just has to be enough 'til they get here."

He scooted himself along the seat, leaned against the sleeping bag, and leaned his head against the passenger door window, eyes closed. His arms were still shaking. His right leg was twitching with fatigue, the quad muscle on the verge of cramping. His left leg ached and throbbed. The toes and foot were cold and wet from the snow. Nausea gripped his stomach. He squeezed his eyes tight shut and tried to relax. "Don't sleep now, old son. Don't sleep. Just rest a while. Get it back together. Get a hold of yourself." The words came out in a raspy whisper. A supplication.

When the truck was warm, he sat up, got the last bottle of Gatorade and a power bar from the cooler, and lit a cigarette. His hands and arms were still tired and shaky, his entire body heavy with fatigue. He washed down two more Advil with the Gatorade and ate the power bar.

Outside the truck, the sun was still shining, the snow glittering. No clouds anywhere in the sky that he could see. "Life ain't real good right now, boy. Not yet. But it's a bit better with that gas in the tank. And the sun is shining. Hang on, and they'll come get ya. Tomorrow or the day after."

He lay on the seat for some time, resting, waiting for his body to relax. Letting his mind go. Letting his body go. Breathing deep and not thinking. Right leg muscles twitching. Arms heavy across his stomach. But he couldn't remain lying here forever.

Hungry again, he made a peanut butter and jelly sandwich. The bread was stiff with the cold and the peanut butter and jelly were nearly frozen. There were a few chips left, and he finished what was in the bag. With the sandwich and chips, he finished the last of the Gatorade.

There was a part of a can of Dinty Moore stew left in the pan. That would make dinner. There was still plenty of meat left in the truck. There was still some bread, plenty of peanut butter and raspberry jam. Two eggs left for breakfast tomorrow. Plenty of coffee remained, a small amount of milk, and all the water he could drink by melting snow. There were three apples and two power bars still in the backpack. "I'm still okay for two or three days. They'll be here to get me before it runs out, even if all I have left is the meat and water. And way more than enough coffee. I can eat elk steaks three times a day for a week if I need to and not touch the meat in the back. I'm sure as hell not going to starve to death. As long as the gas in the truck and the stove hold out."

He shifted around on the seat and pulled the leg up to rest. He took the book from the back of the seat and opened it to read. His attention was continuously drawn to the bright sunlight outside the truck, and he finally laid the book on his chest. Off and on, he dozed but never drifted completely into sleep. From time to time, he turned on the truck to warm up. Mostly he just waited and rested, letting the afternoon drift away. As daylight faded, the snow-covered trees along the ridge glowed a golden orange in the setting sun. He wished he were high on a ridge somewhere, facing west to watch the sunset.

And he remembered the evening he had sat on top of a mountain near eight thousand feet in elevation and watched the sun set over the Seven Devils in Idaho and the Wallowa Mountains in Oregon, the great Snake River canyon between them. The blood red sun painted the bottom of the clouds with vermillion splendor.

At the same time on that evening years ago, to his left, the full moon, its size magnified by the atmosphere, rose above the Salmon River Mountains, a radiant silver disc consuming the eastern sky. He alternately watched them until the sun and its glow were gone, until the moon shrank in the sky and the night surrounded him.

Head turning, body twisting left and right, he had watched them. The sun and the moon. Twin beauties and glories of the sky. And they spoke to him, and he heard their voices.

Tonight, he had the sun's painting of the snow-covered trees along the ridge. And that was good, too.

CHAPTER 25

When the night was nearly full darkness, he came back to himself. "I need to make a deposit on that last cup of coffee," he said, and sat up, feet under the dashboard.

When he opened the door, the cold hit him immediately and hard. Already more than likely below zero, the temperature was no doubt still dropping. He sat on the edge of the seat for a minute, looking across the meadow. Or rather, where the meadow used to be. Now it was just an uneven field of snow. Shadows from the ridges and trees were gone now. The white of the snow glowed in the night.

"Don't just sit here with the door open, dummy," he said and slid out of the truck. When his right foot hit the frozen ground beneath the snow, his leg buckled. He grabbed for the door and caught hold of the armrest on the door. That kept him from falling on his face.

As he stood, taking care of business, he looked back along the side of the truck to the opening where the road out was now a black hole in gathering darkness. "Come on, kids. I need ya as soon as you can get here," he whispered. These words were spoken in the voice of a prayer. A last look at the stars, and it was time to get in out of the cold.

Back in the truck, he rolled down the windows, lit the stove and started a fresh pot of coffee. As the coffee heated and perked, he stared out the driver's side window and the windshield and watched the darkness creep across the meadow and into the trees on the ridge.

When the coffee was done, he sipped from the tin cup, hot in his fingers, and set it on the dashboard where the steam from the hot coffee fogged the windshield in an oval above the cup. He spooned the last of the stew into the small cooking pot and set it on the burner. He lit another cigarette and sipped the coffee as the stew warmed. When the stew was steaming, he ate it directly from the pan and drank the last of the milk. An apple and a power bar made dessert. *Two more apples and one more power bar*, he catalogued in his mind. *And one more Hershey bar with almonds in the backpack"* "But I got a hell lot of lot of meat," he said out loud with a smile.

By the time he had finished eating, it was completely dark. He refilled his coffee cup, lit another cigarette, and sat looking out the windshield. He turned off the stove and closed the windows. He was warm and as comfortable as his situation would allow. *I'm beat*, he thought. His arms were still tired and heavy from holding the gas can. The leg still ached and remained always in his mind. His back ached from the cramped truck cab. Never being able to stretch out was adding to his discomfort. His shoulders slumped, and his head hung forward. *I'm really gettin' beat up right now. Tired and wearin' down. Way down. I could sure use my lumpy old bed for a night or two. And a long soak in a hot bath.*

Sipping the coffee, he realized that old feeling of nature's urges were back. "Damn! I should have taken care of that when I went out earlier." After a pause, he said, "It's gonna be real cold out there now. No cloud cover. The sun gone down and the cold left. Real, hard cold."

For some time, he tried to ignore the urges. But that wasn't going to work. Not this time. And it was getting colder outside by the minute. He wouldn't make it through the night without attending to business. And it wasn't going to happen in the truck. Dejected, he picked up the partial roll of mountain money, gloves, and ski mask. "What's gotta be done has gotta be done. Go get it over with."

Opening the truck door made the cold very real. The warmth in the truck was instantly gone. Cold stung his bare face and hands. Without cloud cover, the temperature was dropping fast and far. "It's cold enough out here now to freeze the lead in a pencil," he said. And it would get even lower as the night wore on. As he slid out of the truck, he picked up the gas cap from the floor and pushed it back in place on the filler hole.

As he turned toward the back of the truck, he saw stars over the ridges to the West. Lifting his head to the sky, he stared at the mass of stars blanketing the dark. "The stars are back," he said. "Man, oh man, ain't that pretty." The Milky Way twinkled across the sky like sequins on a sexy woman's dress as she moved across a dimly lit dance floor. The sight roused such joy in him that he could have stood there for a long time taking it in. *Sure wish I could dance with you tonight, honey. But I've got business to do*, he whispered. He turned away from the stars. The stars were beautiful, but the cold tonight was a killer. "Get done what ya got to do and get out of this cold," he said.

With the cold burning his face, he pulled the ski mask down to cover his head and face completely, settled it in place, pulled on the gloves, and closed the truck door. With the broom under his arm, he moved as quickly as the snow would allow to the back of the truck and around the tailgate. The handle-less shovel was on the tailgate, and he moved it within arm's reach of where he would do his business.

He couldn't do what he needed to do with both gloves on. He removed the right glove and laid it on the tailgate. Closing his eyes, he dropped his pants, gripped the tailgate cable support, moved the injured leg forward under the truck, and did the now familiar one-legged squat in the snow and cold.

His arms immediately began to shake from the strain. His right leg started to quiver, his right quad muscles burning. All that he'd had to do today had taken a serious toll on his strength. *I had to do too much today. And now this.*

As he completed the job, he wondered if he would be able to pull himself up again. His bare skin was burning with the cold. The strain on the rest of his body pushed the pain in the leg aside for now. But it was there. Always there. Pulling with both arms, right leg straining, he growled deep in his chest and gradually pushed and pulled himself to a standing position. His pants were still down around his ankles. His body was shaking with the cold and strain. "Keep goin' boy. Keep goin'. Git 'er done."

He pivoted on the right foot and bent to work his pants up with his left hand. His right hand lay flat on the tailgate. As he leaned forward, dizziness overtook him like a swarm of bees in his head. The truck and the world spun sharply away to his left. He tried to stand up straight, grabbed for the tailgate support wire, and missed it. Body twisting, he fell backward, spinning to his right. The edge of the tailgate struck him in the right ribcage. The truck and the night spun in a narrow arc, and he knew he was going down. And no way to stop it.

As if in slow motion, he toppled away from the truck. He felt it, saw it, and knew in a flash what it meant. He plunged through three feet of snow that did nothing to soften his fall. Snow caved in on his head and body, burying him in a cave of snow, as his already injured left ribcage, hip, and shoulder slammed into the frozen ground. The broken leg bounced. The splint was no protection from the blow, and the explosion of pain followed. The left side of his head bounced hard on the frozen ground with the explosion and glare of a lightning bolt. And he was gone. Deep into the darkness.

How long he lay still in the snow he didn't know. *Have I been out? Yeah. Oh, yeah. No doubt about that.* But somehow, he didn't think it had been very long. The dizziness was still in his head. Snow covered his head completely. It was in his eyes, nose, and mouth. Snow covered his already freezing naked lower body. When he opened his eyes, he saw only darkness and snow. His head and upper body were covered in snow, his lower body partially buried beneath the caved-in snow. The injured leg was out straight in the splint. Overwhelming pain from his toes to his groin ruled his mind. Nausea churned in his stomach. His right leg was bent at the knee and angled across the top of the left leg. Panic exploded in his mind. He took a deep breath and sucked in a mouthful of snow. He gagged and coughed it out again.

Stay here and you're dead, he thought. No plan, no assessment, just get up and move. He rolled onto his back, frantically pushing snow away from his head and upper body. He pushed up with his hands to a sitting position, bare legs and buttocks in the snow, body already shaking and numb. The left leg was still out straight in front of him. He shook more snow from his head and scooted to the right, nearer to the rear of the truck. Groping with his left hand, he found the tailgate support wire. Straining with all that was left in him, he pulled himself partially up, grabbed the side wall of the truck bed with his right hand, and struggled to stand up. The bare skin of his legs and lower torso burned with the cold.

There were no conscious thoughts. He was moving on instinct alone. A gut-level fight for survival. To get back in the truck or die. The world still swam to his left trying to take his vision and focus with it. Dizziness or not, he had to keep moving. He had to get back in the truck. Crawl there half-naked if he had to.

Leaning against the side of the truck, he removed the left glove and laid it on the tailgate beside the right one. When he began working his pants and underwear up his legs, he found the crotch of his pants filled with snow. Fumbling, hands freezing, he scooped as much of the snow out of his clothing as he could. Struggling, he worked up his boxers, then the thermals, then the pants up over his ass and buckled his belt to hold his pants in place. His fingers were too cold to grip the tab for the zipper, so he left it down. He could feel some snow still inside of his clothing, in his crotch and on his upper legs. "It doesn't matter now. Move, you son-of-bitch. Move, now."

Not thinking, he pulled the gloves back on his numb hands, settled the broom under his left arm, and began the trip back to the driver's door of the truck.

CHAPTER 26

In his mind, he reached for his body, groping for his physical self and the world around him. And it slipped through his grasp. Like an old and vague memory, he saw his fall at the back of the truck and felt the snow cave in on him. He felt his head and body slam onto the frozen ground. And he knew he had been completely buried under the snow. He felt it all around him. And he slipped into the darkness.

He knew nothing of the struggle to get back in the truck, neither how he had gotten there nor how long it had taken. But he had made it back into the truck. And then he was gone again. Deep into the darkness. Not knowing if he would make it back to the light.

When he reached for his body again, he felt the cold, wet, pants and underwear that he still wore. And they brought him back to the physical world. Back inside the cab of the truck.

The engine was running and the warm air was blowing, but he didn't know how it had been turned on. He had no memory of starting the truck. And he knew the snow and the cold were still out there, waiting for him.

And the darkness came again, and the world and his body slipped through his grasp and his understanding.

.   .   .

He felt the heat. The scorching and relentless heat. Hot sand burned his feet through his boots. His skin was aflame under a glaring sun. And he wondered if the sun and the hot sand were not real. But they were with him, and he felt them.

His chapped lips were stuck together. When he tried to open his mouth, he had to force his lips apart. His tongue was dried and swollen, rough and clumsy in his mouth. He wished he could swallow, but there was no moisture in his mouth and throat. Sweat ran from his forehead, stinging in his eyes. He had no hat, and the sun lay heavy on his head and shoulders, pressing him down.

Tired and sluggish, he could no longer lift his feet out of the burning sand. He shuffled along, dragging them with each step, leaving twin snake trails in the sand behind him. Searing pain shot from his left leg up to his groin and the small of his back every time he took a step with it.

He felt as if blisters had formed on his bare arms and neck. When he looked at his arms, his skin was bright red, but there were no blisters. He was sweating, but the sweat he produced did nothing to cool his body.

"As long as I'm still sweating, I'm ok," he thought. "If the sweating stops, I'm in big trouble." The word "dehydration" fluttered through his mind.

He struggled through the shifting sand toward the top of a tall dune, seeming to lose as much ground as he had gained in the sloughing sand.

Staggering near the crest of the dune, he slumped to his hands and knees. A bolt of pain shot through his broken leg.

Crawling on his hands and right knee, dragging his left leg behind him, he worked his way toward the crest of the dune. Near the top, he rested on his hands and right knee.

Then, clawing the hot, slipping sand with his bare hands, digging with his feet and knees, he worked his way to the crest of the dune where he remained slumped over. Eyes closed. Head drooping. Gasping for breath.

With effort, he struggled to stand, holding himself on his right leg to look around. His left leg screamed at him with agony.

On the other side of the dune he had just climbed was more sand. Dune after dune rolling like waves on a gray, dusty ocean. For as far as he could see. More sand. More heat. Shimmering and waving to every far horizon. No trees. No rocks. No shade. No water. Just a world of gray sand and heat all around him.

Back bent, shoulders sagging, his right knee wanting to buckle, he lowered himself to sit on the sand again.

Hot sand seared the back of his legs and butt through his pants. He drew his feet and legs toward him and leaned forward with his arms on his bent knees. The pain in his left leg ratcheted up with even that small added weight and pressure.

He wiped sweat from his forehead and ran his fingers through his sweat-soaked hair. It made no difference. Sweat returned immediately and ran down his face and neck. He licked the moisture from his grimy hands and fingers. But that made no difference in his mouth and throat. His shirt was soaked with sweat. He lifted the hem of the shirt to suck what little moisture he might get from the dirty material. But that made no difference either. His tongue and throat remained parched. Numbed and exhausted, he knew he had to move. To remain as he was, was to die. He needed something, anything, to relieve his thirst and agony. But there was nothing. Nothing but to get up and keep moving. And get back in the truck.

Raising his face, squinting his eyes, he looked directly into the glare of the sun. It was exactly where it had been for as long as he could remember. Directly overhead.

He knew he had walked through the glaring heat of the sun for hours. Yet the sun had not moved at all. "And it may never move for me again," he whispered. The heat would never lessen. And the pain would never ease.

Mind fading, body wilting, still he held his determination to go on. To get back to the safety of the truck. "That good ole 'Never say die' heart," he mumbled.

He rolled onto his hands and knees, struggling to get to up. Just to stand again. With more effort than he thought he had in him, he managed to stand by pushing up with just his right leg, both hands pushing down on his right thigh. Pain rolled up his left leg from his foot to his groin. He shuffled forward, down the other side of the dune, the right leg leading with every step, the left leg nearly collapsing with any weight placed on it. Trying to ignore the pain, sand slipping beneath his feet, he moved on.

To where? He wasn't sure. For how long? He didn't know. To what end? Just a vague hope moving through the heat, fading into the heat and pain. How will all of this end? "The heat and the sun are not real. Just an aberration," he mumbled.

Amused, smiling through his cracked lips, he knew it was just a dream, even while he was still in the dream. When I wake up, this will all be gone. The sun, the heat, and the sand. All will be gone. I will be back on the mountain. Back in the snow. Back in the truck. With freezing cold and snow all around me. And the pain. Broken leg and all.

•   •   •

When he opened his eyes and took a deep breath, he knew he was back. The real world was all around him again. He had made it, the lumpy truck seat under his ass and the rolled sleeping bag behind him. The odor of a thousand cigarettes he had smoked back down all the roads he had shared with this old truck lingered, along with the sour odor of the sweaty days and nights. All these told him he was back in the truck.

Despite what lingered in his mind, the cold and the snow and the isolation in the truck were with him. Almost like old friends.

The heat and burning in his leg and the red streak creeping up his left inner thigh made it obvious that what he had feared all along was real. The infection in the back of his head was rotting a little more each day. The gouge left by that dirty elk skull left something ugly behind that spoiled. And that rot-infected head wound found its way through his body to settle in the broken bones and the torn tissue in the leg. And now it was on the move in his blood stream to the rest of his body. Smiling through the sting of his cracked lips and the stink of his sweat, he knew the desert and the blazing hot sun were not real. "Just a dream," he whispered. An aberration caused by the infection throughout his body. "When I wake up, if I wake up, this will all be gone. The sun, the heat and the sand will all be gone. And I'll be back on the mountain. Back in the truck. With the snow-soaked clothes and the cold."

Broken leg and all. And infection creeping through his body.

• • •

There really is no glaring sun. No hot sand.

The mountains are real and the warmth in the truck is real.

The freezing temperatures in the night are real.

But the hot blazing sun is not real.

His fever caused by the injuries was all too real. Consuming him little by little.

The trail he left in the snow by dragging himself to the truck after the fall was real, unseen now under four feet of snow. That trail and the effort to get to the truck would remain with him for as long as he lived, however long or short that may be.

The pile of snow where he had been buried after the fall at the back of the truck? That was real too. And it would remain until the spring thaw.

The trampled snow where he walked around the truck to do his daily duty is real.

The heat of the sun in his mind is not real. The sand dunes and his footprints in the hot sand are a product of his weakening mind.

But the heat creeping through his body is something very different. It is a product of the open wound and infection. And it is real.

The deep cold of the night outside the truck is real. And it is waiting for him.

The blazing hot sun in his mind is just the fever that is now moving through his body.

The trail down off the ridge where he took the bull elk is vivid in his memory and always will be.

The fall on that trail in the snow will always be trapped in his mind. How his foot shot out from under him and his back slammed on the frozen ground. A bit more than a small misstep.

The slimy, sticky mess on the back of his head is a throbbing reality.

The shattered bones and torn flesh in his left leg are agonizingly real.

The symptoms of a serious infection are more real than he would like to admit. But he can't ignore them. And he can do nothing about them.

The sweat-soaked shirt he now wears is real!

The red streak up the inside of his left leg is an omen of reality.

The all-over heat and sweat in his body that gets stronger day by day, hour by hour, are indications of that creeping infection. The reality that he had hoped would never come is glaringly real.

"And if the infection turns to full-blown sepsis?" he whispered. "That all over infection?" That just may be the final reality.

And he knew there was not much more that he could do than what he had done and would continue to do until the end—whatever and whenever that end may be.

•   •   •

By pulsing degrees, he gradually came back to the truck, enough to know, and then was gone again.

Then back to the heat and sand. A fading memory.

A little closer to his body and reality with each change, then gone again. Moving through space and time. Between the dream and the reality. With each shift, a little further back.

When at last he mentally reached for his body, his physical self, he reveled in its feel and existence. And he knew he was all the way back. At least for now.

The memory of the heat and the dream remained with him. The dullness of his mind on that arid dune shivered through his memory. Eyes closed, he waited for it to dissipate. The glaring sun of the dream was still just beyond his eyelids. *It was just a dream. I know it was only a dream.*

Still, he felt the weight of the heat. The sticky sweat on his body. His shirt was damp and clinging. The ski mask was still on the back of his head, sweat underneath it soaking his hair. The gloves still on his hands were now clammy with sweat. His coat was zipped up to his throat. He felt the wetness in the seat of his pants, in his crotch, and down his legs. Cold, wet material clung to his skin. And he remembered the snow caught inside his clothes when he had fallen outside.

The truck was running, and the heater was blowing warm air. He leaned forward and turned the motor off.

"Save as much gas as you can," he whispered.

With sharp clarity, he recalled the dizziness and the fall outside. He felt the pain in his right side where he had fallen against the tailgate on his way down, and the flash of pain when his head slammed on the frozen ground. He felt the snow collapsing over him, burying him, as he fell through the deep drift. He didn't have to reach for the leg to feel the increased pain there.

There was no way to tell if there was more damage to the leg. It wouldn't surprise him if there was, hitting the ground that hard. The only new pain was along his right rib cage. If there was new damage to the leg, the only thing it changed was how long he could last, and whether he died here in the truck or some time down the road.

There was no memory of how he'd gotten back in the truck.

One thing he did know. "I didn't die out there in that damn snowbank," he said out loud. "Nobody's going to find me frozen in a snowbank with my bare ass hanging out, my pants down around my ankles."

He had no memory of how he got back in the truck. But it didn't really matter. Somehow, he had gutted it out and had made it.

"You're one lucky son-of-a-bitch," he said. He knew he could just as easily still be lying out there in the cold and the snow, half frozen. Well on his way to being a block of frozen meat.

At the end of it all. The cold winning.

Fear swelled and swept through him like a roll of distant thunder. Tears filled his eyes. He thought of what those who came to get him would have found if he had stayed out there in the snowbank, half naked. If he hadn't been able to get up, get back in the truck. By midnight, he would have been beyond all knowing. By morning, he would have been a solid block of frozen meat. Not a good way for anyone to find him, especially if it were the boys who came to get him. And the tears washed him with a measure of relief.

When he finally opened his eyes, there was no glaring sun. No hot sand. But the heat still clung to his body. Sweat soaked his shirt. His hair ran with sweat. He pulled off the gloves and wiped his sweaty hands on his pant legs. When he pulled off the ski mask, the material stuck to the back of his head, and he tugged it loose. Bloody liquid clotted the material, and the cut ripped open again. He felt the cut, and his fingers came away coated with a sticky, bloody goo.

"Ah, shit," he groaned.

When he tried to sit up, dizziness swept through him again, and he lay back down, his head against the passenger window. The cut on his head was throbbing and burning. It was cold and dark in the truck.

Not as cold as it is out there, he thought.

Despite the heat in his body and the sweating, chills shuddered through him every few minutes, and he gritted his teeth. With his jaw clamped, face muscles taut, he tried to control it but couldn't.

He knew that at some point the truck had been running and the heater had been on. He had no memory of turning it on. The motor wasn't running now. And he had no memory of turning it off either.

After several minutes, he gripped the steering wheel, pulled himself up, and turned the truck on again. He clicked on the overhead light and looked at the gas gauge. The needle was halfway between a half and a quarter of a tank.

She must have run for quite a bit while I was out, he thought. He had used nearly half of the gas he had put in the tank from the gas can. "That ain't good, boy," he said. "That ain't good at all. But it kept me alive while I was out, and that's a pretty good trade. Even if I don't remember it." He lay back down, unzipped his coat, and waited for the warmth. When he first started to nod and drift toward sleep, he sat up to remain awake until the truck cab was fully warm again.

When the warmth held him firmly in its palm, he turned the motor off.

It would get cold again inside the truck. He knew that. It was inevitable. He could slow it for a while with the truck heater and the stove. But the cold was king here on this mountain. And it was coming for him, a little at a time. But it was coming. If he didn't get out, down off this mountain, the cold would win. The darkness would take him. He could hold it off only so long.

He could not defeat it. When he was gone, either back home or otherwise, the cold would still rule here on the mountain.

His pants were still wet from the snow, and he wished he could change them. But there was no way he could get these pants off and clean, dry ones on again with his leg the way it is. He could cut them off with the knife or scissors. Slit the pant leg of the dry ones and wriggle into them. Even if it was possible, that seemed like way too much effort, using more energy than he wanted to spend. He wasn't sure he could do it anyway.

The pants were twisted around his body, cutting into his waist. Loosening the belt to adjust them, he pulled up his shirt and looked at his right side. There was a wide, oozing abrasion along his lower rib cage that burned. There was no pain in the ribs themselves. "Nothing I can do about that now. It's not so bad. Just another sore spot."

He started to tuck the shirt into his pants again. The outer shirt and the thermal undershirt were both damp and cold, though not as soggy wet as they had been after the fall at the back of the truck. They were gradually drying but no doubt still leaching body heat.

He wrestled the wet shirts off and shoved them under the truck seat. He dug out a clean wool shirt and thermal undershirt from the clothing bag. Struggling into the long sleeves of the undershirt brought his pain to a serious level. He had to rest twice just to get the shirt on and buttoned up. All of that movement increased his pain level in his ribs, his back and the leg. No matter what he did, pain in the leg was always involved. He leaned back against the sleeping bag, head against the blood-smeared window.

"Now that's better," he whispered. He chided himself for not thinking of that until now.

The wet shirt and thermal undershirt had been leaching body heat from the time of the fall over there by the trees, and he hadn't even thought of it. "A serious lapse in thinking that could have cost you your life, old son." He leaned his head against the window.

So, what do you do now, if you run out of gas before they get here? a voice asked him.

"I'll use the stove," he answered.

And if you run out of gas for that, too? Then what?

The options were very limited, he knew.

"Either try to walk out or get into the sleeping bag and wait," he said. Neither choice was ideal. The end results were not attractive to him either way. In reality, walking out was no real option at all. "I told them this was where I would be. If they get here and I'm not, they may never find me at all. Even in the spring."

"Keep doin' what you're doin', boy. They'll make it sooner or later." He took a deep breath and let it out with a long sigh. "But I sure hope it ain't later."

He lay back against the sleeping bag and looked at the glowing hands of his watch. It was 2:15 a.m. Tuesday. *It's Tuesday morning, kids. Tuesday morning. I'm late gettin' home now,* he thought. *Time to come get the old man. I'm gonna need ya to come as soon as you can.*

With that thought still in his mind, he let himself drift into sleep.

•   •   •

"They're here. They're coming. Thank God they're coming." He could hear the roar of the snowmobile engines in the distance. More than one? Maybe two or three. He sat up on the truck seat, twisted to look out the back window, holding to the top of the seat back, arm shaking with fatigue, and saw the headlights flashing through the trees, coming down off the ridge where the logging road came into the meadow.

Panting with joy, eyes wide open, a broad smile on his face, he watched them. Headlights twisting through the trees. The sound of the engines getting louder and louder. Then fading away again. The headlights gone. Then louder engine noise. And lights again, moving left to right in the trees, closer, searching for the opening to the meadow. "Come on kids. Keep 'em comin'. I'm right here. Just follow the road. You'll find me. I've been waitin' for you." In his mind, he tried to direct them along the road, mentally guide them to the opening in the trees to the meadow where they would see the truck. "Almost here, kids. Almost here. Come take the old man home."

•   •   •

His eyes flashed open. He was not sitting up in the truck looking out the back window. He was not seeing headlights in the trees. He was lying on his back staring at the roof of the truck cab in the dark. The cold and the night were all around him. He was still alone in the cold and the dark. Still isolated and trapped. Sweat drenched his face and head, dripped under his arms, on his chest, and in his crotch. A shudder sent a bolt of pain through his body. The air in the truck was cold again. His body was hot, sweaty, and stagnant. Chills rattled him.

In his mind, he could still hear the snowmobile engines. He tried to sit up to look out the back window, but his body was too weak to make it all the way up. His arms gave out. His stomach muscles quivered. And he fell back onto the sleeping bag. The back of his head thudded against the door window, sending a bolt of pain through his body. Tears welled in his eyes. His breath came in shallow gasps, and his heart was racing. Dejected, he wiped the tears away with the heels of his hands and groaned.

Palms still pressing his eyes, fingers gripping the top of his head, he whispered, "Don't get crossways, boy. It's okay. You're still alive, and they will come and get you." He took a deep breath and sighed a long, slow exhale.

"Keep guttin' it out here, old son. You're gonna make it." Concentrating on slowing his breathing, he gradually relaxed and his heart rate slowed. In time, he drifted back to sleep.

CHAPTER 27

Awake again, he lay motionless along the seat, his body a heavy, sluggish weight. Thoughts were ephemeral, sliding away from him as soon as he found them. Full consciousness was fleeting. A fog he couldn't hold on to. There was no dizziness, but it seemed his mind was disconnected from his body.

He had a flash memory of the snowmobiles in the night but knew with a flickering thought that it had not been real.

With rigid concentration, he gripped the back of the seat again and, straining, slowly pulled himself to a sitting position. Head hanging, chin on his chest, bent far forward, head almost on the dash board, breathing hard, he held himself up with his arms. His mind kept fading away with no feeling of actually passing out. Not sliding into the darkness, just not there. Mentally.

Real, full consciousness might be a distant reality if he was able think in those terms. His body was a separate entity, unconnected to his mind and thoughts.

The sounds of the snowmobiles still rang distantly in his head. The vision of the headlights still flickered in his mind. *They're here,* he thought.

Are they here? a voice asked.

"They're here!" he replied.

No. They're not here. Not yet.

He heard the rasping in his throat with each breath he took and tried to concentrate on his breathing. That alone. Just the breathing. *Control the breathing. Just control the breathing. Pull yourself together. Get control one little piece at a time*, he thought.

His arms were tired, shaking, from holding himself in a sitting position. Body weak, he turned toward the front, swinging his legs under the steering wheel. The toes of his left foot struck the clutch pedal. And the explosion of pain brought him back. All the way back. Body and mind coalesced, focused as one on the pain. Solely on the pain. Pain radiated up the leg to his hip, groin, and stomach. Pain in the back of his head. Pain consuming him. Pain taking over his world. Ripping his breath from his lungs. Instant nausea swelling in his stomach. His stomach muscles tightened in convulsions, doubling him over. Retching and gagging, he came close to vomiting.

Screaming, he fell sideways onto the sleeping bag. Body curling, shrinking into itself. His mind sliding into the void. And the darkness took the pain away.

CHAPTER 28

Thirst and cold were the first things he knew when he came back. His mouth was dry. Tongue parched. Throat burning for water. And the cold. Always the cold coming for him.

Eyes still closed, he lifted the lid of the cooler and fumbled for a water bottle. It was as cold as if gripping ice. Looking at it, he saw the water in the bottle was frozen solid. Twisting off the cap, he tipped it to his lips, and a small trickle of water seeped from the opening. Even as little as it was, it felt so very good in his parched mouth, on his dried lips. He moved the water across his tongue and licked his lips. There was none to swallow. None to soothe his burning throat.

He got another bottle from the cooler. It, too, was frozen solid.

Sunlight filled the cab of the truck. The windows were covered with frost, and he could see nothing outside the truck. The leg was throbbing like someone stomping on it timed to his heartbeat. Struggling with his weakened body, he shifted as much as he could and turned the ignition key. The motor turned over sluggishly. Moaning. *Oh shit. Not now*, he thought.

He lay back down, eyes closed, chest tightening. With all that had happened yesterday, all that he had fought through, it now seemed as if everything had piled up on him. And now the truck battery was most likely frozen. The extreme cold may have taken that away from him as well. Frozen. Yesterday had taken him to the very edge and had nearly killed him. *And now the truck won't start?* he thought. *When is enough too much?*

"Only at the end, old son," he croaked. "Only at the end. And this sure as hell ain't the end."

He leaned forward, held the key between his fingers, and whispered, "Come on, baby. Come on, now." Turning the ignition key again, the motor ground slowly and then caught, slowed, fired, and started. *Oh Lord have mercy, thank you, ole girl. Thank you. You're still with me.*

Cold air blew from the heater. He wrapped his arms tightly round his chest, shielding himself from the cold air currents. "It'll get warm," he said. "Give it a few minutes. It'll get warm." He lay back against the sleeping bag and closed his eyes, waiting for the heat, the cold rattling his body.

When the air from the heater started to warm, he switched the controls to the defrost mode to clear the windows. He needed to see out. His confinement and isolation were building a deep fear in him, a fear that threatened to consume him. He needed to see that the world was still out there.

As the windows cleared and the cab warmed, he realized he was still damp with sweat. His pants and underwear were still wet from his fall in the snow and sweat from his body. The wet clothes probably added to his loss of body heat. His body was flushed with fevered heat, and frequent chills shook him. Sweat and chills. He knew there was an explanation for this, but he was unable to find it or understand what it was.

As the windshield cleared, he saw the bright sunlight and glistening snow outside and knew that he had been out for several hours. His watch showed 8:15 a.m. Tuesday morning. "Time's runnin' on, old son. Ya should be home in your own bed right now."

Through his confusion, he tried to think of what he should do. "I just want to lay here. Do nothing. Lay here and wait." But he knew that was not an option. He must eat. He must continue trying to take care of himself. "I've gotta eat. I need water, not water bottles filled with ice. And for that I've gotta move."

Try to maintain some control, boy, he thought. *Know where you are now and figure out how to keep movin' on. Until they get here.*

Last night had been bad. Real bad. Nearly fatal. But by pure instinct and guts, he had made it through. Survived it. He was still alive, and he needed to do whatever it took to keep it that way. Stay in control as long as possible. "No," he said "For as long as it takes. Until they come to get me out."

The leg was more painful and was throbbing. He didn't doubt that the fall last night had further injured it in some way. What kind of additional injury he didn't know, and there was no way to find out. The pain now was a hot, burning pain with the usual throbbing ache. When he looked at it, he saw the splints were still in place.

But his body was heavy, lethargic, and hot. Any movement required concentrated effort. The heavy sweating and chills certainly indicated a fever, probably an infection. His head wound was a burning, oozing mess that showed little signs of healing. There was no need to check it again. He knew what he would find. And he knew he needed a doctor and a hospital. Soon. Very soon.

He realized he didn't have to pee this morning. There was no natural morning urge. A good ole morning pee was as regular as the sun coming up. But not this morning. Without it, there was a problem. It could be caused by the loss of body fluid through the sweating. It could be the kidneys weren't working at full capacity. If he didn't get some water, dehydration was not far away and could become a serious problem. He needed water. Lots of water. No matter how much he wanted to sit and wait, he had to get some water. And that meant getting out of the truck to get snow.

And he needed to eat. He had to keep eating, whether he felt hungry or not. Survival mode was ratcheting up.

"Okay, boy. Don't just lay here. Get up and do something for yourself. Don't stop fightin' now." Straining with effort, he pulled himself into a sitting position. He brought the leg onto the seat to lay flat in front of him. The splint was still in place. The leg was covered with his pant leg that he had taped in place when he put the splint on. "There's no way I want to look at that damn thing now."

He turned off the truck and collected the three water bottles that were full with ice. He removed the caps from all three and held them over the coffee cup. A small amount of water trickled into the cup from two of them, no more than a swallow. He was very thirsty and needed water.

With the water in the cup, he washed down two Advil and sat staring out through the windshield. After a few minutes, he said, "No reason to wait, boy. Check the leg. Then you can eat and get some more water."

He slid his butt against the sleeping bag, the leg lying along the seat in front of him. He pulled the first aid kit from under the seat, opened it, and searched for a thermometer. There was none. He was certain that there should be one, but he couldn't find it. "Well, that's that. I have a fever, and there is no way to tell how high it is," he mumbled. "Knowin' what it is won't make any difference anyway. A fever is a fever. Nothing you can do about it now."

He reached for the leg and laid his hand above the knee. It was hot. Not just warm. Hot! So was the cut on his head. With scissors from the first aid kit, he snipped the tape that held the pant leg together above and below the break and spread the pants material and the thermal underwear as far from the top of the leg as the splint would allow. The bare skin was dark, taut, and ugly. Along the top of the leg at the upper thigh, he found more swelling than there had been before. The swelling pressed against the pieces of the splint. He thought of cutting the tape that held the splint pieces together, but unless it restricted his circulation, there was no need to mess with it.

Spreading more material lower along the leg, he found the darkened flesh had crept up the leg to above the knee. Above the discoloration, the flesh was red tinged. The redness ran higher along the inside of the leg and disappeared under the upper part of the pant leg. "Damn," he whispered. He laid his palm on the upper thigh. It was hot. Hot and clammy. Further down, the leg was hot too. Hot and clammy. Hot all the way to his ankle under the top of the socks. Leaning further forward, he gently gripped his toes and felt the heat through the material of the socks.

Mind numbed, staring at the leg, he said, "Well, there it is. No two ways about it." He understood immediately what the redness and the heat meant. Infection! Serious infection! And infection on the move. That was the red streak running up the inside of his leg. Most likely it had started at the cut on the back of his head and moved to the rest of his body.

A confirmation of sorts. And maybe a sentence as well. His head was infected. The leg was infected, both causing the fever, sweating, and chills. Untreated, it could ultimately become sepsis. Overall body infection. He was more than likely already well on his way to that now. "I need a doctor and treatment. Soon," he said. *Sepsis is a killer.*

"You are in real trouble, old son. Real, big trouble. And the clock is ticking." He slouched back against the seat.

"I need ya real bad, kids. And real soon."

He swung his legs to the floor under the dashboard and found a fourth bottle of water in the cooler frozen just as the other three were. Two additional bottles, both empty, were also in the cooler. He brought them out and laid them on the floor.

He emptied the coffee grounds and used filter into the trash bag. There was a small amount of cold coffee in the pot. "I hate cold coffee," he mumbled. With a paper towel, he wiped out both the large and small cooking pots. He sat all three containers on the floor near the driver's door with the four freezer bags he had used as ice bags. Opening the door to the morning cold, the warmth he needed instantly flushed out of the truck. He slid off the seat, leaned his left shoulder against the door jamb, and looked toward the logging road opening in the trees. The point from which they would come. "When they come," he said out loud.

The sunlight on the snow glared across the meadow, causing him to squint. The cold, still air of the morning burned his exposed skin immediately and held him in its grim and lethal embrace. All was silent. Deadly and silent.

"Don't be standin' around, boy. Load up with snow and keep movin'."

He picked up the freezer bags and packed them full of snow, tamping them down to hard packed. He did the same with each of the cooking pots. He emptied the coffee pot and wiped it out as well. He packed the snow into all three pots as hard as he could, pressing it down with his fist. By the time he finished, he was gulping for breath, his head swimming, hands numb from the snow.

Leaning into the truck, he pushed the pots and bags as far across the floor as possible. Turning, he pulled himself into the truck and slid along the seat, legs beneath the steering wheel. When he pulled the door closed, he rolled both windows down slightly and lighted both burners on the stove. The coffee pot went over one flame and the large pot over the second.

All of his motions were slow and deliberate, survival pushing him forward. "Keep moving, old son. Just keep moving."

Fear was with him now. A rock in his guts. A weight heavier than the hindquarter of a bull elk. Fear had risen from his first look at the now infected leg. Fear, palpable and real, was with him now as firmly as the pain in his leg and the sweat on his body. Fear as real as the snow, the cold, and the silence. "Fear is okay." he said. As long as it didn't paralyze him, he would be okay, as long as he used the fear for focus, purpose, action, and determination. To do nothing was to die. "Work with the fear. Just keep working and thinking, and you'll be okay."

The snow was melting quickly in the coffee pot and the large cooking pot. When the snow in the coffee pot was melted, but not hot, he poured the water into one of the Gatorade bottles and took a long drink. He now had some fresh water to drink. As the snow in the large pot melted, he sat the four frozen water bottles in the pot to melt them as well. The water from the melted snow would melt the ice in the bottles and keep the plastic from melting.

He was getting very hungry and would need to eat soon. First, he wanted to get as much snow melted as he could. Water was more important right now. He had to rehydrate his body and keep it hydrated.

He placed the small pot over the burner where the coffee pot had been. With snow from the freezer bags, he refilled the coffee pot. It also meant that he would use more heat to keep the water thawed, causing a dwindling supply of his precious heat source. This was going to be tedious work melting snow and keeping the water from freezing in the cold. "Maybe I won't have to do it very long," he said.

His window for survival was narrowing.

There were two eggs left, no doubt frozen solid. Like everything else. And no bacon to go with them. He put them in the heating water in the small pot. "Boiled eggs are just as good as fried," he said. "Almost anyway."

The butter and peanut butter were frozen solid. He sat the butter container on top of the cooler near the back of the stove to soften it. The bread was also hard. He pried four pieces loose and slid them under the stove to warm between the collapsible legs that held the stove up. "It won't be toast, but I'll be able to eat it." Soon he would have water to drink and breakfast to eat. Things were looking a little better, and he felt better because of it.

When the water in the small pot began to boil, he eased both eggs in it to cook. He watched the water boil, his mind floating. The concentration it had taken to do the very little that he had done, converting snow to water the past several minutes, had taken its toll on his concentration. His body was sluggish to the point of lethargy. Only by forcing himself to activity had he been able to get some water to drink. Keeping the water from freezing again would require constant effort and attention.

When he thought the eggs were nearly cooked, he opened the butter container, pulled the pieces of bread out from under the stove, and coated them with butter. He removed the large pot of water from the stove with the partially thawed water bottles still in it and sat it on the floor. The water bottles were slowly thawing in the hot water.

All of this water needed to be transferred to the empty water bottles. The air inside the truck was warm and humid. The windows were foggy from the heated water.

He needed to melt more snow, but he didn't want to open the door and let the heat out right now. "And I want some coffee," he growled.

He turned off the burner on the stove, spooned the eggs from the hot water, and set them on a paper towel on the dashboard to cool. The water from the small pot went into the coffee pot with a new filter and grounds. He relit the burner under the coffee pot and a cigarette with the same match. While he waited for the coffee, he lay back against the sleeping bag, brought his leg onto the seat, and closed his eyes. Resting his hands on his stomach, he held the ashtray as he smoked and listened to the sounds of perking coffee pot.

He was tired. Sinking toward exhaustion. Body and mind. And still sweating, though not as much as before. The chills had not come again. Physical movement was still slow and lethargic. "I need to rest for a while. Let the eggs cool and then eat."

When the coffee pot finished perking, he turned off the burner, stubbed out his cigarette, and sat up, shifting his feet under the steering wheel, careful not to smack them on the clutch pedal again. He filled his cup with hot steaming coffee and poured what was left into the thermos. That would keep the coffee hot for some hours. He needed the coffee pot to transfer the water to the bottles. With the eggs peeled, he nibbled at them until they were gone, ate the four pieces of bread and butter, and sipped coffee. It wasn't much, and he wished it were more. "It won't fill me up, but it's something," he said. "It'll fill the hole for now, anyway."

And now he needed to rest. Sleep if he could. It was very warm in the truck now from the constant use of the stove. *Or is it the fever?* "Mostly likely both," he said. Sweat still formed over his body, especially under his coat. He didn't want to take the coat off in case he fell asleep and it got real cold in the truck again. With his current weakening condition, he could not physically afford to expose his body to a deep, freezing cold.

As he slid toward sleep, he had the feeling that his body was sinking, collapsing into the truck seat. As he drifted away, his mind floated into a dark unknown. *Where's the fear now?* he thought. *I should be afraid of this. Especially if it gets real cold again. And afraid of the infection.* And yet, he gave himself up to the sleep without fear. Sleep and the dark unknown. *Will I come back from this one,* he wondered as he drifted away. *Is this my last sleep?* Still he was not afraid. As he gradually slipped below the threshold of consciousness, he thought, *Not this time. I'm not done yet. I'll be back. I'll wake up. They'll come get me.* And then he was gone. Deep into sleep.

CHAPTER 29

The sky above him was bright and blue, a shining crystal sky. Clear of all clouds for as far as he could see. He once had a satin shirt just that color. He had been told by someone that the color was 'French Blue.' He wasn't sure if that was a real color. But he liked it, the color, the name, and the shirt. When the collar frayed from use, it was all he could do to throw it away. He'd never seen another shirt like it. Not that exact color. He always looked for one.

He often thought he would like to have a car that color. Not a truck, a car. A truck was made to wear earth tones. Not ugly macho camouflage like some guys painted their trucks. Just solid, earthy colors. But a car could be French Blue.

Looking at the sky, he knew that if he chose, he could see the entire sky. Not simply horizon to horizon, but all the sky all the way around the world. Wider than existence. Deeper than forever. Cloudless or storm-filled. Sun-filled day or star-curtained night. It was all there for him to see whenever he chose. And, of course, he would much prefer the star filled night.

He heard the voice of the sky and the sun, tickling every nerve in his eyes, ears, and body.

And he smiled.

The ground beneath his feet was more than just soft—loam, a mixture of decayed vegetation and dark, brown droppings of the forest animals, and old loose soil. Topped by tall, waving grass. Each step was like walking on deep foam rubber, or maybe what it would be like if a person could actually walk on water.

The fragrance of the earth rose around him. Rich and hearty. Full and pungent. Wrapping him in the most elemental of odors. Nothing man could make could feel that soft or smell that robust and tantalizing. No perfume could allure him as that smell did. Well, maybe there is, he said. The touch of her warm skin in the night and the perfume she always wore. The feeling of that touch and the aroma of that fragrance washed over him now.

And he smiled.

The voice of the earth filled his nostrils, his skin, and his mind and cushioned his step.

And he smiled.

Gliding across the meadow on strong legs, arms swinging, relaxed at his sides, he felt at peace in every atom of every cell of his body. In all the limitless chambers of his mind.

And he smiled.

Deep within the core of all that was him, he smiled.

As he approached the tree line and the gentle rise of the earth before him, a light breeze brought to him the smell of the pines. His nostrils flared and the sharp tang of the trees' scent tantalized him. With a deep breath, he drank the essence of the pine boughs into his lungs. Deep into his lungs. He felt the fragrance coursing through his blood, settling into the tissue of his flesh.

He had heard that odors were merely atomized particles cast off from the object from which the odor came. He wasn't sure if that were true or not, but he liked to believe it was. In which case, he was now breathing in minute particles of the earth and the surrounding pines. Their DNA was passing into his lungs, his blood, and becoming one with his flesh and his DNA. He liked that idea.

And he smiled.

There had been nights when he had lain beside her as she slept and reveled in her relaxed beauty. He looked intently at her closed eyes, no movement behind her lids. He slid his face close to hers, noses almost touching. Deliberately, he timed his inhaled breaths to her exhaled breaths in her sleep, taking her breath deep into his lungs. Absorbing her DNA with his lungs, his blood, his flesh. He took her inside himself, becoming one with her.

He now scanned the trees all around him. Dark green pine boughs waved their greeting to him. Light green, quivering aspen wagged their fingers at him in mirth. The rustle of the branches. The shimmer of the aspen. A gentle assault on his eyes that soothed him. He drank in their colors and the movement as his soul swayed in unison with them. He heard their voices singing a soft and gentle song in harmony. A song just for him.

And he smiled.

The giggle and chuckle of the stream to his right amused him as if it were a child at play. For the stream was yet a child here high in the mountains, in constant motion like a happy, active boy, rushing headlong through its early life toward the maturity of the river. But up here it was still a child.

He paused to listen to the stream's youthful voice snickering through the brush on its way down the mountainside. His ears soaked up the stream's childish giggles.

And he smiled.

A narrow game trail wound up the grade of the ridge through the trees, and he stepped to where it entered the forest. Mottled shade wriggled on the ground with the slight movement of the boughs and limbs above him. The ground was blanketed with fallen pine needles, pinecones, and aspen leaves. The cushion felt soft on the soles of his boots. As he moved through the trees along the trail, the checkered shadow and light massaged him as it climbed up the front of his body to fall back to earth from the top of his head and shoulders.

He absorbed the flutter of the light and shade with every pore.

And he smiled.

How far the trail would lead him he didn't know. It was not important. Where the trail would end, he had no idea. The answer was moot. He would follow this trail to the end. Wherever it led him. Just to be there when he got there. And see what he would see.

What was important was that he was here, deep in the forest, walking a game trail, the sun shining, the day warm and comfortable.

His leg and body whole and strong.

And he smiled.

Moving through the trees along the trail, he encountered an aged and decaying log lying across the trail, its trunk denuded of bark. Broken limbs scattered along its sides. Through long years this tree had grown, strong and tall, resisting harsh winds, thunderous storms, and deep snow. Until its life was over.

It lay now in its final stage of life, releasing its elements back to the earth from which it had fed and grown.

He straddled the wide trunk, a simple passing to the other side to move further along the trail. But he paused. Feet off the ground, legs encircling the old tree, he tipped his head back and looked up through the branches of other trees, the children of this old decaying log, to the slivers of blue sky above. Slowly, he lowered his back along the uphill tilt of the log and drooped his arms along its sides, fingers skimming the smooth softness of the wood. Eyes closed, he took a deep breath and concentrated on the feel of the log beneath him.

The more he relaxed his body and mind, the more he felt his body sink into the spirit of the tree. He became one with it. Absorbed by it, the ancient tree embraced him and held him close. Drifting with the cycle of its centuries of life, the old tree whispered its ages of knowledge into that ear that listened in his deepest being.

How long he remained there, he didn't know and didn't care. In time, he sat up and looked around him. Scattered across the dappled ground small, twisted pines had pushed their way through the soil, reaching for the sunlight. Sprung from a seed smaller than an ant, these seedlings, too, would straighten, grow tall, absorb the sunlight, and drink of the earth. If left to themselves, they would age, grow weak, and fall to the ground to feed the seedlings they had shed over their long lives.

As his hands pressed flat on the smooth surface of the log, he swung his leg over the trunk, slid to the ground, and stood on the trail on the other side.

And he smiled.

Squirrels in the branches above him chattered their greeting. Crows fluttered from limb to limb before him, announcing his arrival, their wings whistling through the air with each stroke.

From somewhere high in a pine, an owl interrupted his daily nap to ask his nighttime question, "Who? Who? Who?"

"It's only me, old owl." he said. "It's only me. Go back to sleep."

And he smiled at all these voices as he followed the trail.

The trees thinned near the top of the ridge. Large boulders spread left and right across the end of the ridge and down either side like an arm around the shoulder of the mountain. The trail ended abruptly at their base. It turned neither left nor right but ran straight to the base of the rocks. The climb up the side of the rocks was neither steep nor difficult.

The largest of the rocks sat perched high on the pile with a narrow ledge winding around the right side. As he followed the ledge, it widened on the opposite side of the rocks where it was no wider than a chair bottom. The tallest part of the rock formed a back rest if he sat on the ledge with his feet hanging over a drop-off, falling three or four hundred feet to a dark shadowed forest below him.

The view below this perch was a rolling vista of dark green pines spotted with tamarack and aspen. A line of mountains in the distance stretched to his left and right. Other mountain ranges ranked to the farthest horizon, each successive range dimmer than the ones before it.

He sat on the ledge, feet hanging into emptiness, leaned against the rock wall behind him and scanned the vastness of the world before him. The shining sun, the green forests below his feet, and the mountains fading from dark green to light hazy blue stretched into the distance. Far away gossamer peaks silhouetted against the sky.

And he smiled.

He leaned his head against the rock and closed his eyes. The rock cradled him in its palm, and he heard its deep, resonant voice.

All the voices around him sang. In harmony. The earth, the trees, the animals, and birds. The rocks, the breeze, and the warmth of the sun. The distance of the mountains and the vastness of the sky. All their voices, together, sang to him.

And he smiled.

He added his own voice to their chorus.

With the warm sun on his face, soft wind combing his hair, head leaning against the rock behind him, he gradually drifted into sleep. And the voices of the earth faded away.

A soft beat of drums from a far distance rolled across the mountains, the valleys, and the forests below him, gradually increasing in volume, until the very air around him vibrated in time with the drumheads. Overtaking and filling the world around him. Deep-throated drums with the voice of faraway thunder.

Chanting voices rose and kept rhythm with the drums, high, melodic voices.

High on the rocky rim, he rose and stood above the forest, arms outstretched, palms raised to the sky. He swayed left and right in time with the beat of the drums and the chanting voices. He didn't know the language or the words of the singers. These things were old and lost in the ages of long ago. But deep within him, he understood the meaning of the song and the words.

It was a song of thanks for the day. A song of thanks for the hunt. A song of thanks for the sacrifice the majestic elk had made. A song of death, praise, and honor.

The spirit of the drums and the singers enhanced the world around him. The color of the sky was brighter. The emerald green of the forest was deeper. The breeze on his face was softer and more tender. The scent of the pines was sweeter. The rocks and earth beneath him hummed in tune with the drums and the song.

And he smiled.

CHAPTER 30

He lay still, eyes closed, his body still heavy. His mind was like a weight inside his head. The truck seat was beneath him, the rolled sleeping bag beneath his shoulders, the back of his head against the cold passenger door window. No high ridge. No rocky ledge. No sitting perch overlooking the dark forest or the far-off mountains. No warm sunshine on his face nor gentle wind in his hair. None of that was of this world, but only a product of his sleep, a trick of his somnolent imagination.

He was back inside the truck.

Still, the beat of the drums thrummed within him, beating in time with the throbbing of his leg and the beat of his heart. The chanting voices echoed just below the surface.

But now there was no smile.

As the throbbing and pain in his leg rose to his consciousness, the drums and the voices faded away back to the ancient time from which they had come. He was still alone. Still isolated.

There was no smile.

You've gotta get out of here, ya know.

"Yeah, I know," he replied.

Your leg's getting worse.

"I know. I know," he said dejectedly, irritated.

Confusion in his mind was a physical presence. When he tried to clear and focus his mind, he couldn't. Thoughts slid away before he could hold them. The clarity he'd had before he slept was gone. Worry crept into him like the cold that took hold of his body. But he didn't understand what he could do to clear his mind. Even attempts to concentrate were ephemeral, wisps of smoke blown quickly away into a void.

He knew the brief conversation he just had was a conversation with himself. At the same time, the words had the feel of a conversation with someone else. Someone outside of his mind.

That doesn't make sense, he heard. *You're the only one here. You're just talkin' to yourself again.*

"Yeah, I know."

But the feeling of another entity remained. Talking out loud was nothing new for him. He did it all the time, at least when he was alone. Good times and bad. It was not something he worried about. It was just what he did. But a conversation with himself was something else entirely.

These four sentences certainly had a different feel—the sense that he was responding to a voice other than his own, thoughts not his own.

•   •   •

He was sitting up but didn't remember the act of sitting up. When he woke, he had been lying down. Now he was sitting up. A sense of time lost crept through him. His eyes were still closed. And it was still very cold.

When he opened his eyes, he found it was still daytime. The windshield was partially blocked with frost. By the look of the shadows, it was late afternoon. The truck was not running, and the stove was not on. The cold was holding him in its deep embrace.

Turning the ignition key, the truck started immediately. "That's a good old girl. You're still with me," he said.

Feet under the dashboard, the left foot resting on the splint, he leaned against the seat back and waited for the heat to come through. Looking around the inside of the truck cab, he saw the water in the large cooking pot had not frozen again. The bottles of water sitting in the pot were not frozen either. The coffee pot sat on the unlit stove. As he reached for it, he glanced out the passenger door window toward the hidden stream. There was a large oval smear of bloody fluid on the glass. "Oh, man, that's nasty lookin'."

He moved his right hand to the back of his head and felt how hot his head and scalp were. His scalp tingled with the heat. His ears burned with it. His eyes were grainy, and his eyelids were heavy with the heat. The area of the cut was hot and sticky when it should be cool and scabbing over. His fingers came away covered with a bloody goo. He was repulsed by the sticky mess.

The washcloth lay on the floor beside the cooler. It was crusty, dry and blood streaked from when he had washed his hands and the back of his head.

When? Yesterday? Days ago? the voice asked.

"I don't know," he said. "I just don't know."

He soaked the washcloth with water from a bottle and washed his hands again. The water was very cold. Checking his forehead, cheeks, and chest, he found them all hot as well. His shirt was still damp from sweat. Leaning forward, he placed his hand on his upper leg and found it very hot.

It's gettin' worse, he heard.

"I don't even need to look at it to know that."

The coffee pot was nearly full of cold, black coffee. He tried to think of when he had eaten last and couldn't remember. He couldn't remember having eaten at all that day. He couldn't focus enough to remember breakfast. "I slept through lunch, I guess." he said.

He saw the Advil bottle sitting on the dash and couldn't remember when he had last taken a dose.

Softly, in the depths of his mind, he remembered the beat of the drums, the high-pitched chanting. They rose inside him. But now there was no smile. The voices were singing a song of death, not a song of thanks and praise. It didn't touch him. Had no effect on him. His mind and emotions were flat. Dull. And the song faded.

His head was hanging forward, shoulders slumped, eyes closed. Not asleep. Not awake. Lost in the swamp of his fevered mind.

When he opened his eyes, the truck was still running and warm. The coffee pot sat on the truck seat beside him, his hand still holding the handle. How long he had been like that he didn't know. It didn't matter. He set the coffee pot back on the stove and turned off the truck.

How much gas you got left, boy? the voice in his head asked.

"I don't know," he answered. Not knowing didn't seem to matter either. Not now. He didn't look at the gas gauge. Looking at it wouldn't change how much was there. He would use it to stay warm until it was gone or until they came to get him, whichever came first.

•   •   •

Outside the truck, the light was slipping away. It was sliding toward night. The temperature was dropping. Even in the warmth of the truck, he knew the cold was closing in on him. It was out there, seeking its way into him. At some level, he could feel it. Waiting for him. Coming for him.

You need to eat, boy.

"I know. But I'm not hungry."

When did you eat last?

"I don't know. I can't remember."

He didn't feel hungry, physically or emotionally, but he knew he must eat.

The bottle of Advil still sat on the dashboard. He shook out four tablets and washed them down with cold water. He didn't know how much effect they would have on pain this strong, but he took them anyway. Even a slight reduction in the pain might help.

The bag of meat was on the floor near the gear shift. When he tried to pull the meat from the freezer bag, the meat was frozen together and stuck to the bag. He pried it loose and separated the two pieces of tenderloin and laid them in the frying pan. All of his motions were slow and cumbersome. His fingers and hands were clumsy. It was hard to maintain focus with his eyes or his mind. His head kept wanting to droop forward toward sleep. Back rounded against the seat, shoulders slumped, sleep was closing in on him, trying to take ahold of him.

Don't sleep now, boy.

"Why not? I'm tired. I'm worn down to a nub. I need to sleep.

Eat. You've got to eat first.

"Yeah. Ok. Eat first. Then sleep."

The frying pan sat on the unlit stove. The frozen meat was uncooked. The coffee was still cold. More time had slipped away when he wasn't looking. With trembling fingers, he managed to light a match, started both burners, and sat back, waiting for the meat to cook and the coffee to heat. Again, his head slouched forward involuntarily.

You can't sleep now, old son. Ya gotta stay awake with that stove on, the voice said.

He opened his eyes and looked out the driver's window, across the snow-covered meadow. "Roll the windows down, old son," he said. "Roll 'em down when ya got that stove on. Don't kill yourself now." He rolled both windows down about an inch and waited.

His hand groped his shirt pocket and found an empty cigarette pack. He crumpled it, dropped it on the floor, leaned forward, and opened the glove box to get another pack. With stiff, clumsy fingers, he fumbled getting the new pack open.

As he shook the pack for a cigarette, a rattling chill ran through him, and he nearly dropped the pack. His hands shaking, he tried to get a match from the small box with uncooperative fingers. When he tried to strike the match on the side of the box, his fingers fumbled and he dropped the match on the seat between his legs. Body trembling, arms shaking, fingers twitching, he managed to pick it up and light it. The shaking cigarette in his lips would not coordinate with his trembling fingers holding the lighted match. He held the cigarette with his left hand, lit it, and took a deep drag. After a second drag on the cigarette, he laid it in the ashtray where it remained, forgotten.

He put the pack in his shirt pocket and looked at the stove. The meat was sizzling and the coffee was boiling. He turned the meat over and turned off the burner under the coffee. The bottom of the cooked meat was dark, nearly burned, and he turned off the burner to let the meat finish cooking with the heat of the pan. He rolled up the windows and stared across the meadow.

When he reached for the cigarette, he found it had burned completely down to the filter and was out. More time had slid away.

All of his movements now were done as if he were controlled by some force below conscious thought. Or, perhaps, more than likely, a subliminal function of his mind. Both his body and his mind were sluggish and uncoordinated.

The truck cab had gotten very warm from the heater of the truck running earlier and both burners of the stove on. The chills and trembling were fading away. But he was sweating again. With the warmth in the truck now, his physical lethargy was muted. Not gone, but diminished.

But not his mind. It was still heavy and distant. He wanted to sleep. Just lie down and sleep. Let it all go away.

Not now, boy. You didn't eat yet, the voice said.

"Yeah, I know. I gotta eat."

When he tried to lean on his right elbow, over the pan and the meat, he was not able to coordinate his movements to cut the meat. His hands still shook and his fingers were still clumsy. When he sat up and put the pan in his lap, the heat of the bottom of the pan was too hot for his legs. From the clean clothes bag, he padded his legs from the heat of the pan with his folded last pair of blue jeans. He poured a cup of coffee and sat it on the open glove box door, cut all the meat into bite-sized pieces, and began eating.

Two elk tenderloins are a lot of meat for one person. One would be more than enough with a full regular meal for two people. He would eat as much as he could and save the rest for later.

The milk was gone. The chips were gone. The stew was gone. The peanut butter was frozen. The butter was frozen. The bread was frozen. It was just not worth the effort to thaw them. The meat was frozen but easy to cook and eat, and it would have to do. There was plenty of meat. He sipped coffee while he ate the meat. The coffee was day-old bitter, but he drank it anyway.

Cook some more meat for later, boy. You'll need it, the voice said.

"Yeah. Cook some more meat and save it for later," he repeated.

While he ate, he looked at his watch. It was 4:37 p.m. Tuesday afternoon. "They're coming for you. They'll get here and take you out. Hang on. They're coming," he said. That was all that mattered to him now. The only end he wanted to think about.

CHAPTER 31

For a time, how long he didn't know, he sat slumped forward, eyes closed, body sagging and at rest. He was not really asleep but not really awake either. A mental apparition. Time lost in the hot, foggy swamp of his sickness. His neck ached, and he sat up straight, rolling his head around to loosen the cramped muscles. Immediately dizzy, he opened his eyes and stared out through the windshield. Snow-covered trees slowly drifted across his vision. The day was nearly gone. The cold was leaking back into the truck. The dizziness finally slid away and left him.

The memory of snowmobile engines from the past flickered through his mind.

"They're coming to get me," he said.

Not today, they're not.

"No. Not today."

Maybe tomorrow?

"I sure hope so. God, I hope so. I'm in pretty bad shape, and I need a doctor. Soon."

You're right about that. But you can make it.

"Hell, I could walk outta here if I wanted to."

I hope it doesn't come down to that.

"You and me both, old son. You and me both."

He looked at the watch. It was still Tuesday. Just before 6:00 p.m. Time was slipping away more than he had realized. It was nearly dark outside. He turned on the lamp and set it on the dashboard.

"Okay, it's Tuesday evening. Maybe tomorrow. They should be here tomorrow."

What are you gonna do if they don't come tomorrow?

"I don't know." He paused for what seemed a long time, trying to think. "They'll be here. They're coming."

You've always taken care of yourself. Always done for yourself. Not relied on anyone else when you didn't have to.

"That's true. I take care of my own problems. If I get myself in it, I get myself out. That's the way I've always done it. The way it's always been and the way I wanted it. I've always got myself out of every tight corner."

This ain't no ordinary tight corner, old son.

"You got that right. This is the tightest corner I've ever been in. I'm gonna need help with this one."

The heavy weight of isolation and the closeness of the truck cab were always with him now. A trap he couldn't seem to pull himself out of. He hadn't been outside since yesterday, not even to pee.

"This is not the way it's supposed to be," he mumbled. Whenever he thought of dying on the mountain, he had a vision of how it should end—sitting beneath a tall pine with a view of a deep valley and far-off mountains, leaving his elements to the soil of this world that he loves.

But this is the way it is, and there's nothing you can do about it now, the voice said.

"All I gotta do is survive until they get here. Just hang on a little longer."

Cook some more meat so you have something easy to eat when you need it. Warm up the water so it won't freeze tonight.

"Yeah, that's all I can do for now. Get through tonight. Cook some meat. Warm the water. Then get some sleep."

He put what was left of the cooked meat and the cut-up tender loin in a freezer bag and slipped it into the cooler. He rolled down the driver's window and poured out the old, bitter coffee. He left the window partially open and rolled down the other window a little as well. Clean, cold water from two bottles refilled the coffee pot, and he put it on the stove over a lit burner.

The back strap pieces were frozen solid. The only way to cut them into steaks would be with the saw. He slid the stove as far as possible along the cooler top to make a little room for the cutting. From the piece he had cut before, he began cutting new steaks. The frozen meat was cold in his bare hands. When he had several pieces cut, he filled the bottom of the frying pan and set it on the second burner, lit it, and continued cutting until that entire part of the back strap was cut into steaks.

His arm and shoulder ached, his hands trembled, and he was tired from the continued sawing. Sweat beaded his forehead and trickled from his head behind his ears and along his neck. He leaned back against the seat and rested; eyes closed.

Hey, wake up, boy.

"I'm not asleep."

You can't sleep now. The stove is on.

"Okay, okay. I'm not asleep," he growled.

The water in the coffee pot was boiling. He refilled two of the water bottles with the hot water, hands shaking, spilling some over his fingers and on the seat. He screwed the lids on the bottles and set them on the floor beside the thermos. When he put them in the cooler later, the insulation of the cooler would maintain the heat in the water bottles and keep them from freezing overnight. When he looked at the lid of the cooler, he noticed the many scars on the lid from cutting the meat with the saw. "I'm gonna have to get me a new cooler," he said.

He refilled the coffee pot with snow from the freezer bags, packed it down tight, and put it back over the burner. When the snow was melted, he added a new filter and coffee grounds. He turned the meat over in the frying pan to finish cooking. When the coffee was done, he filled the tin cup. What was left he put in the thermos. Resting, back against the sleeping bag, ashtray in his lap, he smoked and waited. Sipping hot coffee, he closed his eyes and rested his head against the cold window.

Don't sleep now, boy. You'll burn the meat.

"Okay, okay. I'll watch the meat 'til it's done. But I need to sleep."

You've got all night to sleep.

When the meat was done, he placed it on a paper plate. The rest of the meat went into the frying pan to cook. While it cooked, he cut up the already cooked pieces and put them in another freezer bag.

None of these movements required thought. They were just what needed to be done. He didn't want to think about the fact that he might not be able to do these things later or tomorrow. He didn't want to know what tomorrow would be like, and especially what his mind might be like. The mind was bad now, and he knew it wasn't going to get better. More than likely a lot worse.

"They'll be here tomorrow."

Yes, they'll be here tomorrow.

The infection had taken over. That he knew. It had brought the fever, sweats, and chills. After the injury, it was the one thing he'd dreaded. And it was here. Big time. Without medical treatment soon, it was only going to get worse. Without any medical treatment at all, he would not make it out of this truck and down off this mountain. At least not that he would know about.

If they're not here by noon tomorrow, you might have to walk out of here, ya know.

"Yeah, I know. At least I might have to try. I'm not gonna sit here in this truck and just wait to die. I don't want the kids to find me like that. If I'm gonna die, I'll do it out there on the mountain trying to get out."

I'm not sure you can make it walking out, old son.

"I probably can't, you know. I'm in pretty bad shape."

You'd better think it over real good.

"Yeah, I know."

The water in the coffee pot was boiling again, and he filled two more bottles with hot water, again burning his fingers, and set them on the floor beside the other two. There were still two more empty bottles to fill. With the coffee cup, he filled the coffee pot with water from the large cooking pot, set it on the stove, and refilled his coffee cup from the thermos.

The second piece of back strap had never been cut and was coiled and folded around itself, frozen. It was going to be very difficult to cut it into pieces to cook, and it wouldn't fit in the pan whole. He put it back in the plastic bag and laid it on the floor again.

"Man, I'm gettin' tired. I need to rest."

Just do the best you can, boy, but keep doing it 'til it's done.

"Okay," he whispered.

He sipped coffee from the cup and lit another cigarette, set the ashtray in his lap, and waited for the meat to cook. The cigarette he was holding woke him when it burned down to his fingers. When he opened his eyes, he saw that a long ash from the cigarette had fallen to his lap, missing the ashtray. "So much for smokin'. Ya can't even stay awake long enough to finish a damn smoke," he chided himself. "More lost time slipping away."

The meat was done. He turned off the stove and put the meat on the paper plate to cool before he cut it into bite-sized pieces. He filled the two final bottles with hot water and turned off that burner as well.

"You're done for now, old son," he said.

Don't go to sleep yet, boy. Ya gotta get this meat and water in the cooler first, the voice told him.

"Okay, okay. Quit pushin' me."

Eyes burning, eyelids drooping, the back of his head burning, and the leg throbbing, he wanted to lie down and sleep. He fought drooping eyelids, continually on the verge of dropping off. He wanted to sleep. Nothing more. Warm or cold, he needed to sleep. When he was asleep, he wasn't confronted with the mess his mind was becoming—a stagnant swamp of a mind. Trying to keep his mind working was frustrating.

Sleep silenced the pain, the pain in his mind and the pain in his body. In sleep, there was no pain.

But sleep did not control the cold. The cold was always there. Coming for him even in sleep. The cold killed his sleep when it woke him with its control over him. He knew that in sleep, the cold might take him. Completely and forever. And yet he wanted to sleep. Needed to sleep. Slip beyond the pain, the mess of his mind, and the constant struggle. If he died in his sleep, he would never know.

But there were still things to do. Survival to hold on to.

He turned on the lamp. Barely able to hold the saw, he cut the rest of the meat into bite-sized pieces and put it in a freezer bag. He moved the stove to the seat and put all the water bottles and the meat in the cooler and slumped back in the seat, legs under the dashboard.

"Now I can sleep," he said.

Not yet, old son. Get that coffee pot ready for some coffee in the morning. Take some more Advil and drink some water. A lot of water.

When he had filled the coffee pot with water from the saucepan, he added a filter and fresh grounds, and set it on the floor. All that was left was to put it on the stove in the morning.

There wasn't much water left in the large saucepan. He dipped a cup of it and washed down four more tablets of the Advil. Then he drank two more cups of the cold water to finish off what was in the pan and set it aside on the floor. The water cooled his lips, rinsed his mouth, and soothed his throat as it went down.

The sun was down, and it was completely dark outside. He turned off the lamp and lay on the seat. A swatch of stars was visible through the windshield. "Hello, stars. You pretty ladies of the night," he said.

The leg was stretched out along the seat, his upper back against the sleeping bag, head against the cold passenger window. It was dark in the truck, and he closed his eyes and gave himself up to the night.

How much gas is left in that bottle in the stove? the voice asked.

"It doesn't matter. I've got meat to eat," he replied. "I can make coffee in the morning. They're gonna be here to get me out tomorrow."

Are they really?

"Damn right they are," he said. "That stove is gonna stay here all winter anyway. I'm not. Now leave me alone and let me sleep."

As he faded into the darkness of sleep, he whispered, "Good night kids. I'll see ya tomorrow." His last thoughts were of his children.

And of her.

Good night, lady.

He slipped into the dark with a slight smile on his lips.

CHAPTER 32

Shivering head to toe woke him to the dark of night. Sweat covered his head and torso. Sweat under his arms, on his chest, in the small of his back, on his butt, and in his crotch. Cold, wet clothing clung to him. The cold had taken over the cab of the truck again. And still he was sweating. Sweating with intermittent teeth chattering and chills. In his mind, he searched for warmth, begged for heat, and found none, mentally lost. What did he need to do to get warm again? When he found no immediate solution, he whispered, "Is this it, old son? Are you done now? Has the cold won?"

Turn the truck on, dummy, he heard the voice say.

"Turn the truck on," he repeated dully. "Turn the truck on."

Trying to lean forward, still trembling in every muscle, he was not able to sit all the way up and fell back on the sleeping bag, banging his head on the window. Pain exploded inside him. Burning pain shot through his head, front to back, and ricocheted around the inside of his skull. Dizziness spun him through the truck cab, ripping orientation from his grasp. The strength he needed just to sit up was nearly gone. His body flopped like a scrap of paper skittering along the ground in a skiff of wind. Both feet banged on the floor of the truck. Agony in the leg overwhelmed him, and the darkness took him away. There was no chance to hold it off.

•   •   •

Wake up, old son, the voice said.

He didn't respond. Didn't know how to respond. There was no understanding in him.

Louder, the voice said, *Wake up, boy. Wake up NOW!*

He opened his eyes and stared at the ceiling of the truck cab. The voice echoed in his head.

Wake up and start the truck.

He didn't respond. Not in his mind. Not with his body.

Start the truck or you're dead, the voice insisted.

"Dead," he said. "Dead. Start the truck. Start the truck or you're dead."

Straining with the little energy he had left, his body still trembling and out of control, he gradually raised himself and gripped the steering wheel with his right hand. Pushing with his left hand on the seat, right hand pulling on the steering wheel, he managed to sit up and slumped forward, his head near the dashboard. His right arm across his chest gripped the steering wheel, holding him upright. Leaning his body to the left, he slid his right hand to the steering column and groped for the keys hanging in the ignition. He grasped the keys between his thumb and the base of his index finger and tried to turn his hand. Weakness and trembling prevented him from putting enough pressure on the key to turn it.

Don't let go of that key, he heard. *Turn that key now. Turn it and start the truck.*

Grunting with determination, he applied pressure to the key and turned it slowly toward the dash. The motor groaned, stalled, and groaned again, and he released the key. *If that battery's frozen, I'll be next,* he thought.

He turned the key to the start position again and the motor groaned. There was nothing left to do. Just hold the key in the start position and wait. If it started, great. If it didn't, that was it. Done. The battery frozen, the motor gone, no more heat from the old truck. Lighting the stove would have gotten the truck warmer, faster, but he wasn't sure he could do what he needed to do to light the burners. Didn't think he could hold a match and strike it with the way he was now. Holding the key in the start position, the motor groaned again, turned over slowly several times, gathered speed, and started.

"Oh, baby, thank you. You good old girl. Thank you, thank you, thank you." He released his grip on the keys and settled back against the seat, leaning to the right. His right arm at his side, hand on the seat, held him up. He was gradually losing strength. He slowly lowered himself to his right side, knees bent, feet on the floor, until his head lay on the sleeping bag. Soft and cool, the sleeping bag pillowed the right side of his hot face and ear. The dashboard and the glove box were right in front of him. The glove box door was still open with the coffee cup sitting on it. The inside of the glove box was crammed with papers, maps, and unknown junk.

"Man, I gotta clean all that crap outta there when I get home," he said. His eyes slowly closed, and he drifted away to the sound of snowmobile engines. Voices were outside the door, shouting, calling his name. Whose voices he didn't know. Voices that had come to get him. Take him home. He sank deeper toward sleep listening to the voices shouting his name.

Don't go back to sleep now, the voice told him. *Wait for the heat. Then turn off the truck.*

The sound of the voice brought him back. Fully awake.

Warm air was blowing from the heater vent. There were no snowmobile engines idling outside the truck. No voices called his name. He was still alone in the truck. Still alone on the mountain. Despite the sweating, his lips and mouth were sticky dry. Shivering chills shook him. Thirst nagged him. His eyelids fought to close, but he forced them to remain open.

Sliding forward, he pushed the stove off of the cooler onto the floor behind it. With effort, he lifted the lid of the cooler and snaked his right hand inside. Groping, he found a bottle of water that was cool and drew it out. He twisted the cap off and lifted the neck of the bottle toward his lips, hand shaking. But he tilted it too soon and poured water on his neck and the seat. It didn't matter. A second attempt brought the bottle to his lips, and he drank deeply. Lying on his right side, his head on the sleeping bag, he sat the bottle against his chest, still holding it.

Warmth was gradually increasing from the heater. The trembling of his body was slowly receding. His eyelids were still heavy, but he kept them open with force and determination and drank from the water bottle. He was afraid that if he slept now, the truck would run completely out of gas while he was out, and he would have no heat for tomorrow. Without heat, he was dead for sure. *Stay awake 'til you're warm*, the voice said. *Stay awake. Then turn the truck off.*

He drank more water and waited. The water was not cold, but it was wet and felt good in his mouth, on his tongue and throat. He took another sip and rinsed his mouth before swallowing it.

The Advil was sitting on the dashboard, and he leaned forward, groped for the bottle, and knocked it onto the floor. Fumbling, he picked it up, shook out four tablets in his palm, replaced the cap, and dropped the bottle back on the floor. He washed the pills down with the rest of the water in the bottle and dropped it on the floor, as well.

When he lay back down, the truck cab was warm again. His shaking body was not completely still but not out of control as it had been. Heavy and weak, he waited for several more minutes, forcing his eyes to remain open, reveling in the warmth of the air around him. Gradually he was sinking back toward sleep.

Turn off the truck and go back to sleep now, old son, the voice said gently.

Out the window, the stars dusted the sky.

He leaned forward, turned off the engine, and lay back down. His eyes closed as his back touched the sleeping bag, and he gently lowered his head against the window. He immediately drifted into the darkness. The warmth of the air in the cab held him gently, and he relaxed in its embrace. He knew no more of the world. And nothing disturbed his rest. No drums. No singers. No snowmobile engines. No voices outside the door.

CHAPTER 33

Hours later, as he rose to the surface of the world, there were no drums or singers. There were no idling snowmobile engines outside the truck. No voices in the night calling his name as he came awake. All was quiet and still. At some level, he knew those things were not a part of the real world. But he wished they were. They were the last vestiges of hope. Maybe the voices would have been the kids come to take him home. When he opened his eyes, it wasn't completely dark, but not light either. Early morning before the sunrise.

Wednesday, he thought.

He closed his eyes and lay still on the seat. No rescue. Yet! His timeline had run out. But he wasn't ready to give up.

The cold had slipped into the truck while he slept. Yet again.

This was his reality. Cold and pain and alone. This was the life he lived. For now. But his world, the world he wanted, was not over yet.

Sit up, boy. A pause. *Sit up now, boy.* The voice was still with him. *Ya gotta keep hangin' in there, old son. Keep gutting it out. Don't give it up now.*

He rolled to his right side, gripped the steering wheel with both hands and, arms quivering, slowly pulled himself to a sitting position, feet angled beneath the dashboard. His body was still hot and heavy. His arms lay across his legs, hands shaking, fingers trembling. The injury on the back of his head burned. The ache in his leg was there. Always with him. Hot and throbbing.

"That leg ain't goin' nowhere," he said.

Nope. Not 'til you do, boy. Now get the stove started and make some coffee. Get some meat out and eat. And get some heat in this truck.

He made no reply to the voice, lifted the lid of the cooler, and took out a bottle of water and a bag of cooked meat. He sat the meat on the floor. A long drink from the water bottle soothed and relaxed him, easing the dryness of his lips and mouth and cooling him.

The stove was still tipped behind the cooler and lay at an angle on the bags of clothes and trash bags. With effort, he struggled it onto the top of the cooler. The coffee pot was sitting on the floor near the passenger door with water, filter, and grounds already in place. His fingers trembling, he fumbled a match from the box. On the third try, the match flared and he lit the burner and a cigarette and waited for the warmth and the coffee. The muscles in his legs, back and stomach still quivered from fatigue and cold. All of his movements were slow, sluggish, and shaky. They required a concentration he had never had to use before.

Now, his mind was a hazy wall. He saw from outside himself his sluggish and trembling body. He knew he could do nothing to change it.

The heat from the stove began to warm the cab of the truck immediately. Ashtray in his lap, he smoked and stared out through the windshield as the frost melted from the glass. Over there, across the empty snow-covered space, was the ridge, the line of trees, and the slight decline where he had slipped and fallen and broken his leg. "On Friday," he said.

"What a long time ago that was." He whispered.

That small place by the trees was the beginning. And perhaps the end as well. Occasionally, he drank from the water bottle.

Images of his time before the fall flitted through his mind. Walks up the ridge through the trees. The sunlight in the forest. Sitting in the shade by the stream. The elk coming up the trail. The mule deer buck in the canyon. The voices of the earth that had spoken to him. All the good that he had come here to be a part of came back to him now. Washed over him and through him. And those memories relaxed him, giving him comfort and a measure of peace.

When he heard the coffee pot perking, he put out the cigarette, set the ashtray on the floor, picked up the tin cup, and filled it with hot coffee. He set the coffee pot back on the stove but not over the flame. He left the burner on for heat. The only movement he made was to sip from the coffee cup now and then. He sat still, quiet and relaxed, staring through the windshield at the snow. Shoulders slumped forward, head sagging. Heavy eyelids drooping. And waited. For whatever this day would bring. It was Wednesday. The last day. The deadline. Time had slipped away.

The truck was warm. The sun was up. The snow glistened across the meadow. The voices of the mountains and all that was here were still silent. He was now detached from it all. Isolated in the truck. Isolated in his mind. And the cold was out there. Waiting for him. Coming for him.

The only voice he heard now spoke to him.

You forgot to roll the windows down when you lit the stove, boy.

He looked at the door windows, the frost melted away. They were both rolled up fully. "It didn't matter," he said. "I'm not dead."

Rather than roll them down now, he turned off the stove burner and started the truck. He took a sip of coffee and set the cup on the seat beside him with his finger still crooked inside the handle. His back was against the seat, head resting on the back window. He closed his eyes and rested, the warmth in the truck holding him. The feeling of being outside himself persisted as he drifted away. Whether to sleep or unconsciousness he didn't know. It didn't matter. Either way he had no control. Time was slipping away.

As the world around him dimmed, the drums and the chanting song rose in him again. The death song kept time with the beating of his heart. No snowmobile engines revving.

They're not here, he thought. *They haven't come yet.* He slid away into the darkness.

• • •

As the heat in the cab cooled enough to notice, it woke him. The motor wasn't running. He didn't remember turning it on or turning it off.

Voices outside the door called his name.

"They're here," he said with a sigh. "They're finally here." He sat up straight, eyes half open, and waited for them to come to him. When no one came, he tried to twist around to look out the back window to the entrance of the logging road but couldn't make the turn far enough to see the opening in the trees.

His body was too weak. Movement was too hard.

No. They're not here yet, old son.

"I can hear them," he mumbled. "I can hear them calling me."

No. Not yet. That's just in your head. They're not here yet.

The sound of the voices blinked out as if they had never been.

"Oh god," he moaned. "They've got to be here. I need them to be here."

I know, old son. I know. Hang in there.

Dejected, he slumped against the seat. His hand knocked the coffee cup onto the floor, splashing cold coffee on the side of the cooler and the bag of meat. His eyes filled with tears, and he sobbed, shoulders shaking. Tears ran from his face and dripped from his chin onto his lap. His nose ran and plugged. Great gasps for breath racked his body. Rocking back and forward on the seat, he let his emotions run free. Sobbing and moaning, he gave himself up for a time to his agony and despair. Gradually it subsided, and he sat still, tears dripping from his chin, wetting his pants.

Okay, boy. Move on now. This isn't gonna change a thing. If they're comin', they'll get here, the voice said. *If not, you're gonna have to hang in there and see it out to the end, whatever that may be.*

He wiped his eyes with the heels of his hands and sat up as straight as his body would allow. "I have to get out of here," he said. "I don't want them to find me when it's too late."

Do you think you can walk out of here?

"I may have to try," he replied. "I just may have to try."

But looking at the more than three feet of snow in front of the truck, he knew that wasn't going to happen. He was in too bad of shape now to walk across the street, much less out of here. He was far too weak and sick to even get out of the truck.

Maybe if he had tried early on after the fall, he might have been able to make it, at least to the county road. If he'd had the crutch and the splints when the snow wasn't so deep and he was in better shape. But not now. Walking out was no longer an option. In reality, it never was. He always knew that. If he tried it now, they would never find him until the summer thaw, if then.

He was here, in the truck, to the end. Whatever that may be. If it came down to it, he could turn the old truck on for warmth, run her till the gas was gone, and they could go out together.

"I'm probably too weak to get out of the truck to just take a piss," he said.

Warm up some meat and have another cup of coffee. You need to eat something. And don't forget to roll down the windows.

He wiped his eyes and blew his nose with a paper towel. With both of the burners lit, he set the coffee to warm over one flame and the frying pan over the other. He dumped the meat from the freezer bag into the frying pan. In a few minutes, the meat and the coffee were warm, and he turned off the burners and rolled up the windows. He poured a cup of coffee and stabbed pieces of meat from the pan with a fork. The meat was good, the coffee perfect.

·   ·   ·

When he opened his eyes, it was daylight. He didn't remember getting sleepy or falling asleep. The sun was higher in the sky than he had remembered. Pushing on toward noon. More time had slipped away. He didn't know what time it was and didn't look at his watch. Time no longer mattered. It was Wednesday, and his time here was near the end. Bright sunlight glistening off of the snow streamed through the passenger door window. His eyes burned with it, and he closed them and leaned back against the sleeping bag.

He came awake without knowing that he had been gone again. Or for how long. The fork was in his hand on the seat, a piece of cold meat speared on the tines.

The smell of stagnant body odor in the truck no longer repulsed him. It was just there. A part of his reality. The pain in his leg and his head were there. As if they had been there forever. Both a part of his reality, too. The heat and the chills in his body and the weight of his stagnant mind were there. Also, a part of his reality.

Of its own volition, his hand raised and brought the fork to his mouth, and he chewed the cold meat. An action delayed, separate from any thought.

His head drooped forward, and his eyes closed. The drums, faint and far away, rose around him. Not in his mind. Not in his thoughts. The air around him gently vibrated with their beat. The voices singing, chanting the death song, echoed through the truck cab.

What are you gonna do, boy? the voice asked.

"Wait for them the come get me," he responded out loud.

Can you get your ass out of this truck and walk out of here?

"No. It's too late. I'm in too bad of shape to make it now." And he waited.

Are you sure? the voice whispered.

"Yes, I'm sure," he said and knew the truth of it. "That's too far of a walk anyway."

The sound of the drums and the singers rose in volume around him. He felt them in the air like a fragrance. Felt their gentle lure and seduction. He wanted to give himself to their song.

The cold skimmed through the cracks around the door and slithered into the truck. Insidious and greedy. The cold was coming for him. Cold like a killer fog crept across the floor. It didn't matter. He had no more strength to fight the cold.

They had not come for him.

"Yet!" he amended immediately.

The vibration of the drums and the chanting voices reverberated through the truck, through his mind, and through his body. Invading all of his space. Gradually increasing in volume. Always more pervasive.

His eyelids sagged closed. His head drooped. Darkness enclosed him, and time slipped away.

Later, how much later he didn't know, the voice spoke again. *So, what are you going to do, old son?*

"Stay warm and wait for them to get here. They're coming," he said. "I believe that. I have to believe that." He lay curled on the seat, head on the sleeping bag, eyes closed. He didn't open his eyes. Wasn't even certain that he had the strength to open his eyes, much less sit up.

The sound and feel of the drums rolled over him. Rose and pulsed through him. The high melodic voices sang with the rhythm of the drums and the beat of his heart. Dancing feet stamped the earth in unison. The singing voices were joined in harmony with all the voices of the earth. And his voice joined them. Blended with them.

Beneath the drums and singers, chanting the death song in time with the beat of his heart, he heard the snowmobile engines again. Racing and revving. Voices shouting. Calling his name. Competing with the death song. Competing with the cold coming for him.

The drums and singers called to him. Chanting his death song. Enticing him to come to them. But he did not join their voices. He did not sing the song.

The cold had come for him one more time, holding him in its tight grip with a promise to take him away from the pain. His will and understanding of how to fight the cold had left him. But he chose not to join their chorus.

The opening in the forest at the logging road beckoned to him. He reached with his mind for the road home.

The cab of his old truck, a good friend for years, held him in its gentle embrace. And he rested in its comfort.

Snowmobile engines idled near the truck. Voices shouted, called his name. Demanded his attention.

All these competing scenes mingled, merged, and whirled like rivulets to a stream. Twisting and turning, they blended together in his mind and in his heart. His determined, beating heart.

EPILOGUE

"Slow down a little," said the passenger. "You need to take the next right. There's a bit of a berm just past the entrance. But it's not too bad gettin' over it."

The pickup was tall and beefy with a jacked-up suspension and a powerful engine. A young man's truck. Its once glistening solid black paint job was coated with dust and mud. The oversized rims and tires made it stand tall above the road's surface. When he'd first seen the truck, he wasn't so sure he could even get in it. He wouldn't have made it up to the seat without the U-shaped step that was welded to the frame and jutted out from beneath the body, below the door. A padded handhold, attached to the door post, helped as he pulled himself into the truck.

With the high suspension, oversized rims, and aggressive mud-treaded tires, it made for a pretty rough ride. By his way of thinking anyway. With the tread on those tires, this truck could go just about anywhere on dirt, pavement, or in mud, sand, or snow. But the washboard ruts at several places along the gravel road had bounced and danced everything in the truck's bed from side to side and front to back. *This truck rides rougher than any truck I've ever been in*, he thought. The tires didn't hum on the pavement. They roared. He had a headache from the noise before they had gone fifty miles.

Even with his warning, the driver missed the turnoff. He skidded to a stop, throwing the passenger forward to brace his arms on the dashboard.

They backed up and turned into the narrow gap in the trees. When they reached the berm, the driver stopped the truck and shifted into four-wheel drive. With more care than the passenger thought the driver had in him, they eased over the low berm and headed up the road through the trees.

As the truck moved up the narrow, gentle grade, sunlight flashed through the tall pines, winking through the windshield. An occasional sapling pine tree and some brush scraped along the undercarriage of the truck.

The fragrance of the pines that grew close along the side of the road drifted through the truck's open windows on the warmth of the air currents. The passenger turned his face to the opening and took a long, deep breath through his nose, scenting the air with his eyes closed. He held the aroma deep in his lungs for as long as he could hold it. A wide smile spread across his thin, angular face and crinkled the crow's feet wrinkles at the corner of his eyes.

The driver looked at him with eyebrows drawn into a frown and a quizzical look on his face. The passenger turned to look at the young man as he let his breath out in a long sigh, his face beaming with unconcealed joy and his eyes wide and sparkling. After a moment, the driver's face opened in understanding.

"Yeah!" the young man said in a soft voice. He, too, took deep breaths through his nose, taking in the fragrance of the pines with a smile of his own, "Yeah!"

A bit under two miles along the road, the driver pulled the truck to a stop. A young pine tree, about eight inches thick at the base, had bent across the road, its top touching the ground on the opposite side of the road, blocking their way. The young man turned off the truck engine and sat looking at the tree.

"Most likely the snow weighed it down this winter," the passenger said.

"Yeah," replied the driver. "You sit tight. I'll get the saw and cut it out of the way." He opened the truck door and hopped to the ground.

I don't think I'll ever be able to make a jump like that again as long as I live, thought the passenger. Remaining in his seat, the passenger watched through the windshield. With a handheld bow saw, the young man cut the small tree near the ground and dragged it to the side of the road. As he climbed back into the truck, he wiped a sheen of sweat from his forehead and wiped his hand on the leg of his pants. "It's warming up out there," he said as he started the truck up and drove up the road again.

"Didn't your old man teach you not to wipe your hands on your clothes?" the passenger teased with a smile.

As they moved along the road, the passenger had never seen this country from this perspective before. He had always been the driver when he had been here in times past. His attention focused on the narrow road. As they climbed the grade, he watched the terrain drop along a steep hillside beside the road. At the bottom of the ravine, through the pines, he caught glimpses of a stream running swift and full with tumbling, clear water. Sunlight flashed off little waves in the stream's current. *My, oh my*, he thought. *How I would like to dip my hands in that cold water and take a long, slow drink. Water up here is the sweetest water found anywhere on God's green earth.* He remembered telling a friend once that this water came out of the best filter ever invented; the side of the mountain. Not some rusty old pipe laid underground years ago.

As they approached the crest of the grade, he turned to the driver. "After you get over the top a ways, the road takes a bit of a turn to the right. That's where the deep washed-out ruts will be. The supra's graded wrong there, and the snow melt runs right across the road. You shouldn't have any trouble getting' past 'em with this truck, but you'll want to pull to the left side of the road and take 'em real slow. You'll tear the front suspension right from under the truck if you take 'em too fast." After a moment, he said, "That wouldn't be a good thing way back here in the high country. It's a long walk to town from here."

As they approached the ruts, the driver stopped, leaned forward over the steering wheel, and craned his neck to look at them over the high hood of the truck. After a minute, he turned off the engine, opened the door, and hopped to the ground. He walked forward and stood looking at the ruts in the road. There were two smaller ones that would be no problem at all. The center rut was about eighteen inches deep and more than two feet wide on the right side of the road. It was shallower and narrower on the left side and getting around it would be no problem for the four-wheel drive. He walked back to the truck, got in, and started the engine. He backed up the road several yards, looked at the ruts again, and swung the truck to the left side of the road as he rolled forward.

With his foot on the brake, he let gravity pull him down the grade until he felt the right front tire drop into the rut and then gave it a little gas to pull up the other side and through the rut. The rear tire dropped into the rut and bounced out the other side as they continued down the hill.

"Piece of cake," said the driver, as they continued down the grade of the road. Gradually the grade lessened, and the road began to flatten out. More or less.

Looking through the windshield, the passenger said, "Would you do me a favor, son?"

"What's that?"

"Before you get to that turn up ahead, could you pull over and stop?"

The driver turned to the passenger and saw unease on the older face. Instantly, tension thickened in the cab of the truck like an unpleasant odor.

"Sure. Whatever you want." After a pause, he asked, "You OK?"

"I'm fine," was the quiet reply.

Something less than a quarter of a mile short of the turn, the driver pulled onto a wide spot on the right side of the road. He put the truck in park and waited. Several minutes passed, and he glanced at the passenger, who remained staring out the windshield. Without speaking, he turned off the truck and sat quiet, hands on the steering wheel, fingers drumming a nervous rhythm.

The passenger sat motionless, hooded eyes staring forward. If he were looking at anything in this tangible world, you wouldn't know it by looking at him. Mottled sunlight and shadow speckled the hood of the truck and the road ahead. A light breeze wafted through the truck's open windows, bringing with it the sharp aroma of the pines. The sound of the breeze in the trees accompanied the gurgle of the creek, unseen now through the forest. A crow in a nearby tree squawked an unspecified complaint to the world. A squirrel scrambled up the trunk of a large pine near the right front fender and sat on a limb flicking his tail, intermittently chirping at the men in the truck.

Gradually, the visible tension in the body of the older man relaxed, and a flicker of a smile graced his lips. He turned his head to the right and scanned the forest of trees and brush. His head still facing away from the driver, he said, "Here's what I'm gonna do." And he paused. He had not said, "Here's what I want to do" or "here's what I would like to do" but "here's what I'm gonna do."

After a long pause, he continued. "You set here for a spell if you will. Maybe an hour or so. Take a nap if you want. We've got plenty of time. I'm gonna walk down there and have a look around. See what I can see." Again, he paused. "I just need a bit of time to myself if you don't mind."

"You sure you're all right?" the driver asked.

"Oh yeah. Sure. No problem," he said with an embarrassed shrug. "It ain't far, and the ground's gentle from here to there." He nodded his head. "I'll be fine."

The driver leaned back in the seat, hands lowered to his lap, and released his own tension. "Okay. Take as long as you need. I'll come on down shortly."

The passenger looked at the younger man and smiled. He opened the door, gripped the handle, and placed his right foot on the step. He swung his butt around and backed out of the door. When he placed his left foot on the ground to take his weight, he winced but tried not to show it. He reached back into the truck, picked up the cane from the floor, and closed the door. Without saying more, he turned and headed away from the truck down the road.

After several steps away from the front of the truck, he stopped in the middle of the road. Turning, he walked back to the truck, passed the driver's door without so much as a glance at the driver, and chucked the cane into the bed of the pickup. Turning again, he headed once more down the road with a pronounced limp and a bit of swagger in the swing of his arms.

The younger man watched him walk down the middle of the road. The older man didn't really seem frail now. He walked with a strong stride despite the limp. But he had changed. A lot. Certainly, he was much thinner.

He had lost more than sixty pounds over the past few months. The muscular shoulders, the broad back, and the thick upper legs were muted now. The bulk of the man he had known all his life was gone now. Hopefully not forever. His pants sagged around the butt and bunched under the belt. His shirt hung loose on his frame. But all in all, he was getting stronger and looking healthier.

He was quieter. More introspective. Not dour or sullen, just quieter. He still smiled a lot. But now, at times, he smiled something within himself. A special secret he kept closely guarded.

As he walked, the man lifted his hat from his head, ran his fingers through his hair, and replaced the cap at a jaunty angle on the back of his head. When he reached the turn in the road, without turning back to face the truck, he raised his right arm in the air and pointed his thumb to the sky as if to say, "I'm okay, and I know you are watchin'."

Back in the truck, the young man shook his head and smiled. He leaned his head against the headrest, closed his eyes, and waited.

·　　·　　·

When the older man reached the edge of the trees where the road opened into the meadow, he stopped in the last of the shade. There, out in the open, near the small stand of trees, sat the old truck. "There she is, old son," he said. "Sittin' there waiting for ya." The old truck had been here all winter buried under the snow. The silent snow. From this distance, it looked no worse for it.

The tarp for the lean-to was twisted on the ground. The end of the rope that had held it up had broken from the tree it had been tied to by the weight of the snow. The tarp that had covered the woodpile was wrapped around the base of a tree where the wind had blown it.

This day was warm, and sweat formed on his brow and under his arms as he walked. Standing in the shade, looking at the old campsite, he shifted his weight to accommodate the leg. It ached a bit, but not too bad for as far as he'd just walked. Debbie, his physical therapist, would be proud of him. But standing too long and walking any distance still brought the leg to mind.

Not that it was ever very far away. He would probably have this limp or some form of it all the way to the grave. Or so the doctor said. Debbie was more optimistic.

He scanned from right to left across the opening from the stream running full and happy, past the campsite and his old truck, past the low end of the ridge, and to the far end of the long meadow.

Tears filled his eyes for all that had happened here during that long week. In some ways, it seemed much longer than that. His mind was now filled with the things he had gained here. And the things he had lost. All the memories he had of his time here. The good and the bad. The beautiful and the ugly. The joy and the sorrow. A lot of each. So many things lived in so short a time. A time that had stretched to a lifetime, nearly to the end of his time. He pulled off his cap and wiped his eyes with the heel of his hands.

I'm glad you weren't with me on this mountain, honey, he thought.

There were things he didn't remember. A lot of things, really. To remember them was no longer important to him. Never really had been. He had no memory of those who came with his sons to get him. He had met some of them since and thanked them for all that they had done. He had no memory of the trip out but had been told of it. He had no memory of the first days in the hospital. He'd been told of that as well. When he first came back to himself in the hospital, he reached out his hand to turn the truck on for the heater to warm the truck. It took a while to understand and accept that he was no longer in the truck.

The worst part of the hospital was the coffee. Strong and bitter. Too much like Dad's hunting camp coffee years ago. Worse, actually.

He'd been told that for days in the hospital, it had been touch and go. But, hell, it had been touch and go from the first moment his foot slipped in the snow and he fell flat on his ass over there on the end of that damn ridge.

Fragments of dreams, or were they hallucinations, flickered in his mind from time to time. He didn't try to draw them out. They came and went of their own volition. Here, now, on the mountain, they seemed somehow closer to the surface. He was almost able to reach out and touch them with his mind. But he wasn't sure he wanted to—at least not all of them.

He thought about that touch and go thing a lot over the past few months. His conclusion was that life was pretty touch and go. Things, good and bad, just happened. Just when you thought things were rolling along fine, something or someone slapped you in the back of the head and down you went on your ass in the snow. Some of those slaps and tumbles are easy to get over, no damage done. Some are not so easy. "And some of them are with you forever," he said in a quiet whisper. "There just ain't no gettin' over some of them at all."

He walked slowly across the open space to the back of the truck. The tailgate was still down. The hinges groaned when he slammed it closed. The meat was gone. Members of the snowmobile club from the town not far away who had helped get him out had come back and brought out the meat, his guns, and a few other things. That's how the people are who live up here in the mountains. If you need help, they just naturally step up and do what needs doing.

Standing by the back of the truck, he looked at the ground near the right rear corner of the truck bed. There were no scuff marks. No indications of what had happened here. The memory of his fall here that night at the corner of the truck in the cold and the snow was clear and vivid up to a point. From there on was where things got pretty much lost to him. Now, he turned his back on that memory. All he wanted to remember of that night was that he had made it. He had made it back in the truck and gutted it out. He had survived. With a bit of help there at the last, of course. He knew how it would have turned out without that bit of help.

He walked along the left side of the truck, running his hand affectionately over the top of the sidewall of the truck bed. He stopped near the front of the truck, his hand on the hood warmed by the sun.

Across the open ground, past the old fire ring, he looked at the end of the ridge. Under the trees, the ground was speckled with sunlight and shadow. He could see the horns of the elk lying on the ground where he had fallen, no doubt still tied to the packboard along with the bones of the front shoulder of the elk. *There's no need to go there*, he thought to himself. *Leave 'em where they lay, old son. You don't need a reminder hangin' on your wall.*

Near the start of the main trail, he saw a white piece of ribbon tied to a tree limb fluttering in the breeze. A part of the trail sign he had marked up through the trees. In his mind, he walked that trail again. Winding through the trees along the ridge to stand where he had taken the elk. He sat again by the log and watched them come up the draw, turning up the trail through the brush, to the place where the bull had made his sacrifice.

He thought of the cow that had sneaked up behind him at the stand.

He smiled now at those memories.

Further up the ridge, he sat again on the large rock and watched the mule deer buck come out of the trees to drink at the stream and nibble from the brush.

And he smiled at another good memory.

In his mind, he saw those blue mountain peaks rimming across the far horizon beyond the dark forest where the big river ran. Another memory in the long chain of all the distant mountains he had seen in his lifetime.

He smiled and nodded his head at all of those memories. Visions and memories never to be forgotten.

After a few minutes, he knelt in the dirt beside the truck and looked beneath it. There was no evidence of leaking antifreeze or oil on the ground. "You got lucky there, old son," he said. They would drain the oil and the antifreeze and put in fresh before starting the truck. None of tires were flat, but all were low on air. They had brought a small compressor just for that reason. He stood and unlocked the driver's door and left it open to air out the cab. *Funny thing*, he thought, *lockin' up a truck that was up here all winter buried in ten feet of snow.*

He walked around the front of the truck, unlocked and opened the passenger door, and left it open as well. He turned to the fire pit and looked at the partially burned logs and ashes. He remembered the back strap steaks with fried potatoes and onions he had eaten there, cooked over an open fire. "As good a meal as I ever had," he said.

He moved past the firepit and the pile of firewood to the tree beside the stream. He closed his eyes and heard the gurgle of the stream and smiled at its familiar voice. He pushed his hat back on his head and looked at the crystal blue sky. He closed his eyes again and remembered the dark sky speckled with millions of twinkling stars; stars you never see in the city. He unzipped and watered the tree one more time.

A few more steps and he lay on the ground by the stream, his head over the water. He laid his hat on the ground beside him, dipped his hands in the ice-cold water, and drank deep of the mountain stream. He splashed water on his face and head, shivered, and drank again, and then shook the water out of his hair.

Getting back up was more difficult than it had been in the past. That leg just didn't work the way it used to. He would have to live with that as well. The most obvious reminder, as if he needed one.

In the shade of a small Aspen on the bank of the stream, he sat astraddle an old log, a log he had sat on many times before over the years. They were old friends and had spoken often. After several minutes, he lay back along the log, pulled his hat down over his eyes, and let his arms hang down on either side of the log. His fingers caressed the smooth sides of the old tree. A few deep breaths and he felt the spirit of the old tree enfold him and hold him close. His own spirit smiled for the embrace.

Above and behind him, a squirrel chattered and scolded him from the branches of a pine. A flock of crows moved from tree to tree calling to each other, gossiping. From somewhere across the stream, an owl spoke his nighttime question, "Who? Who? Who?"

"It's just me, Mr. Owl. Just me come back for the afternoon, the memories, and to get my old truck," he said.

There were no drums, no chanting voices or feet stamping the dry earth in dance. Those were things reserved for dreams, the hunt and the harvest. And the call of the old things deep inside him.

There would be no more hunts for him. Alone anyway. He knew that and tried to accept it. It wasn't easy. But that's just the way it would have to be. The hard work of a hunt would have to be shared with other, younger men or simply dreamed about from his favorite easy chair. He would never again be able to pack the heavy loads. Walk the steepest trails.

But he also knew that he would come back here again, to this or some other high mountain. Alone. To walk what forest trails he could, lay on the old logs in the dappled sunlight, and sit on the high ridges to gaze at the far-off mountains. He would come to listen to the wind in the pines, the squirrels in the trees, and the owl asking his question in the night. He would rest beside the chuckling stream and listen to its secrets. He would come back for all the voices he loved.

All of this was necessary, he knew. Required for his existence. His touchstone to the natural life that was an integral part of him while he was here. For as long as he lived.

As he lay on the log, the breeze brought the aroma of the pines to him, and he heard their voices. He understood them. The voice of the shivering aspen leaves dancing in the sun above him sang to him, and he understood their melody. The rocks and the mountains added their voices to the chorus of the trees, the creek, and the breeze. They all sang in harmony to him. And he knew the song and the melody, and he added his voice to theirs.

These were the things he came here for. The voices he needed to hear with that ear deep inside of him. The things he needed to touch with the fingers of his soul. These were the things he would remember for the rest of his days. The pieces of the world that would remain with him. Forever.

Up in the trees, along the road, the truck engine started. The young man was coming now. They would pack up the tarps and stack the cut firewood for someone else to use. They would put the new battery in the old truck, change the antifreeze and oil, pump up the tires, put in fresh gas, and get it started. He and the old truck had a few more miles to share. He had a few more mountain trails to walk, a few more far-off peaks to gaze at. He sat up on the log as the young man in the big pickup came into the meadow.

"It's time to go, I guess," he said, looking around. "I'll see ya the next time around."

As he turned toward the truck, from across the stream, a large great horned owl stepped off his perch high in a giant pine tree and spread his wings as he fell toward earth. The owl lifted on the breeze to soar just over the man's head, his wings silent as he chased his shadow across the meadow. He watched the owl glide on the currents of warm air and rise sharply to the very top of the pine across the meadow.

And his soul settled with the owl on that high limb.

About the Author

Born at home in Oregon in 1944, Roy Mullen grew up in a large family with very little, developing a passion for written art very early on. From a young age, his short stories and poetry were often submitted for school and amateur writing contests. He adopted his love for the outdoors from his father, who taught him to hunt and appreciate the calm and serenity only nature can provide. Losing his father during a hunt at 16, his connection to the outdoors grew deeper. After college and serving in the military, setting his own wants aside, Roy raised five children in Idaho, dedicating himself to his family and community in numerous ways, such as serving as a police officer. With his children grown, retirement offered Roy the opportunity to return to his own passions, writing and the outdoors.

Note from Roy Mullen

Word-of-mouth is crucial for any author to succeed. If you enjoyed *The Elk Hunt*, please leave a review online—anywhere you are able. Even if it's just a sentence or two. It would make all the difference and would be very much appreciated.

Thanks!
Roy Mullen

We hope you enjoyed reading this title from:

www.blackrosewriting.com

Subscribe to our mailing list – *The Rosevine* – and receive **FREE** books, daily deals, and stay current with news about upcoming releases and our hottest authors.
Scan the QR code below to sign up.

Already a subscriber? Please accept a sincere thank you for being a fan of Black Rose Writing authors.

View other Black Rose Writing titles at www.blackrosewriting.com/books and use promo code **PRINT** to receive a **20% discount** when purchasing.